Antony Maitland Q.C., barrister and detective, has a friend at Scotland Yard, Detective Superintendent Sykes. Sykes is concerned about the following:

A newsagent has been murdered in North London. The police discover a protection racket of which they judge the dead man to have been a victim. They find two young 'salesmen' with dubious records, and they also find enough solid evidence to charge them with murder.

But in court the police evidence explodes. Witnesses contradict their original statements. The defendants then accuse two police officers – one senior and one junior – of threatening them in an attempt to extort money. This is the kind of corruption most hated at Scotland Yard and a very senior officer decides that the full rigour of the law must be applied.

When the trial comes up it is Maitland's uncle, Sir Nicholas Harding, who conducts the defence. Maitland acts as his uncle's junior. Meanwhile Maitland has been making some enquiries of his own in an attempt to find out what has really happened in this immensely complex case. He unearths some information that may be used to weaken the prosecution case.

Once again there is a splendid court scene with Sir Nicholas and Antony working in tandem. And in the end there is a satisfying revelation.

Sara Woods is a modern master of the art of combining the 'Golden Age' plot forms with scenes in court. This story will enthrall her many admirers – and should increase their numbers.

by the same author

BLOODY INSTRUCTIONS
MALICE DOMESTIC
THE TASTE OF FEARS
ERROR OF THE MOON
TRUSTED LIKE THE FOX
THIS LITTLE MEASURE
THE WINDY SIDE OF THE LAW
ENTER CERTAIN MURDERERS
THOUGH I KNOW SHE LIES
LET'S CHOOSE EXECUTORS
THE CASE IS ALTERED
AND SHAME THE DEVIL
KNIVES HAVE EDGES
PAST PRAYING FOR
TARRY AND BE HANGED
AN IMPROBABLE FICTION
SERPENT'S TOOTH
THE KNAVISH CROWS
THEY LOVE NOT POISON
YET SHE MUST DIE
ENTER THE CORPSE
DONE TO DEATH
A SHOW OF VIOLENCE
MY LIFE IS DONE
THE LAW'S DELAY
A THIEF OR TWO
EXIT MURDERER
THIS FATAL WRIT
PROCEED TO JUDGEMENT
THEY STAY FOR DEATH
WEEP FOR HER
CRY GUILTY
DEAREST ENEMY
ENTER A GENTLEWOMAN
VILLAINS BY NECESSITY
MOST GRIEVOUS MURDER
CALL BACK YESTERDAY
THE LIE DIRECT
WHERE SHOULD HE DIE?
THE BLOODY BOOK OF LAW
MURDER'S OUT OF TUNE
DEFY THE DEVIL
AN OBSCURE GRAVE

Sara Woods
AWAY WITH THEM TO PRISON

'Away with them to prison; and the day
Of combat shall be the last of the next month'
King Henry VI (Part 11)
Act I, Scene iii

MACMILLAN

ISBN 0-333-39008-3

First published 1985 by
MACMILLAN LONDON LIMITED
4 Little Essex Street London WC2R 3LF
and Basingstoke

Associated companies in Auckland, Delhi, Dublin, Gaborone, Hamburg, Harare, Hong Kong, Johannesburg, Kuala Lumpur, Lagos, Manzini, Melbourne, Mexico City, Nairobi, New York, Singapore and Tokyo

Typeset in Great Britain by
Bookworm Typesetting Ltd., Manchester

Printed and bound in Great Britain by
Anchor Brendon Ltd., Tiptree

Any work of fiction whose characters were of uniform excellence could rightly be condemned – by that fact if by no other – as being incredibly dull. Therefore no excuse can be considered necessary for the villainy or folly of the people appearing in this book. It seems extremely unlikely that any of them could resemble a real person, alive or dead. Any such resemblance is completely unintentional and without malice.

S.W.

Michaelmas Term, 1975

Wednesday, 1st October

It had been a pleasant interlude. A meeting between two old friends with many interests in common at a restaurant that Antony Maitland was accustomed to think of as the halfway house; that is, roughly halfway between Detective Superintendent Sykes's office at New Scotland Yard and the Inner Temple where he was a member of his uncle's chambers. A meeting moreover that had no ostensible reason other than the fact that Sykes, who had issued the invitation, was not for the moment overwhelmed by work, while Maitland, at the commencement of the Michaelmas Term, had not yet reached the stage where things began to pile up to an uncomfortable extent. All the same, Antony, whose worst enemies could not have called him imperceptive, was aware that behind the detective's usual placidity there lay a rather strange and very uncharacteristic sense of unease. But it wasn't until they had finished their luncheon and coffee was on the table that he brought the matter bluntly into the foreground.

'Out with it, Superintendent. You'd another reason for wanting to get together with me today, besides the mere pleasure of my company.'

For the moment Sykes's attention seemed to be completely absorbed in stirring his coffee, a very necessary process since it contained, as Antony knew without having to count, at least five lumps of sugar. Even when he spoke he didn't answer the implied question directly.

'Somebody told me that Sir Nicholas wouldn't be back in London before the weekend,' he remarked.

'I admit,' said Antony slowly, 'he always objects to my getting what he will insist on calling mixed up with the police, but not when it's a purely social occasion, as this is. Or isn't it?' he demanded with sudden suspicion.

'It is and it isn't,' said Sykes maddeningly. 'You've been away for the best part of two months, so it's natural I wanted to exchange news, but –'

'But I've been out of touch with what's going on here, and there's something or other you feel I should know. Out with it,' he added encouragingly. Sykes's bluntness was a byword, and his present attitude completely incomprehensible. 'It can't be anything personal, I've only been back since Sunday, and the list Mallory provided me with of the briefs he's accepted on my behalf is as innocuous as even Uncle Nick could wish. And damned dull into the bargain,' he added regretfully.

Sykes seemed to make up his mind. 'It isn't personal,' he said, 'but something rather unpleasant has come up that I think might interest you. And I'd very much like your advice. Besides –'

'Come to the point, there's a good chap.'

'Do you remember the time two years back – almost exactly two years as a matter of fact – when you got Jim Arnold off on a burglary charge?'

Maitland frowned. 'Of course I remember it,' he said rather sharply. 'And to be exact, I didn't get him acquitted.'

'One day in gaol which he'd already served,' said Sykes reminiscently. Now that he had started to talk, his unwillingness seemed to have left him. 'It's the first time,' he added, 'that I ever recollect your courting publicity about a case, though it was subtly done, I grant you that.'

'That's all very well, but what about Jim Arnold? You're not trying to tell me he's slipped from the straight and narrow again, because quite frankly I just won't believe you. I've seen him several times since then, and if there'd been anything troubling him he'd have told me. Besides, even if he'd wanted to take up his old ways Jimmy and Doris wouldn't have let him. You know they both brought their families back from Canada because there was some doubt as to whether he'd be allowed to go and join them.'

'Wait a bit, Mr Maitland, wait a bit.' Sykes's tone was soothing. 'I know you've a soft spot for Jim, quite a number of us on the Force feel the same way, and I've certainly heard no suggestions of trouble in that quarter.'

'Then what the hell is all this about? All this circumlocution!' Antony was becoming impatient.

'I only asked if you remembered the case. There was a protection racket involved.'

'That was all cleared up. The chaps who were actually operating it, Alf and Stan – I'm afraid I can't remember their surnames – were convicted, and the chap who'd been organising it all murdered his partner in crime and pleaded Guilty to everything when the case came on.' He paused, and then added almost in a pleading tone. 'It's all over, Superintendent, finished and done with. So I can't understand why you want to drag it up again.'

'Well you see, Mr Maitland, there's been a suggestion that something of the same sort may be happening still.'

'That somebody has taken up where Alf and Stan left off, you mean?'

'Something like that. And I was wondering . . . knowing you, Mr Maitland, I was wondering whether you might not know a little more about the matter than you told us at the time.'

'This,' said Antony rather grimly, 'is where we c-came in.' The slight stammer was warning enough to anyone who knew him as well as Sykes did that he was losing his temper, but the detective, now that the matter on his mind had been broached, showed no signs of discomfort. 'Why s-should I have kept anything f-from you anyway?' Antony asked him. 'I was only too thankful to have the whole thing cleared up and Jim not back in prison.'

'You'll admit there have been occasions –'

'Times when I couldn't be completely open with you because of my client's interests. I've never d-denied that, have I?'

'No, and it was something like that I had in mind. For instance, if you knew of anything that would have made the court a little less sympathetic towards Jim Arnold –' He paused, and added deliberately, 'Would you have told me that, Mr Maitland?'

Antony smiled suddenly. 'No, I can't say I would,' he said. It was no use being angry with Sykes, whom he had to thank for more kindnesses than he cared to remember. 'Will you believe me if I tell you there was nothing? It happens to be the truth.'

'Then naturally I believe you.'

9

'And if I did know something,' Maitland amplified, 'I'd tell you that. Though I might not, of course, tell you what it was.'

'I know.' Sykes looked around for the waiter, but when the man came Antony said quickly, 'I'd like some more coffee,' and waited until it had been brought and poured. Then he said, 'You can't just leave it there, Superintendent. For one thing, unless things have changed in the last two months, I can't see what you're doing interesting yourself in that kind of a case. And for another you're worried, and not just about accusing me of not being frank with the police, which you've done at least a dozen times in the past without any sign of embarrassment at all.'

Sykes put down the sugar bowl and gave his companion his sedate smile. 'I suppose I do owe you some sort of explanation,' he said. 'And perhaps I hoped you'd ask for one. It began with a murder, you see, though that isn't what's troubling me. I'd like your advice, but I don't want you mixing yourself up in this sort of thing.'

'What sort of thing, for heaven's sake? If it's a legal matter it could be very much my business to get mixed up in it. But you say it isn't the murder that's worrying you, so I don't quite see —'

'I'll put it as briefly as I can,' said Sykes. 'Two men were arrested, the witnesses didn't come up to proof, and the case was thrown out in the Magistrates' Court.'

'In that case there's nothing to be done but forget about the whole thing. Unless you've got any other suspects, of course.'

'Unfortunately we can't. I've mentioned Sir Alfred Godalming to you before.'

'The new Assistant Commissioner?'

'The same. He's determined to stamp out all suspicion of wrongdoing among the men under him and a disciplinary inquiry is being held at the moment to decide what to do.'

'But that happens all the time,' Maitland protested. 'The two men are probably as guilty as hell, but if they or some of their friends have subverted the witnesses . . . look here, who was the investigating officer?'

'That's what is worrying me, lad,' said Sykes rather heavily. 'Detective Inspector Mayhew —'

'Mayhew? I don't believe it! That if he was in charge of the case there's any reason for an inquiry, I mean.'

10

'It's true all the same. And I don't believe it either, but I never thought I'd hear you say that, Mr Maitland, not about your nearest and dearest. You've always told me it's the bane of a barrister's life being told, "he wouldn't do a thing like that".'

'Yes, and I meant it. But Mayhew . . . I suppose he's being accused of conspiring to pervert the course of justice. Who is he supposed to have conspired with?'

'Detective Constable Harris, whom I believe you met once.'

'A dark, good-looking chap, very young?'

'That's the one.'

'When will this inquiry finish its deliberations?'

'Within the next few days I should think. But it's even nastier than I've told you so far, the defendants say that the charge was brought with the intention of extorting money from them. Or rather, that they were framed because they wouldn't pay up.'

'That's even more unbelievable.'

'So I think, but if the D.P.P. agrees –'

'The whole matter will be aired in court Even if they contented themselves with a charge of perjury it wouldn't be so bad, but –'

'Sir Alfred is out for blood,' said Sykes bluntly. 'That's why I said I wanted your advice.'

'If they're accused of making false statements intended to be given in evidence in criminal proceedings I think the most they can get is two years, but I can't be sure until I look it up. But if these two men can substantiate what they say about extortion I've a nasty feeling the sky's the limit. But perhaps the Director of Public Prosecutions won't play ball.'

'That seems to be the best we can hope for. Tell me, Mr Maitland, what's your opinion of Mayhew?'

'Well –' Maitland paused to consider the question, and for the moment the Chief Inspector was as clear in his mind's eye as if he had been physically present. Mayhew was a big man, heavily built, with a shock of dark hair and a face so expressionless that until you knew him you might have thought him of a sullen disposition. He had very little to say for himself on the whole, but when he did bring himself to speak (invariably prefacing his remarks with a rumbling cough which always reminded Antony of a grandfather clock nerving itself to strike) did so very much to

11

the point. 'He has a sense of humour,' Antony said as last, 'and – and of compassion. Do you remember that night at Sunbury when I was so worried about Jenny? He was a sergeant then and when the news came in that she was safe he took the time to reassure me before reporting to his superior officer . . . and as it happened to be Conway that took some courage. Come to think of it, you were there, Sykes, I can't think at the moment why.'

'An interested bystander,' the superintendent assured him. 'But go on with your assessment.'

'Since then he's helped me a dozen times with comments apparently made in complete innocence, but in reality very much to the point of what I wanted to know. So when I say I like him I'm bound to admit I'm prejudiced in his favour, not least because I'm inclined to think he likes me, and has a genuine desire for justice to be done . . . and if you say I'm talking about what *I* think is justice at any particular moment in time, Superintendent, I can only say the remark isn't worthy of you.'

'Nothing of the sort was in my mind, I assure you,' said Sykes in his placid way. The amused look that so often surfaced when they were talking together was beginning to be very evident, and Maitland paused again to give him a suspicious look before he continued.

'As for the charge . . . how great is the frustration, Superintendent, when you can't prove something you believe from the bottom of your heart to be true?'

'Very great indeed,' Sykes told him soberly, any humour he had momentarily found in the situation was now obviously in abeyance. 'As I'm sure you know yourself, Mr Maitland.'

'For my sins, yes, I do know. But the law, unfortunately sometimes, is the law. Have you ever been tempted to tamper with it . . . in the interests of what you believe to be justice, let's say?'

'Tempted, I suppose,' said Sykes slowly. 'But never to the extent of yielding to the temptation.'

'No, I'm sure. I didn't really need to ask you that. But suppose that Mayhew – we can disregard the luckless constable for the time being, don't you think, because obviously his position would only be a supportive one?'

'Well, I daresay –' Sykes was answering the implicit query,

without waiting for Maitland to complete it. 'I find it difficult to believe of Mayhew, but it could happen.'

'All right, grant that for a moment. But extortion . . . a charge deliberately framed so as to demand money from the defendants for dropping it. That's a different matter, isn't it?'

'Very different.'

'And it sticks in my gullet, as I gather it does in yours. I'd be unwilling to believe Mayhew guilty of perjury, though I suppose I must admit the possibility that some particularly offensive crime had been committed and he thought that was the only way of getting a conviction. But to frame a charge deliberately, for his own benefit . . . I can't accept that.'

'That's just about what I feel, Mr Maitland,' Sykes agreed. 'But it's out of my hands, there's nothing either of us can do about it. Only I thought . . . I wondered –'

'Whether I might know something helpful that I'd been keeping to myself?'

'Yes. I'm sorry if I offended you about that.'

'Think nothing of it,' said Antony airily.

Perhaps it was the unexpected lightness of his tone that prompted Sykes to persist. 'If you do know anything, Mr Maitland, the police are the people to deal with it . . . not you.'

'I've already told you –'

'Yes, I accept that, of course. The only thing is, knowing you, if anything should occur to you I'd prefer you brought it to me.'

'I wonder what kind of a thing you're referring to.'

'If there were any further ramifications to the protection racket that were revealed when Jim Arnold was brought to trial –'

'I told you, I don't know of any,' Antony interrupted him.

'And I've told you I believe you. The only thing that's troubling me, Mr Maitland, is whether when you come to think about it anything else should come to mind.'

'Meaning –?'

'Exactly what I say. I'm desperately sorry about what has happened –'

'Yes, well, I hope you're not going to leave it there. Tell me at least how the whole unpleasant business started.'

'A man was murdered, a man in a small way of business who ran a newsagents shop, combined with the usual sweets and tobacco, a rack of paperbacks, you know the kind of thing. His name was Goodbody and he was set upon one night practically on his own doorstep and bludgeoned to death.'

'Wait a bit, Superintendent. You've been talking about a protection racket. Was he robbed?'

'No, he'd deposited his day's takings in his bank's night safe on the way home, and what little he had on him was untouched.'

'Then I don't see –'

'Of course you don't,' said Sykes indulgently. 'Mayhew was the investigating officer, and at first he thought, according to his report, that it was a mugging that didn't come off, nothing to do with the shop, just because he happened to be there. Nobody attempted to talk to Mrs Goodbody that night, the neighbours rallied round and the doctor was called and she was terribly upset. But the next morning she came out with this story of her husband having been threatened and of course that changed the whole course of the investigation.'

'Threatened if he didn't pay for protection you mean?'

'What else?'

'Had he been doing so?'

'He had, according to Mrs Goodbody. She said two men had gone to the shop about eighteen months ago and her husband had eventually given her details of exactly what had been said. But then recently he'd said he was tired of paying for nothing, and it was time someone called their bluff.'

'But surely . . . if he didn't intend to go on paying up why didn't he go to the police? Was he . . . had he a record perhaps and was afraid they wouldn't believe him?'

'Nothing like that. As far as anyone knows he was an extremely law-abiding man. The thing was that, according to his wife, he wasn't one to be intimidated by anyone and was ashamed that he'd given in for as long as he did. So he made up his mind that he'd deal with the matter himself.'

'I can sympathise with that, but did he know of anyone else in the locality – wherever it was – who could also have been threatened?'

'It was in North London, the Bowes Park area, and no, he hadn't talked to any of his fellow tradesmen. What he told his wife originally was that two men had been to see him, talked

14

quite pleasantly at first about what a pleasant district it was and what a nice little business he had, that sort of thing. And then they told him that his account was in arrears with the Shadwell Confectionery Company at Bermondsey, but the company didn't want to make trouble for him so they'd accept instalment payments if he made them regularly into the company's account at the Wood Green branch of the Northumbrian and Wessex Bank. That led to a good deal of argument at home, and Mrs Goodbody had told him when he decided not to go on paying that he ought to report the matter, but he said he could deal with it quite well himself. The day he was killed was not long after that.'

'Did they just mean to beat him up, or had they murder in mind?'

'The latter I should think from the extent of his injuries. Which leads us of course, as you've already realised, Mr Maitland, to the inescapable conclusion that there were other people in the area involved, and that the unfortunate victim was being made an example of. I'm telling you now about the reports just as they were filed. Constable Harris was tagging along and he confirmed everything Mayhew said. The Shadwell Confectionery Company really exists, and that was where the first inquiries were made. The Managing Director, who was also the owner – and from what Mayhew said I imagine it's a money spinner – had never heard of an account at Wood Green; the firm's account was kept locally at Bramley's Bank. That seemed good enough to get a court order to examine the Wood Green account, which was fed with regular weekly payments by tradespeople in all the surrounding areas. It had been opened about two years before by a chap called Charles Kingsley, and he had arranged for standing order payments to be made every month to two men whom the manager presumed were agents of the company. Their names were Stokes and Barleycorn, of all things, and we'd better refer to them that way as they both had the same Christian name, James. That sent Mayhew back to Mr Shadwell, of course, who confirmed that Kingsley was the company's Treasurer, at present on holiday, somewhere on the continent he believed. The company employed a number of agents in the London area, their products were popular, but he wasn't familiar with any of their names. And this is the point where Mayhew made his mistake . . .

if in fact that is what happened.'

'He took it for granted, I presume, that the Treasurer had absconded and that there was nothing further to be found out at the confectionery company.'

'That's exactly it. He went back to the bank, and got particulars of the destinations of the standing order payments. That took him to two other branches of the Northumbrian and Wessex, one had James Stokes's account, the other James Barleycorn's, cheques were drawn on both and occasional cash withdrawals were made, but none of the branch staff seemed very familiar with either man. Both lived not far from the branch to which his money was transferred, and cautious inquiries revealed the fact that Stokes was a married man with two children and Barleycorn was single. That was good enough for Mayhew, but of course he realised, as I would have done myself, that it wouldn't be anywhere near enough for the court. So he had them followed, and made a list of the places that they visited in the course of the business day. All were shops with a line of confectionery products, though some of them, like Goodbody, dealt in other things too. Then he started asking questions.'

'Was anyone willing to talk? It seems obvious enough what was happening.'

'Well, he drew a blank as you might expect in the Bowes Park area, nobody was risking being dealt with as the unfortunate Mr Goodbody had been. But he found a man in Palmer's Green who was willing to talk, after a little gentle persuasion I imagine, and he told just the same tale as Mrs Goodbody, that he had been told to clear his overdue account with Shadwell Confectionery by regular payments into the bank at Wood Green. He had a small account with that company, but the two men who visited him were so menacing that he was afraid not to comply and make the larger payments. But his story went a little further than that. He claimed to have seen the murder, and to have recognised Stokes and Barleycorn whom he knew quite well by sight as they called on him every month. So at that point Mayhew felt he had quite enough to go ahead.'

'It certainly seems . . . let's see, Mrs Goodbody, Mr Shadwell – you did say that was the name of the owner of the company, didn't you? – the bank who received the payments, and now this

16

other chap at Palmer's Green. What went wrong?'

'Everything,' said Sykes, rather more dramatically than was customary with him. 'Mrs Goodbody, called by the prosecution in the Magistrates' Court, denied ever having said such a thing. Her husband's death had been a terrible shock, but with so many wicked people about and his coming home late at night she supposed it wasn't to be wondered at. Then the Palmer's Green shopkeeper, whose name was Peele, said the payments he made to the bank were actually to discharge his monthly account with the Shadwell Company and the rest of his story was sheer fabrication, and finally Mr Shadwell got up and said he was sorry to have misled the police but Mr Kingsley had not returned from holiday and confirmed that the account had been opened at Wood Green for the convenience of their customers in North London. Stokes and Barleycorn were among the most successful of their agents and had been taken on by Mr Kingsley to open up the territory.'

'Was he telling the truth?'

'He may have been, as he saw it. It's the sort of arrangement a chap in charge of finance might make without bothering to inform a very busy man.'

'But the others . . . surely they'd all made statements.'

'Certainly they had. Mrs Goodbody said she'd been so confused and unhappy, and the policeman so abrupt in his manner, that she really didn't know what she'd been signing. Peele said straight out he'd been threatened with prosecution – "and don't think I couldn't find something wrong," Mayhew is supposed to have said – and hadn't dared deny the matter until he heard Mrs Goodbody's statement. As for Kingsley, he was the picture of innocence and very convincing too from all I hear. Of course Mayhew had given his evidence right at the start, with Harris to confirm his story, but by that time nobody was believing a word either of them had said. And when the Magistrate threw the case out one of the accused got up and said, "It was all a plot, they said they'd do us if we didn't give them three thousand pounds." And that of course put the cat among the pigeons nicely.'

'I can imagine it would. The thing I'm wondering is, where would those two chaps have been supposed to have got such a sum?'

'If they were innocent, you mean?' Sykes sighed. 'If they were innocent they were honestly employed as salesmen, and making an extremely good income. Extremely good. There's no doubt they could have raised it between them. The question is, why should a respectable company have employed them?'

'They both have records, then?'

'Petty crime, nothing as serious as murder.'

'Nothing involving violence?'

'Not a thing. All the same, if they'd been committed for trial and alleged police misconduct at that stage, their past would have come out in court and might have counted against them in the eyes of the jury. But the point that worries me is how they came to think of such an idea . . . if it isn't true, that is. And that's why –' He broke off there and smiled at his companion, spreading his hands in a rough parody of a gesture Maitland was fond of making.

Antony smiled in his turn. 'That's why you came to me, in case I had secret knowledge of some mastermind who might be behind them.'

'Well, after the business with Jim Arnold it didn't seem unreasonable,' the superintendent protested.

'I'll forgive you.' Maitland's tone was light again. 'So what happened after that?'

'The A.C. saw red. There were consultations with everybody from the Home Secretary down to the legal department, but I wasn't privy to what went on. Then this disciplinary committee was convened, but I'd be very much surprised if some serious action weren't taken.'

'Then you don't know what Kingsley said in reply to further questioning. Whether he had references for these two men for instance?'

'No, I don't know a thing beyond what I've told you. And you might be able to tell me, Mr Maitland, supposing they decide that dismissal from the force isn't enough, supposing they take the matter to court. If Sir Alfred has his way, I think that's what they'll do, he'll want to make an example. I suppose they could be charged with perjury, both of them.'

'That's certainly a possibility.' Maitland spoke slowly, thinking it out. 'I'd have to look it up because they will keep changing the law, but certainly conspiracy to accuse of a crime for the purpose of extorting money would be a more serious charge, though it might be more difficult to prove. But I'm pretty sure that if it could be proved it wouldn't matter a scrap whether the two men accused of murder in the first place were guilty or not. Why not come to dinner one day next week, any day but Tuesday, and I'll have an answer for you then. Come to think of it, the end of the week might be best. If the inquiry decides to send its findings to the D.P.P., whose consent would certainly be necessary for any further action, it'll take a few days for you to know what's happening.'

Sykes's answer was rather oblique. 'I shall be happy to see Mrs Maitland again,' he said primly. 'Would Friday evening suit you?'

'Excellently well. I suppose . . . oh, well, it's no use conjecturing. But Mayhew . . . no, I don't see it.'

'That's my instinct too, but like you I don't altogether trust it,' Sykes told him. 'You know as well as I do that the police force isn't recruited entirely of saints, and I'm sure you can imagine the temptations that arise.'

'As well as the next man,' said Antony rather dryly. It was only a year since his ancient feud with Chief Superintendent Briggs of the C.I.D. had come to a head, and been settled once and for all. The episode had led to Briggs's retirement, though not very long before he would have left the Force in any case, and Sykes, who had seen the whole thing from close quarters and been distressed by it, was perfectly well aware that Antony, though the other man's animosity had frequently aroused his anger, bore no lasting malice for what had happened.

The friendship between Sykes and Maitland had grown steadily over the years into one of complete trust, though as their conversation that day had demonstrated, the Superintendent wasn't above accusing Maitland of hiding things from the police on occasion which he felt would have been better brought out into the open. The detective was a squarely built man with dark hair now beginning to be flecked with grey, whose north country origin was apparent the moment he opened his mouth, though it was only in moments of emotion that he now resorted to a really broad dialect. His attire was perhaps more suited to country life than to the town; he looked in fact like a prosperous farmer, and (Antony would have added) one who had done a good deal at market that day. Now he was signalling for the bill, and beginning a string of rather formal and long-winded farewells. Antony interrupted with ill-concealed impatience.

'Yes, Superintendent, I've enjoyed it as much as you have, and I appreciate your confidence, even' – he smiled faintly as he spoke – 'if the purpose of this meeting was a lingering distrust of my openness with you two years ago. I'm desperately sorry about Mayhew though, and that young lad who's got mixed up in the matter as well. I only wish there was something I could do to help.'

'If there is I'll tell you,' Sykes promised, and paused a moment before he added, 'So long as it's nothing to get you into trouble.' Thinking it over later, Maitland reached the conclusion that the sentence hadn't originally been intended to end that way.

A few minutes later they parted on the pavement outside the restaurant, each understanding the other well enough. Antony walked back to chambers, and occupied his mind as he went with the problem of the best way to approach his uncle concerning the matter when Sir Nicholas returned to town that weekend.

Monday, 6th October

As it happened, Sir Nicholas and Vera didn't return home until fairly late the following Sunday, and though Antony and Jenny met them at Heathrow there wasn't much in the way of significant conversation that night. The following evening, however, Mrs Stokes, Sir Nicholas's housekeeper for many years and much more amenable since his marriage a little over four years ago, had prepared a special celebratory dinner, to which their nephew and niece were invited.

This involved no more than descending two flights of stairs from their own quarters, as they occupied what was always referred to as a flat, though it was in fact the two top floors of Sir Nicholas's house in Kempenfeldt Square. After so many years it is doubtful that any of them even remembered that the arrangement had originally been considered a temporary one, and certainly the fact that their domain was far from self-contained caused no trouble to anyone.

Vera, Lady Harding, the former Miss Vera Langhorne, was a barrister in her own right, and had practised on the West Midland circuit before her marriage, so perhaps this had helped her to fit comfortably into the household. Antony and Jenny had only one complaint, that her arrival had made it very unlikely that Gibbs, Sir Nicholas's aged butler, would ever condescend to retire, an end towards which they had all been working for years. He seemed to approve of Vera (perhaps she was the only person in the world of which this could be said) and as for years now he had done as little or as much work as he chose, and in any event thoroughly enjoyed playing the martyr, the matter was now considered hopeless.

Before dinner their talk was mainly of the vacation that had passed, and it wasn't until the meal was over and they were settled in the study, which had always been Sir Nicholas's favourite room and now was really the only one available since Vera had rearranged the big drawing-room to house her stereo equipment, that Antony had the opportunity of mentioning his talk with Superintendent Sykes, and the unfortunate Chief Inspector Mayhew's predicament. For once in his life his uncle heard him out without interruption, a fact so unusual as to make Maitland a little nervous.

When he had finished Sir Nicholas allowed the silence to lengthen for a moment and then asked pertinently, 'That leaves us with just two questions, Antony. What do you think about this charge?'

'I like Mayhew, and the only time I saw Constable Harris I thought he was a very good type with lots of promise. I'm desperately sorry for what's happened.'

'That was not exactly what I meant. Do you think there is any substance in the allegations that have been made?'

'That isn't so easy to answer, Uncle Nick. I'm sure you realise it isn't a thing that would ever have occurred to me, but I suppose it's possible that Mayhew might have been tempted to – to embellish his facts a little, to ensure that justice was done. But the other business . . . three thousand pounds is a lot of money, but not, I should have said, sufficient to jeopardise your whole career for. If that part is true I think we must also suppose that he'd been making a habit of it, that there'd be a lot more cases involved if we only knew about them. I wouldn't have thought it of him but no one knows better than I do that it's quite impossible to be absolutely sure what any other person will or will not do.'

'Yes, I suppose that's as far as I can expect you to go,' said Sir Nicholas, leaning back in his chair with every evidence of enjoyment. He was a tall man, rather more heavily built than his nephew, and with thick hair, so fair that the white in it was almost unnoticeable. He was, as usual, immaculately turned out (the havoc he would already have wreaked among the papers carefully arranged on his desk against his return to chambers was another matter again) and his features were sufficiently regular to make the newspapers' description of him as handsome, which

22

occurred with distressing regularity when one of his cases was being reported, not an unreasonable one; though it roused his extreme ire on the occasions when the offending article hadn't been removed by the female members of his household before he could see it.

Again he allowed the silence to lengthen, and it was Vera who broke it, saying in her abrupt and elliptical way, 'Very clear, very sensible.' The words were accompanied by a grim smile, but their intent was obviously complimentary.

'Quite so, my dear,' Sir Nicholas replied and turned again to his nephew, in whom first his silence and now the gentleness of his manner were occasioning extreme disquiet. 'But there is still the other question, Antony.'

'What is that, sir?'

'As your aunt says you gave us quite a clear account of your talk with the Superintendent. The question is, just what did you leave out of it?'

Antony, who had been sitting decorously enough on the sofa beside his wife, got up and took a turn the length of the room, to the window and back again. 'I told you everything that was pertinent,' he said. 'I thought you'd be interested.' There was another pause while Sir Nicholas looked at him. 'I told you he wanted my advice on the legal aspects, and besides, we hadn't seen one another all summer.'

'This was last Wednesday, you said?'

'Yes, Uncle Nick, it was.'

'Your advice on the legal aspects could hardly have been pressing until this inquiry was over, and then perhaps not even necessary. But the question remains –'

'If you will have it, sir, I'll tell you. I don't think Sykes really believes this extortion business any more than I do, but he didn't think the two men who were accused could have thought it up by themselves. All he wanted to know was whether there was any information about the protection racket that was going on at the time Jim Arnold was being victimised that I hadn't found it necessary to reveal at the time.'

'I might have known it!' Antony and Jenny were both waiting for an explosion, but surprisingly it didn't come. 'As long as you're on your feet, Antony, you may as well do the honours,' said Sir Nicholas. 'It is of course distressing that even your friend Sykes should have so little confidence in you, but it so happens that what you have told me fits in very well with something I was about to discuss with you this evening.'

'You might say,' said Jenny, abandoning for the moment the role of listener to which in this intensely legal household she was so often condemned, but which actually suited her nature very well, 'that it was because Inspector Sykes –'

'Superintendent,' said Maitland automatically.

'– because he trusted Antony that he talked to him at all.'

'I could say so, of course, if you wish me to, my dear,' said Sir Nicholas obligingly. 'The matter seems to have been settled more expeditiously than might have been expected, and it has been decided to press charges.'

'They'd have to get the D.P.P.'s consent.'

'Certainly, but I imagine in a matter of this sort a certain amount of overtime might have been worked by all concerned . . . don't you?'

'I suppose Halloran heard about it and told you,' said Maitland, frowning a little. Bruce Halloran, Q.C., was a close friend of Sir Nicholas's and of all the legal fraternity in London most likely to be familiar with what was being said on the grapevine.

'I have spoken before,' said Sir Nicholas, 'of this habit of yours of jumping to conclusions. I haven't heard from Halloran today.'

'Well then –?'

'It was Mallory who was my informant. He had a telephone call from Mr Bellerby this morning. He is acting for both the accused, and wants me to take the brief.'

'Heaven and earth! Are you going to accept it?'

'Why not? It seems to me, to use a phrase that is so often on your own lips, that the matter may prove intriguing. Or does your surprise mean to imply that you feel somebody else might be better able to conduct the case?'

'You know better than that, Uncle Nick. It was just that I wondered suddenly if that was another reason – the real reason perhaps – that Sykes wanted to talk to me. If the old fox knew what Mayhew was likely to do if they decided to prosecute . . . he's got it all wrong of course, but he may have felt I'd have some influence in persuading you to take the case.'

'I'm glad to see you have so proper an appreciation of the possibility,' said Sir Nicholas, picking up his glass of cognac and eyeing the contents with an air of suspicion, rather as though he felt some substitution might have been made since last he tasted them. 'But as for Sykes, in view of the well-known amiability of my temper –'

'That's just it, Uncle Nick,' said Antony, the humour that was never very far beneath the surface of his thoughts suddenly taking command of his tongue, 'where you're concerned nobody ever knows which way the cat will jump, and Sykes is as well aware of that as anybody.'

His uncle's glass went down on the table beside him again, and he closed his eyes for a moment as though unwilling to regard any longer a world where an associate of his could express himself with so little regard for the refinement of the English language. 'I should be unwilling to credit our friend the superintendent with such an error of judgement,' he remarked in a failing voice. 'Or do you think it is possible, my dear,' he added opening his eyes again and looking at his wife, 'that Antony is deliberately trying to provoke me?'

'Should think it very likely,' said Vera gruffly. She was herself not above laughing at her husband, a fact which Maitland had realised, not without surprise, some time ago. (It was perhaps equally surprising that Sir Nicholas showed no signs of resenting the fact.) 'Knows you even better than I do,' she went on now. 'But you've intimated that you're taking the case, and you're quite right, it sounds interesting.' Vera was a tall, rather thick-set woman, with a mass of dark hair, now liberally sprinkled with grey, that was constantly escaping from the pins that should have held it in place. She had very little dress sense and favoured loose-fitting clothes, but under Jenny's gentle persuasion the cut and style were improving, and she was learning which colours suited her.

'That's all very well, Uncle Nick,' Antony protested, 'but what's the charge? I've been looking it up since I lunched with Sykes, and if they really want to throw the book at them –'

'Must you?' queried Sir Nicholas faintly.

'– I imagine they'll make it perjury rather than conspiracy to

25

obstruct the course of justice or whatever it is. The Perjury Act of 1911 can make that pretty tricky, and I know the two men who were being accused of murder were not exactly exemplary characters, but there are the witnesses at the Magistrates' Court hearing as well. The court believed them then, there's no reason why they shouldn't again.'

'The maximum sentence in that case would be seven years,' said Sir Nicholas thoughtfully, 'as they had got to the point of giving their evidence on oath.'

'Yes, but . . . I know the two men originally accused say the charge was rigged because they wouldn't submit to extortion, but I don't see how they're going to prove that.'

'I have yet to hear the full details of the case against my clients,' said Sir Nicholas, 'and you keep talking about extortion, Antony, but under the Theft Act of 1968 –'

'Oh, good Lord, we're not coming up against that are we?'

'Certainly we are, though I can't see why that should distress you.'

'It doesn't really, except that when I first read the wretched thing I was under the impression that all crime of every kind had been abolished under it.'

Sir Nicholas looked at him for a long moment. 'Even for you that seems to imply an excess of stupidity,' he said in a repressive way. 'However, since then perhaps you have – ah – come to terms with it?'

'I've had occasion to.'

'Well, I can't see that the Theft Act had anything to do with the matter at all,' said Jenny indignantly. 'That isn't what poor Inspector Mayhew is being charged with.'

'The offence he's been charged with comes under that Act, love,' Antony explained, 'if the prosecution are really going that far. And Uncle Nick's only trying to point out that I shouldn't have said extortion, I should have said blackmail.'

'Well, I think extortion is much more expressive of what's supposed to have happened,' said Jenny sticking to her guns in a quite un-Jenny like way. 'And if you want my opinion I'll give it to you now. From what you've told me I don't believe for a minute that he'd have done such a thing.'

'That, my dear, is your privilege,' Sir Nicholas assured her. 'It is our duty, however, to consider every possibility in order to be able to advise our client to the best of our ability.'

'Our client?' said Antony suspiciously. 'Are you trying to tell me Bellerby's been talking about my "special talents" again?'

'The matter was mentioned, my dear boy,' said Sir Nicholas smoothly. 'I didn't disillusion him, though I admit nothing of the sort was in my mind. But you have been involved twice before in cases where an accusation was brought against a member or members of the Force and as you pointed out yourself this may have been what was in the Superintendent's mind when he spoke to you the other day.'

'Those cases were quite different . . . wrongful arrest. Well, one of them led to a charge of murder, but there's still no resemblance.'

'I should say myself that there was every resemblance,' said Sir Nicholas. 'Except that the Force themselves – with the agree-ment, as you pointed out, of the Director of Public Prosecutions – are bringing the case against their own men.'

'Think it's a good idea,' said Vera. Her eyes went from her husband to her nephew, two men as different as possible in appearance and character, but with an occasional similarity of expression, very evident at this moment, that made them look for an instant a good deal alike. Maitland had dark, unruly hair and a taste for the casual that had to be severely repressed on occasions when his professional duties made it unsuitable. He had a sense of humour that was inclined to surface at the worst possible moments, and far more sensitivity to other people's troubles than was good for him, though this latter attribute was as well hidden as he could manage and it had taken her some years to realise that for better or worse it was part and parcel of his make-up. 'Nicholas would be glad of your help, Antony,' she said.

Maitland gave her his sudden smile. 'You mean he wants somebody to do the dirty work,' he asserted. 'I don't need to point out to you, Vera, that he doesn't like my meddling, as he calls it.'

'May not be necessary in this case.'

'No, of course not. We don't know much about it yet, do we? But there's a more serious objection, which I'm sure has occurred

27

to both of you, and probably to you as well, Jenny love. As I understand it from Sykes, the new Assistant Commissioner (Crime), Sir Alfred Godalming, is a prime mover in this business, bent on cleaning up his department and making an example of Mayhew. You know what he thinks of me, very much what Briggs did . . . that I'll do anything at all, legal or otherwise, to get an acquittal. If he finds me appearing for the defence, even as your junior, Uncle Nick –'

'As an arrest has already taken place – I promised to attend the Magistrates' Court hearing tomorrow morning myself – I don't think that objection is valid,' Sir Nicholas told him.

'Then I'll put it even more bluntly. I don't think associating with me will do you any good in his eyes, Uncle Nick.'

'My dear boy, our association, as you call it, has been going on for thirty years. I admit Godalming is only interested in the period since you were called to the Bar, but he knows of our relationship perfectly well.'

'But –'

'The decision of course is yours, Antony, I shan't try to persuade you. I propose to call on Stringer, in any case, to assist us. If you think being involved in this matter would do you any harm –'

'It isn't that, Uncle Nick, you know it isn't that. You and Vera are the ones who are always uttering sibylline warnings about my getting involved with the police.'

'In this case, acting as my junior instead of leading for the defence, I don't think Sir Alfred will be in a position to find any cause for complaint. It may even,' he added, 'do your own reputation some good in his eyes if it is seen that I have no scruples about working with you.'

'Circumstances quite different,' said Vera. 'That is, if you're sure you were telling Sykes the truth when you said you knew nothing more than was revealed in court about that previous protection racket.'

'I was telling him the truth.' He caught Jenny's eye and laughed aloud. 'Don't they remind you of the Duke and Duchess of Plaza Toro, love?' he asked.

'I don't quite see –'

'The Duchess, actually. *I present any lady whose conduct is shady or smacking of doubtful propriety. When Virtue would quash her, I take and whitewash her, and launch her in first-rate society.*' (Vera grinned at that, and even her husband was surprised into a rather austere smile.) 'If you really think, both of you . . . but we don't know anything about the case yet really, it may be only a matter of appearing in court,' Maitland went on.

'That is exactly what I am proposing,' Sir Nicholas pointed out. 'However, if it's agreeable to you we'll leave the matter open. Attend the conference with our clients tomorrow afternoon in chambers, and see what you feel like after that. If you don't want to act I'll call on Derek, as I said, and we'll manage without your invaluable assistance.'

'All right, sir.' No use arguing the subject further, and perhaps his uncle and Vera had a point. 'But this blackmail business, that only stands on the words of the two men who were being accused of murder.'

'Patience, Antony. It's obvious they must have something more, and presumably Bellerby will be able to tell us about that tomorrow.'

'I can't see why the prosecution can't be content with perjury. I'm not saying I believe it, but it should be much more easy to prove.'

'To quote you, because Sir Alfred Godalming is out for blood. It is a matter of the possible sentence, you said you'd been looking it up so you should be familiar with what I'm trying to tell you.'

'Yes, but I thought extortion was out, because I didn't think there was any confirming evidence.'

'Very well then. Where conspiracy is concerned there is no limit to the fine or imprisonment that can be imposed, but only in exceptional circumstances should they exceed the normal sentence for the crime concerned. The key words there are "exceptional circumstances", which are certainly present where the police are accused of taking advantage of their official position. But think of your own first reaction, the jury will feel very much the same. If they were charged with perjury I might put up an argument on the lines you did – that is, if they decided to plead guilty. But where blackmail is concerned, nobody, including the judge who passes sentence, will have any sympathy at all.'

'Yes, I see.'

'In any case the maximum sentence for blackmail is fourteen years, where in the case of perjury it's only seven. But it's no use going on discussing the subject, Antony. You have been able to tell me a little more than I knew already, but we shall neither of us have any real knowledge until we have seen our clients and Bellerby tomorrow. Do you agree to be present?'

'Yes, of course I do, Uncle Nick.' Maitland gave the assurance without hesitation, and it was only much later, when he and Jenny were alone together upstairs, that he reverted to the subject. 'I should like to help, love, of course I would. But I can't help feeling that before we get to the end of this business Uncle Nick and I will be at cross-purposes in some way or another.'

Tuesday, 7th October

I

Sir Nicholas's request for bail had been successful, to Maitland's relief. Not that he had really doubted that it would be granted, but to be absolved from the necessity of visiting Mayhew and Harris in prison was undeniably a great relief.

The conference was called for three o'clock, and he went down the corridor to his uncle's room at about a quarter to the hour, not having seen Sir Nicholas at lunchtime and having only a message delivered through old Mr Mallory as to the time and place of the meeting. 'Is there anything I ought to know before we start?' he asked.

Sir Nicholas removed his spectacles and pushed aside the document he'd been perusing. 'I reserved our defence,' he said. 'Until Bellerby gets the papers from the prosecution I know no more than the bare outline that Sykes gave you.'

'But the blackmail, Uncle Nick. The D.P.P. would never have sanctioned a case being brought without some evidence to back the complainants' statements.'

'Two witnesses claim to have heard Mayhew instructing his younger colleague in the matter. A couple who were dining at the next table.'

'These conversations overheard in restaurants! Don't you think that's suspicious in itself, Uncle Nick? Mayhew would know better. Anyway, when did this occur?'

'Bellerby would have the exact date; after the murder, and before the charge against Barleycorn and Stokes was brought.' Sir Nicholas gave his nephew a long, considering look. 'It sounds to me, Antony, very much as though you were already half convinced that that other charge – the one against our clients – is a mistaken one. May I remind you, for perhaps the hundredth

31

time, that it is a mistake to go into any case of this sort with a pre-conceived notion of what really happened.'

'You don't need to remind me, sir, I know it well enough. You said a couple –'

'A man and his wife, Mr and Mrs Protheroe. He gave his occupation as a building contractor, and she described herself as a housewife. If you're really interested in them, it was her birthday – which is why they're so clear about the date – and they'd come up to town to have an early dinner together and go to the cinema afterwards. The film they wanted to see was being shown somewhere near Victoria, and that is how they happened to be in that district. I must tell you, Antony, they sounded to me to be a perfectly respectable couple, well-spoken and obviously well-read. They had not known, of course, that the two men they were listening to were police officers until they discussed the conversation later and decided that must be the case. Even then it wasn't until they read the account of the Magistrates' Court hearing that the full significance dawned on them, and they thought it their duty to come forward and make a statement, though I gather not immediately.'

'I see. Well, let's see what Mayhew and this other chap have to say for themselves before we pre-judge the matter,' said Antony, not altogether wisely; he watched his uncle stiffen and braced himself for a thunderbolt. Perhaps it was fortunate that at that moment the phone rang, and Hill announced apologetically from the clerk's office that Mr Bellerby and his clients had arrived.

Robert Bellerby was a solicitor whose motto, Antony always maintained, was kindness to clients, but for all that he knew his job and was extremely satisfactory to work with. He had always held a favourable view of Maitland's capabilities; not altogether undeserved, but sometimes a little exaggerated. He bustled in now with his two clients in tow. There was no need for introductions, except in the case of the constable, whom Sir Nicholas at least had never encountered. Maitland gave him a reassuring grin, and said, 'Considering the circumstances of our previous meeting, I remember you very well,' before retreating to his favourite place near the window overlooking the court below, where he propped one shoulder against the end of the bookcase and prepared to listen without committing himself to taking too

32

great a part in the proceedings.

Detective Constable Harris was frankly nervous, but seated himself obediently enough at Sir Nicholas's invitation. As for Detective Chief Inspector Mayhew, his expression was no easier to read than it had ever been, and it occurred to Antony suddenly to wonder whether he could be brought to fluent speech even in his own defence. He too seated himself, moving his chair slightly so that both Maitland and his uncle were within his line of vision, a fact of which perhaps Sir Nicholas alone was aware at that moment. Mr Bellerby, having got his charges safely bestowed, took a chair at the end of the desk nearest the door, which happened to be a favourite of his, and eyed Sir Nicholas expectantly.

'I imagine that in the short time since we met this morning nothing further has occurred that needs reporting to me,' said Sir Nicholas. 'I have asked my nephew to attend this meeting in the hopes that with his knowledge of police procedure there may be some way in which he can help us. But I have to make it clear that he has as yet accepted no brief in the matter, so if either of you gentlemen object to his presence –' He paused, letting his eyes move from Mayhew to Harris inquiringly.

The Chief Inspector gave his warning cough. 'I know Mr Maitland very well,' he said. 'Except for yourself, Sir Nicholas, there's no one I'd rather have in my corner.'

'And you, Mr Harris?'

The question seemed to release a flood of pent-up speech. 'Of course I'm glad he's here,' said Harris. 'We need all the help we can get, and the talk at the Yard is that he's sometimes pulled off acquittals where the cases seemed nearly hopeless. But it's all so damned unfair – every one of the witnesses was lying, and as for that man and woman at the restaurant I swear I never saw either of them before, and in any case the conversation they mentioned never took place.'

'We'll come to that all in due time, Mr Harris. The restaurant they mentioned was –?'

'Hartley's,' put in Mr Bellerby.

'Thank you. Yes, Hartley's. Have you ever been there?'

'I have, often,' Mayhew rumbled. 'Whenever I happen to be near the Yard when I'm working late. And while we were investigating this case and Harris was helping me I took him there more than once.'

'Including the day in question?'

'That I can't tell you. I'd have to consult my diary at the office and even then I could only say it was probable that we went there or that we didn't. It was all sprung on us you see: I knew there must be something because of the blackmail charge but I didn't know what it was.'

'The Protheroes didn't appear at the disciplinary inquiry?'

'No. The Magistrates' Court hearing when Stokes and Barleycorn were charged with murder was last Monday –'

'The twenty-ninth of September,' Mr Bellerby put in.

'And the Protheroes must have taken the rest of the week getting up their nerve to come forward, because apparently they didn't appear until the hearing ended at noon on Friday.'

'And when did you know you were to be charged?'

'Not till yesterday.'

'The whole affair seems to have been very rushed,' Mr Bellerby put in, a severe expression on his normally amiable face. 'I can only suppose that the decision had been made before, and that the actual nature of the charge was changed after the Protheroes came forward.'

'But it was all lies!' Constable Harris protested. Mayhew said nothing, but for a moment his eyes strayed from the group near the desk towards Maitland, still standing near the window.

'I should explain to you, Antony,' said Sir Nicholas (not that he imagined for a moment that his nephew's attention was straying, but it was possible that the two policemen might think so) 'that my clients pleaded Not Guilty in court this morning. Blackmail was added to the indictment as well as perjury, and as Mr Bellerby says, I imagine this was a last minute decision.'

Mayhew gave his warning cough. 'You'll believe me, Mr Maitland,' he asserted. 'I know there's been talk of police corruption, and where it occurs I'm all for its being stamped out, but this –!'

'My uncle has told me of the evidence given by the prosecution witnesses this morning,' said Antony, thinking it better not to mentioned his talk with Sykes. 'The thing we have to consider is what answer can you make to their charges?'

34

'Nothing but our word.'

Maitland smiled at him. 'You know enough about the laws of evidence, Chief Inspector –'

'You shouldn't call me that, I've been suspended.'

'Very well then, I'll try to remember. You know enough about the laws of evidence to know that we shall have to look for some support for what you say. Will you tell us now exactly what happened? I know you've been all over it already with Mr Bellerby, but it's important that Sir Nicholas and I should hear it for ourselves.'

'Yes, of course. But frankly, Mr Maitland, I don't see where this corroboration you talk about is going to come from.'

Antony didn't retort, as he might have done, you're the detective. He said only, 'Let's worry about that later,' and came across the room to join the group. There was no vacant chair except the arm chairs near the fireplace, a little removed from the rest of them, so he perched himself on the corner of the desk, to Sir Nicholas's annoyance. If Mayhew was going to regard him in the nature of a lifeline, a role he didn't appreciate in the slightest, it would be best to set the two accused men at ease as much as possible. 'Begin at the beginning,' he advised, 'and none of this I was proceeding down Piccadilly stuff. We're not in court yet.'

Mayhew smiled at him rather uncertainly and then turned back to his counsel again. 'Is that what you want, sir?' he asked.

'My nephew has his own ways of expressing himself,' said Sir Nicholas, 'but certainly that is what I want.'

'It started with the murder of a man called William Good-body,' said Mayhew. 'He kept a shop in the Bowes Park area; do you want the exact address?'

'Mr Bellerby will give us that,' Sir Nicholas assured him.

'Well, he sold sweets and tobacco and magazines and newspapers. A comfortable little business I should think, and that was borne out by what we saw of his home.'

'You haven't told us how he died,' Antony pointed out.

'No, it was a messy business. He was assaulted on his way home that night, it was a Monday, and beaten to death with repeated blows to the head. No one saw what had happened, or rather no one came forward then to admit having done so, but he must have died quickly from what the doctor said, and had been found within a very few minutes of the occurrence. The local chaps called us in right away, but they'd already searched the whole area pretty thoroughly, and though we went over it again no weapon was ever found. A door-to-door inquiry along the street was no more helpful, nobody had heard anything. One man did say he'd heard a car draw up with a squeal of brakes, but he hadn't noticed the time. It might have been the assassin or assassins suddenly spotting their victim – I had a feeling myself when I saw the body that more than one man had been involved, but there was nothing at all to prove that – but that was hardly helpful in identifying them. Detective Constable Harris was with me in all my inquiries –'

'Wait a bit!' Maitland interrupted him. 'You haven't told us –'

'No, but this part of the inquiry wasn't really relevant, nobody denies the poor chap was killed, and you'll see later why none of our colleagues can back up our stories.'

'Sorry. Go on.'

'This all happened in the evening at about seven-thirty.'

'Did he run the shop alone?'

'No, he had an assistant, but as Monday was always slack he'd given him that day off. A policewoman broke the news to Mrs Goodbody, and alerted the neighbours so they could see she was all right, and we didn't question her until the following morning. Policewoman Cole had told us she was hysterical, so it wouldn't have been much good going there before, but she was quite calm when we arrived. A neighbour, a Mrs Gower, was with her but she went home, rather thankfully I thought, when we arrived. I daresay she had affairs of her own to attend to.'

'You used the phrase "quite calm", Mr Mayhew. Would you agree with that description?' Maitland asked, turning to Harris. 'Not that I doubt your word,' he assured the older of the two detectives quickly, 'but you may have got the wrong impression and it's something we must be sure about.'

Mayhew nodded stolidly. It was quite impossible to tell what he felt. 'Oh yes, sir, that's exactly how she seemed,' said Harris quickly. 'I'm not saying she was – was callous or anything like that, she'd had time to get hold of herself, and some people are good at hiding it when they're hurt. But she was certainly quite calm, quite rational.'

36

'Thank you. Then we can get on to the point of what she had to tell you.'

'She said that her husband had been – scared out of his wits is how she put it – for the past year or eighteen months. At first she couldn't get out of him what was wrong, but then he told her that he'd been threatened with injury, or worse, if he didn't open an account with the Shadwell Confectionery Company and pay for what he'd bought regularly, not later than the first business day of each month, into their account at the Wood Green branch of the Northumbrian and Wessex Bank. If the account was rather larger than he expected he wasn't to complain to the firm, just pay up. It turned out the extra amount – goods he was billed for in excess of what he'd actually bought – wasn't a large sum, fifty pounds a month, but he was the sort of man, she said, who it galled to be put upon like that, and he was always threatening not to pay only she begged him to go on doing so. She didn't know whether he had made the payment the previous Monday, that is, the first of September, but she couldn't think of any other reason for anyone hurting him, so perhaps he hadn't done it after all. She was very vehement about that, that he had no enemies, and when we told her there was five pounds in his wallet and some silver in his pocket she said that would be about the most he'd ever carry on him. Saturday's takings would have been paid into the night safe at their bank, and he'd have left the small amount they took in on Monday in the safe at the shop. Sure enough, the money we found there tallied with the tape in the cash register. And that was really all she could tell us, I didn't want to put her to the trouble of coming down to the station, she seemed to have suffered enough already to my mind, so I asked her if it would be all right if Harris wrote out her statement then and there for her to sign. She agreed, and he did – exactly what she'd told us, isn't that so, Harris? – and that was that. Out next move naturally was to go to the bank she mentioned where the protection money had been paid.'

'Having first, I suppose, obtained a court order to examine the account,' said Sir Nicholas. 'But you haven't told us, Mr Mayhew, whether Mr Goodbody ever had dealings with this confectionery company or not.'

Again Mayhew smiled faintly. 'That would be to take my story out of chronological order, Sir Nicholas,' he said. 'Mrs Goodbody knew nothing at all about the business except what she'd just told us . . . or so she said,' he added rather doubtfully. 'Later . . . well, we had to change our opinion about the lady. We went back to the shop afterwards, of course, in the light of this new knowledge, but at the time I felt it was more important to confirm that there was such an account at the branch bank she mentioned. Then it would be time enough to obtain an order to examine the account in detail.'

'You're quite right, Mr Mayhew, take each step in order,' Sir Nicholas agreed.

'The manager was quite ready to confirm the mere fact that they had such an account there,' said Mayhew, 'and to give me the address of the company in Bermondsey, which in any case I could have found from the telephone book. We therefore went straight there and saw Mr Charles Shadwell, who both owns and manages the firm. He told us that they banked at the local branch of Bramley's, and that he knew nothing of the account at Wood Green. I can see now that we should have taken our inquiries straight to the accounts department, though even if we had done it would have made no difference to the conclusion we reached, but at that point examination of the account seemed urgent and I set in motion the necessary moves for getting permission to do so. Meanwhile – it was now fairly late in the afternoon – we went back to the shop. It had been under guard until we could get round to that, of course, and the assistant had been sent home when he arrived that morning.'

He paused there and Maitland took a moment to consider the implications of this uncharacteristic loquaciousness on the part of the silent man he knew. Something was prompting him to tell the story in as much detail as he could (it never occurred to Antony that it might be a desire to give him as much material to work with as was possible, if he decided to look into the matter himself). But whatever the cause, they were certainly getting their money's worth. 'What did you find there?' he prompted.

'Some of the products of the Shadwell Confectionery Company,' said Mayhew. 'Bars of chocolate, packages of sweets, not a great deal. And monthly receipts from the same company dating back to the beginning of 1974 and amounting to something in the

38

region of ninety pounds a month. Mrs Goodbody had mentioned fifty pounds as the protection payment, so I was beginning to smell a rat' – Maitland's eyes went involuntarily to his uncle's face, but Sir Nicholas remained unmoved – 'so I thought it was time we talked to this David Lindley, the assistant, so see what he could tell us. But first we looked in the back room –'

'The premises had been gone over previously, I presume, by your experts?' said Sir Nicholas.

'Yes, of course, but there was nothing to find, and we hadn't really expected there would be. The only papers in the desk in the little room he used as an office were bills and receipts, all very neatly docketed. We looked in the back room, a sort of storeroom, as I said, and among the packing cases waiting for disposal was one from Shadwell's, not a very large one.'

'And did this Mr Lindley have anything further to tell you?'

'One or two things. He had nothing to do with the ordering, or with the paying of bills: Mr Goodbody did all that himself. But they had a regular order from Shadwell, and it was one of his jobs to unpack it along with the other things that came in. It varied a little from month to month, according to the season, and according to how much they'd sold of the last one, and he'd never taken the trouble to work out how much what was there would cost, why should he? Could he list the contents of the last box he had unpacked, which he assured us was of more or less the same size as usual? Yes, he'd try, and we waited patiently while he did so, and even longer while he tried to remember the retail price of each item. That didn't get us very much further, because, of course, we'd none of us any idea what sort of discount these companies give their customers, but I was beginning to have a feeling we'd have a few more questions to ask Mr Shadwell. But there was one very funny thing.' He paused again, looking from one to the other of his hearers, and Antony obliged with the question that seemed to be needed.

'What was that, Chief Inspector?'

'Well, it was only later that we realised exactly how queer it was, but it fits in at this point so I'd better tell you. The previous Thursday Lindley had been in the office; Mr Goodbody had asked him to find a fresh roll of paper for the cash register, and that meant going to one of the drawers of the desk. He happened to notice a letter on top of it and read it – he says without thinking. It was on the Shadwell Company's letterhead, but hand-written, and it said something to the effect that they wished to remind Goodbody of the fact that his account was in arrears, and went on to say something about being unwilling to take further action because of their good relationship in the past. He was a bit surprised, because though he didn't know the exact amount of each month's order he was pretty sure it wasn't very large, and Mr Goodbody made something of a fetish of paying all his bills at the end of the month so it seemed odd that that one had been overlooked.'

Sir Nicholas frowned over the information. 'I think I begin to see how your mind was working, Mr Mayhew,' he said. 'Was the letter signed?'

'Yes, but Lindley didn't try to decipher the signature, all he could tell me was that it was a rather long one, and underneath it said 'Salesman'. The letter has never reappeared from that day to this, and the best he could give us, as I say, was a paraphrase of its contents. So we called it a day, and went back to the bank the next morning as soon as we had the necessary order.'

'This part at least of your story can be substantiated, I assume,' said Sir Nicholas. 'Other than by your young colleague, I mean.'

'Of course it's true,' said Harris, adding 'sir,' as an after-thought. 'I was with him all the time and I have to admit I didn't catch on to what was happening as quickly as the Chief did, but once we got the whole story it was perfectly clear.'

'Thank you, Mr Harris. You haven't anything to add to what Mr Mayhew has told us so far?'

'No,' said Harris. He sounded doubtful but went on more confidently, 'It's all exactly as he said except that . . . you didn't tell them, Chief, that David Lindley knew all the salesmen who called on them, at least by sight, and said he could identify the two men from Shadwell's.'

'That's right, so he did. Well as far as the bank was concerned the account was all fair and square. It had been opened by a man called Martin Kingsley, who described himself as the Treasurer of the Shadwell Confectionery Company and said it was for the convenience of some of the small local tradesmen who found it easier to pay in cash than to send the company a cheque. The manager admitted that it seemed to him an unusual arrangement, but obviously everything was above board, because all transactions were naturally entered in the account, and a statement was sent to the Head Office in Bermondsey, by arrangement, on the third business day of each month. He had naturally asked Mr Kingsley exactly how it was going to work from the company's point of view, and he said the accounts rendered could easily be checked against the statements. The manager gave us a list of all the people who used the account for paying in. Mr Goodbody of course was among them, and when he looked up the payment that he had made at the end of the previous month it was for thirty-eight pounds, seventeen.

'I see,' said Sir Nicholas. 'So your next stop, I imagine, was Bermondsey again.'

'Certainly it was. We asked for Mr Shadwell, and confronted him with what we had been told at the bank, He looked appalled, I think as a matter of fact that was quite genuine, but he confirmed that Martin Kinglsey was the Treasurer of the company, also the company's Secretary and acting as Personnel Officer. So of course I asked to see Kingsley.'

'From your expression, Chief Inspector,' said Antony, 'I gather we're getting to the really interesting part of the story. What had this descendant of Pooh Bah to say for himself?'

For a moment Mayhew looked puzzled, and Harris said in an urgent undertone, 'Gilbert and Sullivan, Chief. He was the Lord High Everything Else.' Which well-meant bit of helpfulness might easily have put anyone less stolid than Mayhew completely off his stride, but instead he remarked with the first touch of melodrama that he had introduced into his narrative.

'That's just it, Mr Maitland. He'd disappeared!'

'You'd better explain that a bit further,' Antony told him. 'Do you mean disappeared from his usual haunts and from the bosom of his sorrowing family?'

'No, he'd gone on holiday, and his wife with him. They had no children. The trouble was nobody seemed to know exactly where they were, though he'd talked about the Algarve in the office before they went. So that's when we got the accounts department into the act, with special reference to the statements received

41

from Wood Green.'

'How many people were concerned there anyway?'

'Twenty in all.'

'It doesn't sound –'

'Now *you're* going too fast, Mr Maitland.' Mayhew seemed pleased, in spite of his worried air, to be able to make the accusation. 'Wood Green wasn't the only branch of the Northumbrian and Wessex Bank involved: there were ten others as well, north of the river, and all with the same amount of people paying into them.'

'I have the details here,' said Mr Bellerby.

'Just at the moment, and with your permission, Uncle Nick, I think we can do without them.' Sir Nicholas smiled to himself, he was only too glad to see his nephew taking an active role. 'But what did the books disclose?' Antony demanded.

'None of the bigger chains of stores or supermarkets were involved in this rather unorthodox way of paying their bills, just the little shops on the corner, the ones that had to stay open to all hours to make a living at all,' said Mayhew. 'As far as all the members of the company were concerned – except one whom I'll come to in a minute – it all seemed above board. The salesmen send in their orders addressed to the packing department. There they're put up ready for despatch and a copy of the sales slip is sent to accounts where it's dealt with in the usual way.'

'Does the same person always make up the same orders?'

'Not necessarily, but the foreman in the department can allocate the work as he likes, and the others told me he always insisted on putting certain of the orders up himself. They just thought it was because they were the small ones, and involved less work than the others.'

'Well, what had he to say for himself?'

'That's the trouble, Mr Maitland – he was in an accident on the Tuesday night, the day after Goodbody was murdered. A car ran him down in Tower Bridge Road, and he died of his injuries.'

'An accident?' Antony's tone was incredulous.

'Hit and run,' Mayhew amplified. 'That's what they thought at the time, and there doesn't seem to be any hope of proving different. It would have been nice to question him, of course, but in a way it didn't set our inquiry back too much. There seemed

42

nothing out of the way with any of the accounts which were paid by cheque in the usual manner, but when we compared the different corner stores – the ones who paid directly into the bank and the ones who paid their accounts by cheque – you only needed half an eye to spot the difference. The pay-by-cheque ones would probably have a bill of around forty to fifty pounds a month, whereas the Goodbodys would be paying nearer a hundred, and some larger shops even more. It didn't need too much intuition to realise that they were paying protection money in addition to their genuine account. In each case the salesmen concerned were the same men I've mentioned, Stokes and Barleycorn.'

'I see. Have you made any calculations about this? And do you know what sort of commission they would be paid?'

'As for the calculations, Harris has done them.' Mayhew turned to smile at his younger companion, who pulled out his notebook.

'They weren't really difficult,' he said, 'if we rounded everything up to fifty pounds a month, which is the amount Goodbody was paying. A hundred and twenty little shops were involved, and the commission was twenty percent, less the amount of the transfers from Wood Green, which were supposed to represent a minimum amount on which to live in case they made no sales. Stokes and Barleycorn would be getting at least twenty-four thousand a year between them, in addition to their commission on the genuine sales. Not at all bad to my mind.'

'Not bad at all.' Antony smiled at him. 'What about the other eighty percent?'

'Swelling the firm's profits at the moment.'

'Kingsley didn't take it with him?'

'No.' Mayhew took up the tale. 'He went away for his holidays on the eighth of September, so we couldn't prove he'd skipped, but my theory was that he'd heard of the murder and decided to stay away. If that hadn't happened . . . well, the firm would be in a fine healthy state, and when he thought there was enough there to be worth the picking the Treasurer would be in the best position of anybody to take advantage of the fact.'

'Yes, that's very reasonable. But what about the small shops in other districts, whose payments were dealt with in the usual way? Wasn't a difference noticed between the size of their accounts and the ones we're talking about?'

'There was some speculation about it in the accounts department, but it was supposed that Stokes and Barleycorn were particularly good salesmen. Besides, of course, none of them knew the size or location of the stores that were turning in these large orders.'

'That would apply to Kingsley too.'

'Yes, I realise that now. Well, I realised it at the time too but the trouble is – and I still think I'm right about this – somebody at the company must be involved. If Stokes and Barleycorn were acting completely on their own they'd have no way of getting at the bulk of the profit, and Kingsley seemed and still seems to be the obvious person.'

'What about the foreman in the packing department, whatever his name was? How was he being paid off?'

'That's something we never discovered though he was certainly getting a rather larger bonus at Christmas than seemed to be justified. I assume he was involved, he had to be, and I'm afraid I decided that his share must be being stored up for him, probably to be paid out in a lump sum when Kingsley decided to make his exit.' He looked rather desperately from Maitland to Sir Nicholas and then at his solicitor. 'I told you, Mr Bellerby, I know it was guesswork but I believed that because it had to be true.'

'I'm sure Sir Nicholas and Mr Maitland will understand,' said Bellerby soothingly.

'And when they took their inventory,' said Antony rather quickly – he knew well enough his uncle's opinion of anything that seemed to be mere conjecture – 'wasn't it obvious that goods were being paid for that hadn't actually left the premises?'

'Apparently they expect some discrepancies. They make weekly deliveries to the larger stores, but the corner shops we were interested in dealt mainly in various kinds of sweets and chocolates. Mr Shadwell seemed resigned to the fact that some items like that would go missing, and was pleasantly surprised but not at all suspicious when a different situation was revealed. They'd take stock between Christmas and the New Year, while the rest of the operation was closed down, so there's only been one such occasion since the Wood Green account and the others were opened.'

'Were the other accounts you referred to opened at about the same time?'

'Yes, within a week or two.'

'Then I expect your next move was to chase up these two marvellous salesmen.'

'Stokes and Barleycorn,' Mr Bellerby put in.

'Yes, thank you. And you had a list of a hundred and twenty shops in various parts of North London –'

'That was the first thing we did, Mr Maitland – get inquiries started there. But as it was really Goodbody's murder we were investigating, not the protection business which it seemed must exist, we reserved the twelve stores in his neighbourhood who had been paying into the same bank for ourselves.'

'Naturally enough.'

'Yes, only as things turned out it wasn't such a good thing. No one was talking. They all dealt with the Shadwell Confectionery Company, the things they bought from them were very popular with children, and the grown-ups appreciated being able to buy a box of good chocolates, or something of the sort, when an anniversary was coming up, or something like that. They put in their orders each month, and received the goods and paid their bills, and that was that.'

'What about Stokes, then, and the man with the improbable name?'

'We looked in records first, and found them both there. They'd both been in trouble from time to time though nothing very serious. They're both in their early thirties; Stokes is a married man with two children and Barleycorn is single. Stokes has been had up twice as a pickpocket – he seems to have a good deal of manual dexterity because in neither case was the theft discovered till later, so goodness knows how many other similar instances he may have been involved in. The first time he was put on probation, and the second time – which was within the probationary period – he was sent down for six months.'

'Wait a bit! If he wasn't caught in the act –'

'Yes, I should have explained that. He doesn't seem to be a very bright character, because besides taking the cash, and the second man had quite a considerable sum on him as I remember, he tried to make use of the credit cards, which was where he

45

tripped up. In neither case did he try to deny his guilt once we caught up with him.'

'It's a fair cop,' said Antony smiling, 'but I don't suppose anybody says that any more.'

Mayhew took no notice of this attempt to lighten the atmosphere. 'Barleycorn was quite a different matter, a big bruiser of a fellow, a much tougher proposition. The only time he was ever inside was when he was in his late teens, and we managed to make a charge of breaking and entering stick –'

'That was presumably before your favourite, the Theft Act of 1968, was passed, Antony,' said Sir Nicholas with gentle malice.

'Yes, sir, of course it was.' Mayhew, not unnaturally, looked a little bewildered. 'All of thirteen or fourteen years ago. The thing was the M.O. He cased the joint, of course, and thought the owners would be away, but they changed their minds at the last moment. They came back from an evening out just as he was leaving with what cash he'd been able to find, and some small items of jewellery the lady wasn't wearing. But he'd been in the house for some little time, in the drawing-room apparently. There was an empty tumbler that had contained whisky beside one of the chairs, which hadn't been there when they went out, and the record on the hi-fi had been changed.'

'A musical burglar,' said Maitland, amused. 'That's a new one. Tell me, Mayhew, what are his tastes in music?'

'He seems to have a taste for military bands. That's why we're pretty sure he's been involved in a number of incidents since, always working alone . . . at least unless his companion took the trouble to wash up his glass. But no proof could be found at all. In each of the later cases, though, the owners of the house were actually away; sometimes there'd be cash to take, the people concerned said they liked to be sure of having something to come back to if they arrived at the weekend and couldn't get to the bank. Otherwise he'd take small items, easily disposed of.'

'Did any of them turn up again?'

'No. Which means, as you're about to point out, Mr Maitland, that he was in touch with a fence.'

'Yes, of course. So you went to see them?'

'We did, and I don't need to explain to any of you gentlemen that we were by now pretty sure there'd been a protection racket going on, in which they were employees rather than the prime movers because they'd no way open to them of getting at the funds in the firm, and that provided the motive for Goodbody's murder. I think it was a mistake now, but at the time it seemed we'd no choice but to put Mrs Goodbody's statement in front of them, and the other things we'd discovered about the differences between their accounts and other people's. We talked to Barleycorn first and took jolly good care he didn't have a chance to speak to his partner before we saw him too. But they both told precisely the same story. Mrs Goodbody was upset by her husband's death, gone a bit dippy was the way Barleycorn put it, and as for the rest of it they were salesmen for Shadwell and Company, working on commission though with a small guaranteed salary, and had been engaged by Mr Kingsley at the beginning of last year.'

'And what then?'

'We asked why they worked as a team instead of singly and Stokes said he preferred it that way. Jim Barleycorn would go over the stock with the owner, and he'd write down the items required as they were called out to him. Barleycorn, he said, was a shocking writer, but he was pretty good at pointing out what items any given shop was getting short of. As for Barleycorn, he says Stokes wasn't very bright mentally, but he found him very useful and had asked to take him on as a sidekick when Mr Kingsley offered him the job.'

'You asked for alibis, of course?'

'Naturally. Stokes said he'd been at home. The children were in bed, and the missus had gone to the bingo. Barleycorn had been doing a solitary pub crawl, nowhere near the place Goodbody was killed. Well, I don't need to tell you that. But though one or two people remembered him at the places he mentioned later in the evening, it didn't by any means constitute an alibi. I was a bit puzzled by that as a matter of fact, because usually these chaps can come up with somebody who's willing to swear to anything they may want to say.'

'Yes, that is interesting,' said Maitland, reflectively, and his uncle gave him a sharp look. 'You searched the houses, of course.'

'Of course, in the circumstances it wasn't difficult to get warrants, but there was nothing to be found in either case, nothing to connect them with the murder, that is.'

'Anything to show how they were spending the rather considerable sums of money they were earning?'

'Nothing at all. I'd say they were squirrelling it away, in the same way that I suspect Kingsley was doing, only in his case it was still safely in the firm's account where it couldn't be regarded as incriminating to him.'

'With the unfortunate Mr Shadwell paying tax on it, I presume. But that will wait. What had they both been doing before they went to work for that company?'

'Barleycorn said he'd been unemployed for nearly six years and before that he'd been a chucker-out at a pub down near the dock area which is no longer in business. Stokes had worked sporadically as a waiter – we were able to confirm that – though not in the best restaurants.'

'I can imagine,' said Sir Nicholas, 'that at this point you found the whole business rather frustrating. What did you do next?'

'Started on the list of people who had also paid into the Shadwell account at Wood Green and we were halfway down the list before we struck oil. This was a man called Peele, Andrew Peele, who actually lived in the same street as Goodbody, though his shop was a little further away. He didn't come out with it straightaway, but finally admitted that he too had been adding fifty pounds to the amount he really owed Shadwell's each month. I admit I was a bit surprised about that, because what had happened to Goodbody must have given the rest of the people in the same position a pretty good scare, but when he went on to say he'd actually come round the corner and seen the killing take place but been too afraid to say so before, I thought I saw daylight. If Barleycorn and Stokes were under arrest for murder they wouldn't be in a position to harm him, and he confirmed that a moment later by saying that he hadn't thought anybody would believe him, but now that it seemed we obviously suspected them perhaps we would. He knew both of them quite well by sight, of course, and was in no doubt at all about their identity. There was still some daylight left and he got a good look at them. It wasn't a busy street at the best of times, and at that hour most people had already got home and were having their supper. I asked if we could look over the shop, but there was nothing out of order there any more than there had been at Goodbody's. Still, I thought the point had come where we could put the statements up to the D.P.P. Peele came down to the station to sign his, and again it was Harris who drew it up. Not that that mattered much the way things went.'

'The arrest took place – let me see if I've got this right – on the twenty-sixth of September,' said Sir Nicholas. 'And at the Magistrates' Court hearing the following Monday –'

'It was . . . unbelievable,' said Mayhew, and paused as though at a loss for words to continue his story. 'Our first witness was Mrs Goodbody, and she appeared draped in black, the very picture of misery.'

'Like Niobe, all tears,' murmured Antony, and again was amused to see that though Constable Harris took the reference immediately, his superior officer looked momentarily puzzled.

'Well yes,' said Mayhew at last, 'but she wasn't crying too much to tell her story. And it wasn't at all the same one she'd given us. Just how she waited and waited for Willie that evening, and how dreadful it had been when someone came to break it to her that he was dead. The neighbours had been very kind. And of course next morning she'd have been only too glad to help us, only she was quite sure he hadn't had an enemy in the world, and when we'd asked her about his dealings with a certain firm – she seemed vague about the name, but agreed when she was reminded that it was the Shadwell Confectionery Company – all she could tell us was that she knew he'd had an account with them, and had told her their sweets were particularly popular with the neighbourhood children. Hawthorne, who was conducting the prosecution, produced her statement at that point and got permission to read it to her. She just looked round and said she'd never said anything like that, and when she was shown the signature she agreed it was hers, but she'd never read it over because she was quite sure the police wouldn't have put in anything she hadn't said. You can imagine the result that had.'

'I can indeed,' said Sir Nicholas seriously. 'You said, Mr Mayhew, that she was your first witness.'

'I'm sorry, sir, I meant after I'd made my statement of facts as we had discovered them, and Constable Harris had confirmed what I said. So then Mr Shadwell was called, and he did confirm

49

his statement insofar as it was the truth as he knew it at the time. Mr Kingsley had returned from holiday the day before, knowing nothing of what had been going on, perhaps he could best explain the matter. Which he did, and you know, sir, it might be an unusual arrangement but there was nothing illegal about it. He'd taken on Stokes and Barleycorn in the usual way, and if they were rather more successful than some of the other salesmen that was the firm's and their good fortune, and possibly because they were breaking new ground in North London. He hadn't felt it necessary to mention the arrangement to Mr Shadwell; the books were open to the auditors and the entire accounts department knew of it. At this point Mr Hawthorne asked the stipendiary Magistrate – it was Mr Nolan, I expect you know him, sir – if he might have time to confer with me, but Nolan wasn't having any of that. He asked how many more witnesses were to be called, and was told one, Andrew Peele. So he said something like, by all means let us hear what he has to say, and I don't mind telling you that put the fat in the fire properly.'

'Yes, Mr Mayhew, so I gathered, but I think we must trouble you to tell us exactly what his evidence was.'

'He said his dealings with the two defendants, and through them with Shadwell and Company, had all been perfectly above board. The products were popular, and he bought freely. As for the story of seeing the murder, if that had been true he'd have been at the police station right away. And he knew he'd signed a statement to that effect, but the officers who had taken it knew as well as he did that there wasn't a word of truth in it. The fact was, he'd been terrorised.'

'Was he alleging physical violence, or –'

'Something rather more subtle, sir. He said that though his dealings with most of his suppliers had been quite honest, as they had been with Shadwell and Company, he had taken part in certain cash transactions, the profits from which had not been declared for income tax. His shop dealt in groceries as well as sweets and tobacco, and sometimes there'd be a carton of canned goods for sale cheap . . . though he denied knowing where they came from, the obvious inference was that they were the proceeds of a hijacking or something like that. We'd threatened to expose him – he implied that he was more afraid of the income tax

50

authorities than he was of a charge of receiving stolen goods – if he wouldn't go along with us and sign the statement. But later, so he said, his better instincts prevailed and he realised he couldn't go on helping to frame two men he knew on such a serious charge.' Mayhew paused again, and again his glance went round the assembly. 'That's really all there was to it,' he said at last. 'Not unnaturally, they weren't committed for trial, and the disciplinary inquiry was convened the following day.'

'And when that was over –?'

'That was about midday on Friday. I understand the Commissioner and the A.C. were going to see the Home Secretary, to get his reaction to taking the matter to the D.P.P. I knew we were for it, and I thought the charge would be perjury, which was bad enough in all conscience, but then, of course – I'm not quite sure when – the Protheroes came forward. But there wasn't a word of truth in what they said, Sir Nicholas,' he added earnestly. 'Only of course the date they gave was after we'd seen Barleycorn and Stokes, when I was feeling, as somebody said just now, rather frustrated, and before we went to see Andrew Peele. I forgot to tell you that after we'd got his statement we did go to see the rest of the people concerned – I think I mentioned that he was about halfway down our list – but all of them denied there was anything irregular about their accounts at Shadwell's.'

'Was the matter of the accusation the two men made against you at the end of the Magistrates' Court hearing not brought up at the disciplinary committee?'

'Yes, sir, it was. That's what took so much time. But why I said I thought they'd stick to perjury was because there was no proof, until the Protheroes came forward.'

'Yes, I see.' Sir Nicholas's tone was quiet and even Antony couldn't have told you what his uncle was thinking. 'Well, it's a nasty business, and after we've discussed it there may be some more questions for you. Meanwhile, I should like you both to think the matter over very carefully, and see if there isn't someone – one of your colleagues for instance – who can confirm what you say. Not in all particulars, perhaps, but in part at least.'

'I discussed it with Superintendent Sykes while our inquiries were in progress,' said Mayhew, 'but he only knows what I told him. And the other men who went out on inquiries, I explained to you that none of them found proof of anything wrong, so I don't see how that would help.'

'Neither do I at the moment.'

'Just a minute, Uncle Nick, there are a couple of questions I'd like to ask,' Maitland put in. 'The first one is, have the Goodbodys any family?'

'Yes, two sons and a daughter, and a number of grandchildren – I'm not quite sure how many.'

'I see. And the other thing is, have I got the date right? It was in January of last year that this rather unorthodox way of making payments was instituted by Martin Kingsley?'

'Yes, I'm quite sure of that. Do you think that might help?'

'I'm sure my uncle will do whatever can be done with it,' said Antony smiling from him to Harris. 'With the fact that it was a rather unorthodox proceeding, I mean. But I'd be lying if I told you to rely too much on that; the rest of it is pretty damning, and it seems we have only your word, your account of what really happened to put against it.'

'Yes, I realise that. I'm only sorry . . . but that's beside the point. What do you think though, now that you've heard what we have to say. Are you going to take a hand, Mr Maitland?'

'That depends on Mr Bellerby.'

'Yes, of course I know that, but –'

'I'm sure Sir Nicholas told you, Mr Maitland,' said Bellerby, 'that I feel there may be some use here for your special talents.'

To which Antony replied, 'Very well,' meekly, and tried to avoid his uncle's eye.

II

A quarter of an hour later, when the three visitors had gone, Antony went back to his post beside the window again and watched until he had seen them cross the court. Then he said without turning his head, 'It's what Sykes would call a moocky business, Uncle Nick.'

Sir Nicholas had remained seated at his desk, and a parade of ducks, each one wearing a policeman's helmet, was beginning to form on the pad in front of him. He said without looking up, 'But one in which I gather you have decided to involve yourself.'

'That's what you wanted, isn't it?'

'Yes, I think so, if it were just a matter of appearing with me in court.'

'Bellerby's expecting something more than that.'

'Yes, and I have the uncomfortable feeling, Antony, that something has struck you, that you've seen some opening in what otherwise seems a perfectly blank wall. Heaven knows I don't want to go into court with nothing but our clients' denials, but what exactly are you proposing to do?'

'I told you what Sykes said to me the other day. About this business he had some small facts wrong, which isn't surprising when he'd only heard the story at second hand, but I meant that he wanted to know about the money that was being extorted for protection from various sources up to the time Jim Arnold was arrested. He'd been a victim, and when he was tried in October 1973 there was a good deal of publicity.'

'Which you, if I remember rightly, engineered yourself,' said Sir Nicholas rather coldly.

'Only to get public sympathy on his side, Uncle Nick. I thought it might do some good,' said Antony quickly. 'But don't you see where that leaves us?'

'If you're going to tell me that Sykes was right, and you did know something more about the background –'

'No, sir, nothing like that. I'm just thinking that up to two years ago there were those two people organising the business, if you can call it that, with just the two employees, Alf and Stan, and then all of a sudden one of them was dead and the other three in prison, and the field was wide open for someone else to step in.'

'I don't quite see what you have in mind.' Sir Nicholas sounded more cautious than irritable now.

'In this day and age there's more than one gang operating in London, and one at least I know of whose operations have a very wide scope. I wonder Sykes didn't think of them himself, but he's always so busy wondering what I'm hiding –'

'I might have known it!' said Sir Nicholas despairingly. 'When I asked you to join me in this matter, I had your assurance that you knew nothing relevant. It was not my intention that you should mix yourself up with the criminal classes. Also I think – if you'll forgive me saying so, Antony – that you are reading rather too much into the conjunction of dates. Just because the operations of the previous –'

'Gang,' said Antony helpfully, when his uncle seemed to be hesitating for a word.

'Gang then, if you must have it so.' Sir Nicholas sounded tried almost beyond endurance. 'You are suggesting that because their operations concluded in October 1973, and this man Martin Kingsley may have commenced a similar activity in January 1974 . . . I have to tell you frankly that even for you that is carrying conjecture rather too far.'

'Don't you see, sir, it's a possibility.'

'A possibility, perhaps,' said Sir Nicholas, stressing the word. 'Is this what was in your mind when you agreed to take a brief in this matter?'

'Partly,' Maitland admitted. 'And partly what I know of Mayhew, and what I observed of his attitude today.'

'You're going too fast for me, Antony. I admit I don't know the Chief Inspector as well as you do –'

'No, but have you ever known him so talkative?'

'On the occasions I have met him he has generally been in a subordinate position, when silence was only to be expected. He's quite capable of giving evidence in court, as I know from my own observation, without too much hesitation.'

'Yes, I know that. I've seen him in those circumstances too. And I'll tell you what I think, Uncle Nick, and you can blast me as much as you like for jumping to conclusions when I've finished. I think if Mayhew had any funny business in mind, Detective Constable Harris is the last person he would have chosen as his partner in crime.'

'That is certainly carrying the facts as we know them to a rather far-fetched conclusion.' But it was obvious that Sir Nicholas's interest was caught. 'I think you'd better explain yourself, Antony.'

'I don't think I can at the moment, but all the same I'd lay a small bet you'll find I'm right. And that being so I think, sir, that a few inquiries might be in order.'

'If you can see any scope for such activities,' said Sir Nicholas,

'I should like very much to know what's in your mind.' He laid a hand for a moment on the pile of papers Bellerby had left behind (before they left chambers to go home they would be scattered in a glorious confusion over his desk). 'As far as I can see, every conceivable witness is being called by the prosecution, leaving you with no-one at all on whom to exercise your talent for asking questions.'

'I wouldn't say that. We've one witness, Uncle Nick, with one small shred of evidence, Goodbody's assistant, David whatever-his-name-is. But I really meant I'd rather like to talk to Mrs Mayhew, and it might be interesting to see Harris separately. He very properly kept in the background today, but he may have some helpful ideas on the subject.'

'If he has I've no doubt he would have confided them in the Chief Inspector. However I can see no great harm to either of those two interviews, even if I can't see any good either. I should be obliged, however, if you'd be a little more open with me, Antony.'

'You won't like either of the other two things I have in mind,' said Maitland frankly.

Sir Nicholas smiled with one of his swift reversals of mood. 'I've no doubt you're right about that,' he said, 'but all the same I should like to know. After all, if anything comes of these ideas of yours you'll have to tell me sooner or later.'

'Yes, but if nothing comes of them . . . what the eye doesn't see the heart needn't grieve over.'

'If you must be quite as trite as that you might at least be accurate,' Sir Nicholas told him. 'It doesn't seem as though you're going to give me the opportunity of seeing anything.'

'Well, sir, though Father William has a high regard for you I imagine he'd talk more openly if I saw him alone . . . don't you think?'

'That old reprobate.'

'I like him,' said Maitland simply. 'And I think he has a certain affection for me, though I daresay you'd say that was misplaced. Anyway he knows a good deal of what goes on –'

'In his own line of business,' said Sir Nicholas. His tone was repressive again. 'I've never heard that he'd mix himself up in anything quite so unpleasant as this seems to be . . . if we are to

55

believe our clients, that is.'

'He hears a good deal that goes on,' repeated Maitland stubbornly.

'Do you think, in the circumstances, it's a very good idea for you to see him just now?'

'I don't see why not. A social call, that's all. Nothing to do with the matter in hand, even if I am hoping he might give me a lead.'

'And the other line of inquiry you feel might be worth following?'

'I have to see Sykes again about that. Not that I think he'll help me – he refused point blank to do so once on a similar occasion.'

Sir Nicholas's eyes narrowed with suspicion. 'I've said already that the last thing I had in mind when I suggested your joining me in this case was that you should mix yourself up with the criminal classes. Father William is one thing, he may harm your reputation but he won't do you any physical damage. The last time you went north it was to investigate a contract killing. The man concerned is dead but . . . am I to understand you feel Sykes might put you in touch with his associates?'

'No, I don't think he will, but there's no harm in asking. All he would tell me was that they were completely unscrupulous, and they engage in pretty well every kind of racket – oh, well, activity if you prefer it – that might have some profit in it. But even if he refuses I've just one lead. Porson – that's the man I came up against in Arkenshaw – was married, and I may be able to trace his widow, perhaps with no more difficulty than by looking in the phone book. Sykes admitted he felt she knew something about her husband's activities, but even if she didn't she must have known who his friends were.' He broke off and added with rather an apologetic look, 'I told you you wouldn't like it, Uncle Nick.'

'That,' said Sir Nicholas, 'is the understatement of the year. You said yourself that these people were not the only ones in London indulging in organised criminal activity, and to expose yourself on what is no more than guesswork –'

'That's all very well, Uncle Nick. Don't you think Mayhew and Harris have their point of view?'

'Of course they do, but this is sheer lunacy.'

'I don't think it is, but in any case it's the only lead I've got, so I must play it for all it's worth.'

'You sound unusually sure of yourself, Antony.'

Maitland thought about that for a moment. 'I suppose I do,' he said, 'and I can't for the life of me tell you why. But there can't be any harm in at least some preliminary inquiries, and in asking Bellerby to put Cobbolds or some other firm of inquiry agents on to finding out a little more about Martin Kingsley. We can neither of us see him until we get into court, but there's at least a possibility he might lead us to his principal.'

'You don't think then that he himself might be the prime mover in this matter?'

'No, I think it was somebody already up to his neck in dirty work who read about Jim Arnold's trial and saw the possibilities for one more profitable line of business. And that's guesswork too, Uncle Nick, so you needn't point it out to me. But what I started to say was that if I find any reason at all to believe I'm right, Cobbolds can take it from there.'

'I still don't like it, Antony.'

'Come now, sir, you've always told me when we've worked together before that you won't go into court with nothing but a bare denial on the part of your clients.'

Sir Nicholas smiled without much amusement. 'That's true enough,' he admitted. 'May I point out to you, however, that I should also have the greatest objection to having to get up in court and announce that my learned junior was unable to attend because he was either in hospital or in the morgue.'

'I've no intention of doing anything foolish, Uncle Nick. Just a few preliminary inquiries,' he added persuasively. Suddenly his uncle laughed.

'I see there's no turning you from your intention,' he said, 'though like Superintendent Sykes, I can't help feeling you know rather more than you're telling me.'

'No, really, Uncle Nick –'

'Very well, we'll leave it there for the moment. But you must understand this, Antony. I shall want a full report of every step you take and if I don't like what's going on –'

'You'll issue an ultimatum,' Maitland agreed. 'That's fair enough.'

'It would be if I thought it would be the slightest use,' Sir Nicholas grumbled. 'Well, I brought this on myself and I supppose I shouldn't complain. Knowing you I should have guessed how it would be. If you want to see Harris again and talk to Mrs Mayhew you'll have to see Bellerby, so can I leave it to you to make the arrangements with him about putting the inquiries you mentioned in hand?'

As this was just what Maitland wanted he agreed quite readily. 'As for the rest of it,' he said, 'who lives may learn. But I don't think we need mention my own inquiries to Jenny or Vera . . . not just yet at least.'

III

Tuesday evening was by long tradition the night when Sir Nicholas dined with the Maitlands, and since his marriage, of course, Vera had also been a member of the party. Sir Nicholas and his nephew, therefore, left chambers together, and being informed by Gibbs – who was as usual hovering at the back of the hall hoping for something to complain about – that Lady Harding was already with Mrs Maitland, they made their way upstairs immediately. Jenny had long since got used to legal shop, and would in fact have missed the arguments which so often raged about her; while as for Vera, her own career had left her with an insatiable appetite for such matters. Besides, both men valued her opinion, so it was natural that the talk turned almost immediately to the day's events.

For once in his life Maitland was relieved to find that he had no explaining to do. Sir Nicholas related the story succinctly, and finished by saying, 'Antony, as we might have expected, made up his mind on no grounds at all that our clients are innocent, and decided to associate himself with me in their defence. Unfortunately for him the matter gives him no scope at all for meddling, but I shall be glad of his help as well as Stringer's in preparing the case.' After that the subject was dropped, Sir Nicholas having decided long since that the dinner table was not a suitable venue for such discussions. Afterwards Vera announced that it was an evening for Beethoven and Antony was glad enough to oblige her. By the time the Hardings finally left the matter of the case against Mayhew and Harris hadn't once been reverted to.

Jenny returned to it, however, as soon as they were alone together. 'I thought Uncle Nick was rather offhand about it,' she said. 'Does that mean he doesn't agree with you that they're innocent?'

'He'd tell you he was keeping an open mind,' Antony assured her, 'and actually it's much more sensible than my own attitude, because I can't explain what persuaded me that they are.'

'It isn't like you to be so sure,' said Jenny, who knew her husband very well, and was quite aware of the difficulty he usually had in convincing himself that his instinct was, on the whole, reliable. She realised, though he did not, that it was generally himself he was doubting, rather than the person or persons he had decided to put his trust in. But on this, as on so many other matters, Jenny kept her own counsel.

'Well, I hope you'll be able to get them off then,' she said. And began to clear away the coffee cups and glasses. 'But you know, Antony,' she added, not looking at him, 'I did get the impression somehow that Uncle Nick was worried about your taking part.'

'Not worried exactly,' said Maitland, who would have admitted to some scruples about telling a direct lie, even in a good cause. 'He doesn't see what we can do, and he hates going into court with no evidence at all to back up his clients' plea. Besides,' he added, seeing her sceptical look and realising that a measure of frankness might serve his purpose best, 'I want to go to see Father William – there's just a chance he might have heard some gossip that would be helpful, and you know how Uncle Nick feels about that.'

Jenny gave him a long, candid look. 'Well, give my love to Father William when you see him,' was all she said, and picked up the tray in a determined manner. 'I know he's an old sinner, but he is rather a dear.'

Downstairs, Vera had been putting her husband through much the same kind of catechism, and had succeeded in being answered with rather more candour. 'Thought it was all for the best when we suggested he should join you,' she said sadly, 'but there's no stopping him if he's got the bit between his teeth, I know that.'

She was the only person close to him from whom Sir Nicholas would accept colloquialisms without protest. Now he only said, 'I think it very likely he won't get anywhere, so we must just hope for the best. Though whether it's the best for Antony or the best for our clients,' he added doubtfully, 'I really can't tell you.'

Wednesday, 8th October

I

There were a number of things awaiting Maitland's attention the following morning in chambers, though none of them would take him into court before the following week at the earliest. A certain show of diligence was, however, desirable in the interests of keeping old Mr Mallory happy.

Antony sometimes wondered how he would have felt when he joined his uncle's bachelor establishment at the age of thirteen if he had realised how many people, already well set in their ways, his coming was going to affect over the course of the years. Mrs Stokes had taken the upheaval fairly well, his only complaint about that being that whenever he came within her orbit she insisted on his drinking vast quantities of milk, and after his marriage he had suffered the same treatment for several years from Jenny, who had apparently been terrorised into believing that this regime was necessary if he was to maintain his health. Gibbs however, a saintly looking man with a far from saintly disposition (unless you could so categorise his obvious enjoyment in playing the martyr) had disapproved from the beginning, his disapproval reaching a sort of crescendo when the upstairs flat was made; and though of course the matter was never brought into the open he had a variety of different ways of showing what he felt.

Sir Nicholas's clerk, Mallory, whom Antony always thought of as old, had probably really been quite young when first he knew him; in any event his appearance hadn't changed in the slightest over the years. He had borne with apparent equanimity the boy's frequent visits to chambers during his school holidays, but later when Maitland left the army and started reading law he would shake his head sadly and tell his cronies, 'That young man is going to be a disruptive influence.' And how right he had been, as Antony, if he had heard of it, would have been the first to agree. But he bore up well enough under all this weight of disapproval, and only when he was tired and the nagging pain in his shoulder that never quite went away had become almost unbearable did it sometimes seem to him rather more than anybody could be expected to bear.

So this morning, in the interests of peace, he settled himself at his desk and allowed half an hour to pass before he picked up the telephone and asked Hill to connect him with Mr Bellerby. The clerks' office had an awkward habit of knowing everything that was going on, but a discussion with the instructing solicitor in a case in which his uncle was also involved could hardly be taken amiss. While he waited he riffled through the pages of the telephone directory, reciting the alphabet to himself as he did so, until he found the names beginning with the letter P. And sure enough he came across *Porson, Edwin* and an address in Fulham. There was a chance of course that the widow had moved, but it hadn't been quite a year. . . .

His reflections were interrupted by his call coming through, and he jotted down the address while he exchanged greetings with the solicitor. Mr Bellerby sounded cheerful, but that wasn't surprising. He was an optimist by nature, and, Maitland sometimes thought, of altogether too charitable a disposition for the profession he had chosen. Or perhaps credulous would be a better word. It was odd really that he had elected to develop a mainly criminal practice, but it was undeniable that he was extremely successful, certainly on his clients' behalf, and probably also on his own.

'It's good to hear from you, Mr Maitland,' he said as soon as his first exuberance had expended itself. 'You know I was relieved when you took the brief. What can I do for you?'

'One or two things, but I think I ought to explain to you that I don't feel the matter leaves us with very much scope for inquiry.'

He could imagine well enough how Bellerby's round, cheerful face fell into an expression of gloom. 'But you know Chief Inspector Mayhew,' he protested. 'He was so very sure that you at least would hear his story sympathetically.'

'Well I did, though I don't know why he should have come to

61

the conclusion that I'm unusually credulous,' said Antony a little sourly. 'However, that isn't the trouble. At present we have a case – and I haven't looked yet at the papers you left with my uncle but I'm sure they'll bear me out – with a long list of witnesses for the prosecution, and nobody at all to speak for the defendants except themselves. And Mr Goodbody's assistant, of course, but his evidence only confirms theirs on one tiny point. A few character witnesses too, I daresay, but you know how much good they are.'

'Yes,' said Bellerby despondently. 'But I must say I hoped, Mr Maitland, that with your ingenuity you would be able to come up with some line to follow.'

'A couple of things, as I said, but not exactly ingenious,' Antony told him. 'First, I believe you use Cobbolds when you want any inquiries done.'

'Yes, I do. They're very reliable.'

'I know that. The thing is, Mr Bellerby, I can't approach this man Martin Kingsley myself for obvious reasons, but if we take Mayhew's story as true and assume that a protection racket has been going on, he's one person who must have been involved in some way. I'd like to know a little more about him, and about the head of the firm too, I suppose, though I'm not so sure he's involved. Will you put that in hand?'

'Certainly I will. But is that all we can do?'

'Cobbolds's report may suggest some further lines to follow,' said Antony in as reassuring a tone as he could manage. It was odd that so experienced a lawyer as Mr Bellerby should arouse in him a sort of protective feeling, as though the other man was in some way vulnerable. But one thing was certain, he wasn't going to mention Father William, and he wasn't going to say a word about the gang Porson had belonged to until he had a good deal more to go on. 'There are two things I'd like to do as soon as possible though; see Mrs Mayhew, and talk to Detective Constable Harris on his own.'

Bellerby chuckled, immediately reassured. 'I always knew you had a theory that people spoke more freely if you saw them alone than when a third person was present.'

'How well you know me. If I was acting alone in this case, and not with my uncle, I'd have told you what I was doing, of course, and then made my own arrangements. But Uncle Nick is such a stickler for propriety – ' He broke off there, and did not add that at the moment Sir Nicholas had an additional worry concerning his own standing with the police, and in particular with the Assistant Commissioner.

'I should have thought he'd have been used to your ways by now,' said Bellerby, who was one of the few people who never seemed to object to Maitland's excursions into the unorthodox from time to time. 'However, I think we can get round that easily enough. If I make appointments for them to come here – could you manage this afternoon? – I can easily make up some excuse for you to be alone together.'

Antony's thanks were cordial. 'This afternoon would do splendidly,' he added. 'If you can arrange it will you phone and leave a message as to the time?' They rang off a few minutes later, each understanding the other well enough.

Sir Nicholas wasn't in court either, and true to his forebodings Antony found the desk strewn with an untidy litter of papers when he went along to see if his uncle was ready to go to lunch. None of the clerks ever dared to deal with this confusion, but over the years Antony had fallen into the habit of straightening things up himself, and after the first rather vehement protests Sir Nicholas had suffered his ministrations quietly enough, so that Maitland could only suppose he found them useful. Today he separated Regina vs. Mayhew and Harris from a case connected with an alleged insurance fraud, and one concerning public mischief. 'It ought by rights to be affray,' said Sir Nicholas, watching him, 'but the prosecution's case is so weak I imagine they felt the jury might be more likely to convict on a lesser charge.'

'It sounds faintly improper,' said Antony sanctimoniously. 'Are you ready for lunch, Uncle Nick?'

'That would be very pleasant, so long as you don't intend to edify me over the meal with your wild ideas about the Mayhew case.'

'I won't even mention it. In fact the only thing there is to say about the matter can be done in thirty seconds. I've arranged with Bellerby to talk to Mrs Mayhew, and to Harris – not together, of course – at his office this afternoon.'

'That sounds innocuous enough,' said Sir Nicholas, getting to his feet. 'Very well then, let us fortify ourselves. I don't imagine you'll enjoy either interview very much.'

II

Sir Nicholas was right about that, Maitland wasn't looking forward to the afternoon with any pleasure at all. He walked straight round to Mr Bellerby's office when they had finished their meal, and found that Mrs Mayhew had already arrived. That in its way was a relief, at least he'd be getting the worst over first.

The solicitor was as good as his word, he had done no more than perform the introductions when his phone rang, he answered briefly, and then excused himself on the grounds that some unexpected emergency had arisen. Antony repressed a smile, having a theory – privately held for the sake of peace and quiet – that anything urgent in a solicitor's office was automatically put away in the back of the safe for three weeks or so to mature. He made some appropriate remark however and watched Mr Bellerby go with satisfaction.

Mrs Dorothy Mayhew was a tallish woman with dark curly hair and a momentarily solemn expression superimposed on a face that looked as if it were made for laughter. She wore no make-up, and her navy blue dress had a faintly dowdy look. She turned to Antony eagerly as soon as the door was closed. 'I'm so glad to meet you, Mr Maitland, and to know you're going to help Laurie. I've heard so much about you from him.'

Ordinarily that was the sort of remark that would have annoyed Antony intensely, even if he managed not to show it. At the moment, however, his main feeling was one of curiosity. 'Heaven and earth!' he said blankly. 'What on earth could he find to say about me?'

'He doesn't talk about his cases at home,' she assured him. 'Only sometimes when they're over. But he did tell me about the trouble you've had over the years with Chief Superintendent Briggs, and how it all ended. It used to worry him, because he was quite sure of your honesty.' She broke off and added with a laugh that somehow succeeded in sounding extremely embarrassed, 'I'm putting that badly, I don't mean to offend you. But when all this came up he said he was sure you'd be the one person who could help him.'

One thing Antony was sure about, this woman wasn't trying to soften him up. For once in his life he found himself at a loss for words. 'I didn't know Mayhew's name was Laurie,' he said, rather as though some important fact had been revealed to him.

'It's Laurence actually, but everyone calls him Laurie. I am glad to meet you, as I said before, Mr Maitland, but how on earth can I help?'

'I don't know that you can.' He spoke slowly and refrained from adding what was foremost in his mind, I don't know if anybody can. But it wasn't fair not to warn her. 'It's a difficult matter, and there's very little to go on. I'm not saying something may not turn up, but I don't want you to count on it. When we get into court my uncle's as good as they come. That's a thought to hang on to, more than anything I can achieve beforehand.'

'Very well, I will.' She looked at him more closely for a moment. Mayhew had always spoken of him as a man with what some people thought of as an exaggerated sense of humour, but there was something else as well . . . a sensitivity . . . and some emotion stronger than both those things that worried her, though not, strangely enough, for herself or her husband.

Antony was almost unaware of her scrutiny. He was himself assessing her as he would have done a witness in court, and liking what he saw. 'Did your husband talk to you about this case, the one that's causing all the trouble now?' he asked.

'Not until after the Magistrates' Court hearing where those two men were charged. He had to then, everything went wrong, and then for them to get up and say that he and Gerry had tried to get money out of them – ! I'd known Laurie was engaged in the case, of course, because he works all hours when there's something important like that. I knew he was worried about it, too, but not so much as he was about the inquiry later, and then the charge, with two witnesses coming forward to say they'd heard him telling Gerry about the blackmail.'

'Gerry? Is that Constable Harris?'

'Yes, it is. I'll tell you something, Mr Maitland. Laurie's almost more sorry about having dragged him into this than he is about the charge against himself. We've saved a bit of money, having no children of our own, not much, but enough to start a small business . . . perhaps the traditional country pub that policemen are always supposed to retire to. But Gerry – it's Gerard really, but like Laurence that's such a mouthful – is just starting out, and to see his whole career wrecked is rather dreadful.'

'I . . . yes it must be.' She didn't realise – she couldn't talk like that if she realised – that what was involved for both men was not just dismissal from the Force but a really hefty prison sentence. Not that he blamed Mayhew for keeping that aspect of the matter from her as long as he could, though he remembered suddenly that for years he had done the same sort of thing with Jenny until he realised that the unkindest thing he could do was to keep things from her. Which was just what he'd been doing in this case, but that could be remedied. However, as between the Mayhews there was nothing he could do. 'You know Constable Harris fairly well then?' he asked.

She smiled faintly, as though the question or the answer she was about to give gave her some pleasure. 'In a sense I've known him since he was born,' she said, 'though I hadn't seen him since I married twenty years ago until he was transferred to Central. My father was Head Gardener to his grandfather,' she added in answer to Maitland's inquiring look, 'and always thought the world of the family. It's queer how things work out, Gerry's the only survivor and hasn't a penny to bless himself with, while Dad has his own nursery business and is doing extraordinarily well.'

Antony was aware of a sudden sinking of his spirits. 'Are you telling me that Detective Constable Harris comes from a wealthy family who have somehow lost their money?' he asked, but went on, apparently taking her assent for granted, 'How did that come about?'

'Death duties,' she said simply. 'His grandfather died – well that was in the course of nature as they say, he was an old man. But then his father and two older brothers were killed in a motor crash, one of those pileups on the M1 in a fog, when Gerry was in his last year at school. I shouldn't have said he was the only one left, because there's his mother, and there was enough when everything was sold up to buy her a tiny annuity. But he supports her now rather than the other way round. I don't know what got into him to join the Force, but someone must have seen right from the start he was an intelligent boy. I think he was transferred to the C.I.D. as an aide quite quickly, and when the posting was confirmed he was transferred to London. That's when Dad gave him our address and told him to get in touch with us. Of course Laurie couldn't show him any favouritism at work, he takes his turn with the routine jobs the same as anyone else and it was just bad luck that he happened to be what he will call Laurie's sidekick on this particular job. But of course there was nothing to say we couldn't know, him socially, and he was as homesick as anyone I've ever seen when he first arrived in town. In a way,' she went on, and gave Antony a quick look as though wondering what effect her words would have on him, 'he became the son we were never able to have. I wonder if you understand that, Mr Maitland.'

'Very well indeed,' said Antony with truth, and he was thinking of Jenny as he spoke. But the brief silence seemed to disturb Dorothy Mayhew, and he went on quickly and as casually as he could make the words sound, 'I suppose he was expecting to go to university and train for one of the professions.'

'Yes, that's right. Your own line, Mr Maitland: he wanted to be a lawyer. Come to think of it I daresay that's why he chose the police when there wasn't any money left for his training and after a while I don't think he regretted it too much, or didn't until all this happened. For all his education there've never been any airs about him.'

'Why should there be?' He smiled at her. 'I'm sure he's appreciated your kindness, Mrs Mayhew.'

'It wasn't all one-sided, he's a good boy,' she insisted. 'But you see now why Laurie's so upset, wrecking everything for him before he's even got started.'

'Yes, of course. There's something I forgot to ask your husband, Mrs Mayhew, and it may seem like a great impertinence but I assure you it's important for my uncle to know it before we go into court. Did the police ask permission, or get an order to examine your bank account or accounts? And look into your financial affairs generally.'

'Yes, they asked, and we gave them permission readily enough knowing there was nothing out of order.'

'I'm sure there wasn't. But you see this – this dereliction of duty your husband's accused of, if it were true it would be unlikely that it was an isolated incident. That's why it's important.'

'There were just the two accounts,' she told him readily enough, 'both in our joint names. The current account, well there's not much there, and though I told you we've got a bit put away on deposit the passbook shows it's gone in over the years in dribs and drabs. And that's the whole story, we've never gone into any investments as such. Laurie always says it's something you'd have to devote a lot of time to, which is a thing he's short of. As for me, I haven't the head for it.'

'Neither have I,' Antony confided. She left a few moments later and he heard Mr Bellerby's voice in the corridor bidding her adieu. A moment later the solicitor bustled back into his office.

'A nice woman,' he said. 'Was she able to help you, Mr Maitland?'

Antony looked at him almost blankly for a moment. 'I agree with you about the niceness,' he said, shaking himself out of his abstraction. 'She told me two things, one which may be helpful, and the other which definitely isn't. But do you realise she thinks the worst that can happen to our clients is dismissal from the Force, not a prison sentence which may be very long indeed.'

'I don't think she's quite as simple as that,' Mr Bellerby told him. 'But very few people have any idea of the kind of sentence the judges consider appropriate for a given crime. I did gather she felt her husband might get a year or two, but that probably young Harris would get off with probation or a very light sentence, being considered to have been led astray. You didn't enlighten her I hope,' he added anxiously.

'It wasn't my business. If the worst comes to the worst though –'

'Let's hope it won't. What were these two things she had to tell you, Mr Maitland?'

'That everything that they own in the world besides material goods is in two bank accounts in their joint names, which the police have examined and found to be in order. I think something can be made of that fact, because if the charge is true it's unlikely to have been an isolated incident.'

'If you'd read your brief, Mr Maitland –'

'I haven't had time. Besides, Uncle Nick's still sitting on all the papers rather like a broody hen,' said Antony, with a singular lack of respect. 'Is the same true about Constable Harris? The financial side, I mean.'

'Yes. He just has a current account, with enough in it for month to month expenses, and regular payments by standing order to his mother. That was all looked into while the inquiry was still taking place. I imagine it was hoped to find some evidence to support the charge of blackmail which had been made, before the Protheroes came forward.'

'Yes, I suppose so too. The other point may also be in the papers with the brief, although it's hardly the sort of thing Harris would think to tell you, I imagine. He was brought up in what must have been at least extremely comfortable circumstances – his grandfather employed a Head Gardener and so on – and he had every intention of embracing our profession. But the family was wiped out financially when he was nearly ready to leave school, by a motor accident in which his father and two older brothers were killed. As there'd been death duties to pay when his grandfather died not long before. . . . I say, it never occurred to me, but your brethren must have had a field day over that business. I mean, if they were all killed together –'

'Unless one or other of them survived for a short time I imagine the court would take the view that the father, being obviously the eldest, was the first to succumb to his injuries. I don't know the contents of his will, of course, but even if Harris shared equally in his father's estate with his brothers, there can't have been much left after the government had taken their share.'

'That's what Mrs Mayhew said. She seems very attached to the young man.'

'And you're afraid the prosecution will insinuate that he, feeling himself badly used by fate, took advantage of his official position to recoup his losses to some degree.'

'That's exactly what I think, though I suppose he couldn't have been at it long enought to have done much in that direction. However, it's as well to know the worst. Who will be prosecuting, do you know?'

'Mr Hawthorne. As he was dealing with the Magistrates' Court hearing when Barleycorn and Stokes were arrested, I imagine it's felt that he knows more about the matter than anybody else.'

'Yes, I imagine so, too. The only consolation is that he's an extremely fair-minded man, not likely to exceed the bounds of propriety in pressing his case. On the other hand, if what is alleged against our clients were true, you couldn't blame anyone for feeling a sort of righteous indignation at such a breach of trust.'

'No, that's one of the most unpleasant points we have to contend with.' The phone rang at that moment, and when he put down the receiver he announced, 'Constable Harris is here.'

After the visitor had been shown in very much the same charade was played. Harris grinned at Maitland as the door closed behind the solicitor. 'I've always heard you had a weakness for talking to witnesses alone,' he observed. 'I understand it's regarded as unorthodox.'

'Then I'll add to your knowledge and tell you it's a practice my uncle disapproves of, particularly where one of our clients is concerned. Hence the subterfuge I arranged with Mr Bellerby. If you object of course –'

'No I don't, why should I? There's one thing I'd like to ask you though. Do you still resent the circumstances of our first meeting?'

This time it was Maitland who smiled, with genuine amusement. 'You were shadowing me,' he said, 'but why should I hold that against you? If you remember, you were very useful to me later as a witness.'

'Well, as long as you take it like that –' Harris didn't attempt to finish the sentence but his relief sounded sincere. 'But about this meeting, you've gone to a good deal of trouble over it and there's nothing at all I can tell you beyond what Laurie – beyond what Chief Inspector Mayhew told you the other day.'

'About the facts of the case, no, I'm sure there isn't. I was surprised by his fluency.'

'Yes, he is inclined to be silent in the ordinary way, unless it's something he feels strongly about. But you had to know the details after all, and I expect he thought it was more his place to give them than mine.'

Antony left it there, though in his own mind his next words were not completely irrelevant. 'I've just been talking to Mrs Mayhew,' he said.

Harris's face lit up. 'She's a darling, isn't she?' he asked, speaking perhaps for the first time that day with complete spontaneity. 'They've been so good to me since I came to London, and –'

'She made her affection for you quite clear,' Maitland assured him. 'But talking to her made me wonder . . . you do understand, don't you, that if we lose this case the consequences will be very serious for both you and Chief Inspector Mayhew? You see, Mrs Mayhew seemed to think –'

'She understands we may have to go to prison, though not for how long. I think Laurie –' He started again to correct himself, but Antony interrupted him.

'While we're talking like this just use the name that comes most naturally to you,' he requested. 'Yes, Mr Bellerby explained the position to me but I wanted to make sure that you understood it too. I understand what's in Mayhew's mind only too well, and though I'm not at all sure that he's right to keep her in the dark it's a matter between the two of them, no one else.'

'I wouldn't interfere.'

'No, I realise that, not so long as you understand the position, as I see now you do. Tell me, Mr Harris, do you like your job?'

'Very much indeed. I expect Dorothy told you I'd always thought of myself as having a legal career, at the Bar to be precise. But my disappointment about that was only a secondary consideration. After the accident . . . I . . . we were rather a close family, and besides there was my mother to consider.'

'If we lose the case –'

'I shall go to prison, I suppose,' said Harris. Antony took a moment to wonder how much the matter-of-fact tone cost him.

'I meant, what will you do after you come out?'

'I'm trying not to think of it. I don't want,' said Harris 'to seem to be playing on your sympathies. But Laurie has a great deal of faith in your ability, and a great deal of respect for Sir Nicholas as an advocate.'

'Don't expect miracles, that isn't my line.' If Maitland's tone

71

was suddenly sharp it was because the constable's words gave him, though unwittingly, an unwelcome feeling of responsibility for this young man for whom he was beginning to feel a good deal of liking, and for his old friend Chief Inspector Mayhew.

'I won't but –'

'As long as you understand that. Tell me, Mr Harris, how did you feel when every one of your witnesses got up in the Magistrates' Court and denied everything that you and Mayhew had said?'

The younger man thought about that for a moment. 'Flabbergasted,' he said at last. 'And yet in a way that isn't true; I couldn't believe my ears at first, the astonishment came later. The point was they were all lying, they must have been, except perhaps Shadwell . . . he struck me when we first saw him as the sort of man who wouldn't bother much how things got done as long as he didn't have to trouble himself about them.'

'And the Treasurer of the firm, Martin Kingsley, came as a complete surprise to you?'

'A complete and utter surprise. I mean, it seemed so obvious what had happened and that he was up to his neck in it. We never dreamed he'd turn up again.'

'Another thing I forgot to ask you, was there any record of his having left the country?'

'No, but there wouldn't be. Even if his destination wasn't a Common Market country he could hop over to France and go on from there.'

'So he could. How did *he* strike you?'

'A very smooth character.' Harris smiled again. 'Not quite so haughty as Pooh Bah, but quite as capable of concocting a reasonable sounding story.'

'That's what I was afraid of. Let's think about the others though. You wrote out Mrs Goodbody's statement on the spot, and she signed it?'

'Yes, I'd taken down what she said in shorthand.'

'Are you sure she read it over first?'

'I'm quite sure she took the sheets of paper I'd written on, and held them up as though she were reading them for quite long enough for her to have done so,' said Harris precisely.

Maitland laughed. 'I have to agree with Mrs Mayhew, you did

miss your calling,' he said. 'But isn't it more usual –?'

'Yes, of course, I was only showing off. I read it through to her, and then as far as either of us could tell she read it. There's no doubt about that at all.'

'No probable, possible shadow of doubt,' said Maitland rather gloomily. 'We all know where that got the Chief Inquisitor. What about Mr Peele?'

'The answer would be exactly the same, except that as he signed his statement at the station it was typewritten. And he didn't deny signing it, you know, just said he'd been coerced into doing so.'

'I hadn't forgotten. Did you know he'd been doing a fiddle with his income tax?'

'No, but as so many people seem to nowadays I don't suppose I'd have been very surprised if I had known it. But you know Laurie, Mr Maitland –'

'If you ever join the ranks of the legal profession,' said Antony, thinking as he spoke how very unlikely a contingency this was, 'you'll know that the words "he wouldn't do a thing like that" are anathema. In this case I'm inclined to agree with you, but don't get it into your head that that means the jury will. Just think for a moment how it will look to them. You're engaged in a murder inquiry, and stumble on to a protection racket that seems to provide a good motive. You have Mrs Goodbody's evidence, and the rest of your inquiries seem to suggest that her husband was delinquent in his payments, as far as the extra money was concerned, but that gets you no nearer to proving that he was killed by the two men you suspect. I'm afraid people will be only too ready to believe there was some funny business in obtaining Mr Peele's evidence, particularly as all your colleagues engaged on similar inquiries turned up a blank. It was bad enough when the two accused, now no longer prisoners, got up and started talking about blackmail. When the Protheroes came forward . . . were they in court by the way?'

'I don't know. I'd never seen either of them then and might not have noticed. They came forward, as Laurie told you, after the disciplinary inquiry ended.'

'Have you ever known anyone of that name?'

'No. He's a building contractor he said, at *our* hearing.'

'There's no reason then for them to have had a motive for shopping either of you?'

'Neither Laurie nor Dorothy had ever heard of either of them before.'

'Then – think carefully about this one – the evening they say they overheard you plotting in Hartley's restaurant, did you notice anyone at a nearby table who seemed to be trying to hear what you were saying?'

'I'm not even sure whether we were there that day, but I thought you understood –'

'I'm not questioning what you told me. As for the date, if you've forgotten, it was the twenty-third of September, a Tuesday. But you say you went there quite often, so I suppose it's difficult to distinguish one visit from another. Or even to be sure if you were there that particular night, unless it was because you were doing overtime and one of you kept the bill.'

'No, I do remember that Tuesday, because Dorothy was out of town visiting her sister, and that's why Laurie wanted to eat in town before going home. But I didn't notice anybody particular, certainly not anybody listening to us. I'm pretty sure we'd be discussing the case, and we'd both have shut up if anyone had been within earshot.'

'Yes, I see.' Mayhew at least, he reflected, would have been on the lookout for any eavesdropper if confidential matters were being discussed. 'Even so, are you sure that nothing was said between you that could have been misconstrued?' But he answered his own question before the other man had a chance to do so. 'Of course not, it's obvious, assuming your plea of Not Guilty to be a true one –'

'I thought . . . have I said something to make you doubt that?' asked Harris, sounding more anxious than angry at the possibility.

'No.' Maitland gave him an amused look. 'I was merely emulating your own caution of a moment ago. And what I was trying to say was, the only explanation is that you were deliberately framed. All the same it's a little difficult to understand. You'd been to see Barleycorn and Stokes, and because they'd been asked for alibis they must have known they were suspected, but they must have known too that the murder

74

'couldn't be proved against them on the evidence you had at that point or I imagine Mayhew would have been a little more demanding. So wouldn't it have been sufficient to terrorise Mrs Goodbody – as I suppose they must have done – into denying her story?' He was speaking slowly, thinking it out as he went. 'Then when Martin Kingsley turned up and confirmed that they were *bona fide* salesmen . . . you could have suspected as much as you liked, but couldn't have proved a thing.'

'But after that we saw Peele and that made all the difference.'

'Certainly it did. But he too could have been intimidated, which seems to have been what happened, as he as well as Mrs Goodbody went back on his story and the whole thing was thrown out of court. That didn't get you off the hook as far as the authorities were concerned. If the witnesses were telling the truth now you'd both committed perjury. Wasn't that enough for them? I'm talking now about whoever was behind all this. Why did they go that one step further?'

'Spite?' said Harris rather tentatively.

'Yes, perhaps. Even so, I think there must have been some stronger reason. Something one of you knew,' he added slowly.

'I've told you everything I can think of. As for Laurie . . . like you I was surprised that he had so much to say at the conference in your chambers. It could have been because there was something or somebody he suspected . . . but how could there be?'

'That,' said Maitland, 'is the question. How long since you were transferred to Central, Mr Harris?'

'About two years.'

'You'll have made friends in that time.'

'Yes, of course, but on the whole we're kept pretty busy.'

'Following innocent barristers around London for instance,' said Maitland. Rightly or wrongly he felt their conversation at this stage should be kept on as light a note as possible.

'Things like that,' Harris responded in the same vein. 'I get on pretty well with my colleagues. Sometimes we have a night out together or a double date. But the senior ranks naturally I only know to say Yes, sir and No, sir to, and if you're thinking of anything in the way of professional jealousy, that would be something aimed against Laurie, wouldn't it?'

75

'That wasn't exactly what was in my mind. Friends outside the force for instance . . . the dates you mentioned.'

'I can't afford to get serious about anybody yet,' said Harris, 'so I've been working on the principle of there being safety in numbers. I find it awfully difficult to take this conversation seriously, Mr Maitland.'

'You're probably right and it will get us nowhere fast,' Antony agreed. 'All the same . . . is there no one girl in particular?'

'Yes, but . . . I don't understand.'

'That makes two of us. But tell me her name, there's a good chap.'

'Alice Harper.'

'Did you meet her on one of those double dates you mentioned?'

'No, I met her because Mother gave me some letters of introduction when I came to town. One of them was to her parents.'

'Now you do begin to interest me.'

'But this is just nonsense. Mr and Mrs Harper are perfectly ordinary people, and I only went to see them, and the other couple who'd been friends of my own parents, to please Mother.'

'Tell me about them,' Antony invited.

'If I must, but you can take it from me we're wasting our time, Mr Maitland. I don't want to seem ungrateful, but –'

'Then tell me,' said Antony again.

'Well, there were the Harpers, they live in Bayswater and he's an architect. His name's Colin and hers is Janice, and they've had me to dinner a few times, well fairly regularly as a matter of fact. I think that was her idea rather than his. I met them once when I was out with Laurie and Dorothy Mayhew, and I think Mrs Harper felt Mother wouldn't approve of my being so close to them and perhaps she could persuade me into making more "suitable" friends. That's all nonsense, of course, but at least I was able to see Alice, besides taking her out whenever I could afford it.'

'Did the Harpers know you were taking their daughter out sometimes?'

'I don't know the answer to that question; I didn't make a point of telling them and I never asked Alice about it. But I never discussed my work with them, I had a feeling they'd think it was somehow demeaning.'

'Obviously Alice doesn't,' said Antony with a smile.

'Alice is different. I could talk about anything with her.'

'Good. And what about the other introduction your mother gave you?'

'I never actually visited them because they happened to be with the Harpers the first time I went there, and after that I met them there fairly frequently. In conversation I learned that their names were Paul and Alex – Alexandra I suppose – and my mother had already told me that he was a newspaper man, and she gave lessons in flower arranging, which sounds a silly sort of occupation to me. I suppose it's a hobby really. Alice calls them Aunt and Uncle, but I don't think they're related. But whatever all this has to do with –'

Maitland didn't let him finish. 'Can you think of anybody else you've been in contact with since you came to live in this area?'

'The girls I spoke of weren't very important to me. I rarely saw any of them more than once.'

'Well, you can do something for me Mr Harris, if you will. Give Chief Inspector Mayhew some details about our conversation, and ask him if he can think of anybody, anybody at all, even one of his closest friends, who might have some reason for wanting to see him put out of circulation for as long as possible.'

'A friend wouldn't do that.'

'I hate to remind you, but your youth is showing. You should try to develop a more cynical attitude. Friends talk to each other, and sometimes things may be said that mean nothing at the time but may prove inconvenient if remembered later.' He paused, looking rather hopelessly at his companion. 'Will you do as I say?' he asked, 'and make Mayhew realise I'm deadly serious about it. I'll have to see him myself, but it will save time if he thinks about things first.'

'Of course I will. I know you want to help, Mr Maitland, but honestly I think you're barking up the wrong tree.'

'When you see my uncle again mind your language. He has the greatest aversion for slang.' He was coming to his feet as he spoke, and Harris followed suit.

'Is that all?' he asked.

'All I can think of for the moment. Don't think too badly of me,' he added. 'We none of us know what may prove to be important until it jumps up and hits us.'

Detective Constable Harris made his farewells politely enough, but he was frowning as he left. 'He thinks I'm mad,' Antony confided to Mr Bellerby when the solicitor joined him again. 'The trouble is, I'm not altogether sure he's wrong,' he added reflectively. 'But if we're going to get anywhere in this affair we've got to try everything.'

III

The study door being invitingly open when he got home, it didn't need Gibbs's, 'Sir Nicholas would like to see you, Mr Maitland,' to tell him that his uncle wanted an account of his afternoon's activities. He said, 'Thank you,' rather absently and went across the hall, turning over in his mind the rather meagre information at his disposal. He declined a drink on the grounds that Jenny would be expecting him, and embarked on a brief account of his talk with Mrs Mayhew and then with Constable Harris. 'Sounds a nice woman,' said Vera gruffly when he had finished. 'Hope you didn't enlighten her.'

'As to the length of sentence her husband actually faces, no I didn't. All the same –'

'You don't quite agree with his leaving her uninformed,' said Sir Nicholas. 'There might be a lesson there for you, Antony.'

'Yes, sir, I made a mental note of it. Roger's coming round tonight,' he added, with apparent inconsequence, but both his hearers understood well enough what he meant.

'Something you've been keeping from us?' said Vera, looking suspiciously from one of her companions to the other.

'You must acquit me of any such intention, my dear, it was at Antony's instigation. However as he seems to have decided on a policy of frankness I suppose I may tell you that his idea of defending our clients includes pursuing a gang,' said Sir Nicholas blandly, conveniently ignoring the fact that he had ignored his nephew's wishes by speaking fairly plainly to her before. 'I should

78

myself prefer the phrase "criminal organisation," or something of the sort, but at least the word gangster is preferable to racketeer.'

'Don't like the sound of that,' said Vera, as though it was the first she had heard of it.

'Well, I don't like it much myself,' Maitland admitted, 'but if those two are innocent, and I'm increasingly of the opinion that they are, somebody had to persuade Mrs Goodbody and Peele to change their stories, and – what may have been much harder – persuaded Martin Kingsley to return home.'

'You don't think there's any chance that Kingsley was behind the activities of the two – shall we call them collectors?' said Sir Nicholas.

'No, I don't. I think he was recruited by whoever heads the organisation,' said Antony, with unusual deference to his uncle's high standards in the matter of English usage. 'When the people who were preying on Jim Arnold among others were put away, and he saw an opportunity of turning a dishonest penny along the same lines. But I've been thinking –' He stopped there and didn't attempt to finish the sentence.

Sir Nicholas sighed. 'Where you're concerned, my dear boy, that statement always fills me with apprehension,' he said. 'I will grant you your gang if you like,' he went on distastefully, 'but beyond that I'm not prepared to go.'

'It was just something that occurred to me when I was talking to Harris,' Maitland explained.

'I don't like what you've had to tell me about that young man,' said Sir Nicholas thoughtfully, apparently ignoring the statement, though his nephew knew well enough he would return to the point later on.

'He's a nice young chap, Uncle Nick.'

'That is hardly the point. It's bad enough that he seems to be a close friend of the Mayhews, but the rest of it is infinitely worse. A young man brought up with certain expectations and finding them thwarted through no fault of his own, may well be held to feel that he has a grudge against society.'

'Yes, sir, that point had alreay occurred to me. I discussed it with Bellerby and we both think it's something the prosecution – Hawthorne's taking it by the way – will stress. Having been present at the fiasco in the Magistrates' Court when Barleycorn and Stokes were accused he's considered to know more about the case than anybody else.'

Sir Nicholas acknowledged the information with a slight inclination of his head. 'And what was this thought that occurred to you, Antony?' he asked.

'That Mayhew and Harris were in quite enough trouble when the case against Barleycorn and Stokes was dismissed without the further accusation that they'd been trying to make money out of it.'

'That certainly gives your argument of the existence of a criminal organisation of some sort further weight. The two men must have been told already that they'd be looked after if any of their plans miscarried to have come up with that statement so readily.'

'Yes, but that isn't exactly what I meant. Not all of it, anyway. They'd been primed, that's certain, but the question is why? And the only answer I can come up with is that either Mayhew or Harris knows something about whoever is running things, and that the safest thing would be to put them out of the way for as long as possible, to get them an even longer prison sentence than a perjury charge would have brought.'

'I think you're carrying that argument too far. The statement may have been made purely out of spite.'

'And backed up by the Protheroes? I don't know much about them but –'

'According to the papers Bellerby sent me, which I would recommend to your attention as soon as you have a moment to give to them, they're a respectable couple with a good address in Putney.'

'That's all very well, Uncle Nick, I still say the whole thing must have been arranged beforehand, while Barleycorn and Stokes were still in custody on the murder charge. They'd plenty of time to approach the Protheroes after they were released, but I simply won't believe they'd have made that statement and *then* set about trying to find someone to back it up.'

'So somebody else instigated it,' said Sir Nicholas slowly. 'And from that you conclude . . . what do you think of his conclusions, Vera?'

'First glance, a bit far-fetched,' said Vera. 'Known him to be right before, however.'

'That's true, but I think myself that I should have stopped after the first sentence,' said Sir Nicholas smiling at her. 'But the idea that it must be someone known to our clients . . . are we to be reduced again to referring to Mr X, Antony?'

'I should have hesitated to suggest it, but it's certainly shorter than "the head of the criminal organisation", which is what I suppose you'd prefer,' Maitland told him. 'However, it needn't necessarily be somebody known to them socially. I didn't stress this with Harris, because if it was something learned in the course of their professional duties it would be far more likely something that Mayhew knows. But I do think a friend or acquaintance is far more likely. In the case of a criminal investigation every statement is weighed carefully, whereas something said in casual conversation can be forgotten for months, and then suddenly come to mind and assume a significance you hadn't given it before. And if you think I'm being wrong-headed about this, Uncle Nick, just look at it from my point of view. I have to start somewhere.'

'I must have been mad,' said Sir Nicholas bitterly, 'to think I could interest you in this matter without having you run amok.'

'But you do see the force of my argument, sir,' Antony insisted.

'It has a certain weird validity,' his uncle admitted, 'and whatever I say it's obvious you're going to take your own line. I can only ask you to leave as much of the actual inquiry as you can to other people, and content yourself with providing me with some ammunition to use when we get into court.'

IV

The hardest part, of course, was still to come, and in what he recognised as a cowardly way he postponed it until after dinner when Roger Farrell arrived to give him moral support. It was easy enough to provide an excuse to do this. 'Roger will be interested,' he told Jenny, 'and as I've already been over the whole thing with Uncle Nick and Vera I don't want to have to repeat it for a third time.'

81

Roger and Meg Farrell were perhaps the Maitlands' closest friends, though it is possible the claim might have been disputed by Bill Cleveland whom they had both known all their lives. Bill farmed in Yorkshire, and they spent the greater part of each long vacation with him, but certainly the Farrells were the friends they saw most often. Roger in particular, as Meg was an actress and a popular one at that. When she was working, which was practically non-stop, Roger was in the habit of coming round to Kempenfeldt Square in the evening after he had left her at the theatre. For the last few months however, to her husband's great delight, she had been resting; ever since, in fact, the man who was playing Othello to her Desdemona had been taken ill. It may be that she'd enjoyed this unexpected freedom as much as Roger had, in any case all the parts that had been offered to her since then had had in her eyes something wrong with them. So it was not unnatural that Antony's greeting that evening should include an inquiry as to her whereabouts.

'I'm afraid there may be something in the wind again,' said Roger in a resigned tone. (He was a stockbroker, and Maitland was always amazed to see how much free time he was able to award himself, without apparently affecting his financial position at all. But then that had been pretty secure in the first place.) 'She's been terribly secretive about it, even with me, and she swears whatever happens isn't going to happen for some time. Jeremy Skelton is mixed up in it somehow, but I've a sort of feeling the play isn't even written yet.'

'That sounds a bit odd. I mean if it was anyone but Jeremy I'd say it was a mad idea. But I expect she can trust him by now not to turn out a complete fiasco. However, I've got a story to tell you, not a very edifying one on the whole.' He was busying himself pouring his friend a drink as he spoke and didn't look round. 'I'm afraid it's rather a long one, because I'll have to start from the beginning for your benefit, and Jenny doesn't know the last bit either so she's all impatience.'

Jenny, looking anything but impatient, was curled up in her favourite corner of the sofa with the lamplight gilding her brown curls. 'It's rather a sad story really, Roger,' she told him, 'because it concerns that nice Inspector Mayhew. I can't remember if you've met him, but you've certainly heard Antony talk about

82

him and we've always thought a lot of him, but now he's in dreadful trouble and is going to be tried for something Uncle Nick won't let us call extortion. It's an awfully complicated story,' she added.

'Then I'm glad I shall be hearing it from Antony and not from you,' said Roger smiling at her. Jenny's explanations were notorious for their lack of coherence, but she had long since stopped minding being teased about that. They had known Meg longer than they knew her husband, but by now he was just as much a part of the family . . . not always an advantage, as he himself would have pointed out, because to Sir Nicholas, who had also accepted them, this merely meant that he felt at liberty to speak his mind freely when he considered it necessary.

Neither Antony nor Jenny ever stopped to think about it now, but there was no denying that Roger was something of a paradox, both in character and in appearance. He was one of those men who could never come into a room without completely changing the atmosphere, without giving the company an immediate awareness of his presence; but apparently at will he could change all that, and efface himself so as to be practically unnoticeable. He was by inclination a man of action, but at the same time extremely sensitive to other people's moods. And Antony who, not being given to introspection, never realised that that last description might equally well have been applied to him, trusted his friend as he did himself, and came nearer to speaking freely to him about certain subjects that were generally forbidden than to anyone else in the world. Since the injury to his shoulder he had had to accept physical help in small matters from any number of people, but Roger was the only one of whom he would openly ask such assistance.

Maitland had by now finished serving the drinks, making several journeys between the tray on the writing-desk and the circle round the fire, as was his custom. 'So I hope you're in an attentive mood,' he said, 'because Jenny's quite right in calling it complicated and you're going to have to explain the whole thing to Meg. I'm damned if I'm going to go through it again for her benefit.'

Roger had seated himself in the chair that was usually reserved for Sir Nicholas, and received the glass with a murmur of thanks.

'Am I to gather that you're mixing yourself up in Mayhew's affairs,' he said, 'and that Uncle Nick doesn't approve?'

'Uncle Nick is acting for him,' Antony said. 'And Bellerby having offered me the second brief I've accepted it, with I may say my learned relative's complete agreement. He and Vera had some nonsensical idea in their heads that it would be good for my image if we acted together . . . something like that.'

Roger nodded. 'The Assistant Commissioner, Sir Alfred Godalming,' he said.

'As Meg isn't here to complain I shall say, precisely,' said Maitland. 'Only now' – his eyes flickered a moment to his wife's face – 'Uncle Nick isn't so sure he hasn't got a tiger by the tail.'

'I take it you're trying to tell me that you want to go further into the matter then he thinks is wise,' said Roger. He paused a moment, but the implications of that quick glance at Jenny hadn't been lost on him. He knew perfectly well, what Antony had only learned painfully over the years, that though Jenny would be upset by any idea of danger in her husband's activities, being kept in the dark about them was for her a far more painful experience. 'I also take it,' he said deliberately, 'that whether or not you're right you both feel there may be some danger involved.'

Maitland's glass was forgotten on the mantelpiece. He knew these two too well to pretend to an ease he didn't feel by seating himself. '*If* I'm right,' he agreed. 'When I've finished you can tell me what you think about that. Though Jenny forgot to mention that there's another person involved. So conspiracy is also involved. Do you remember my telling you about Detective Constable Harris?'

'I don't remember the name.'

'Briggs put him on to tail me once, but I made good use of him as a witness when I was trying to find out what had happened to Harriet Carr.'

'Oh, that chap, of course I remember.'

'Well, he was involved with Mayhew in all the inquiries, and other members of the Force too, but as it turned out their evidence was of no value, and if Mayhew was working a fiddle the only way he could have done so was with Constable Harris's help. But I'd rather begin at the beginning . . .'

It wasn't all news to Jenny, of course, though quite a lot of it was, and she had so far heard nothing of what had happened that day. When Antony had finished there was a moment's silence, and then Jenny said, quietly enough, 'Mrs Mayhew sounds a nice person. I hope things are going to turn out well for them. I suppose in any case Constable Harris – Gerry did she call him? – would be let of more lightly because he'd be supposed to be under the Chief Inspector's influence?'

'I would expect so, certainly, but – to echo Uncle Nick – I didn't much like what she told me about his background. Don't you see –?'

'Oh, yes, you made that quite clear. The prosecution will say he had a grudge against life because things didn't turn out exactly as he wished. Perhaps they may even try to imply that it was he who influenced the Chief Inspector.'

'Well I do think, Jenny love, that as far as Mayhew's concerned . . . if he had been blackmailing criminals instead of charging them this wouldn't be an isolated incident.'

'That seems reasonable,' said Roger.

'Yes.' Antony turned to him eagerly. 'What do you make of it all?' he asked.

'I only know of the people concerned by hearsay,' said Farrell slowly. 'When you first heard the tale from Sykes, Antony, what was your reaction?'

'I found it difficult to believe of Mayhew, though I can see the temptation for a detective to fake evidence against someone he's sure is guilty. But the other . . . I found that still harder to believe. And when I thought it through further –'

'Assuming the innocence of your two clients I find your arguments very convincing,' said Roger. 'But then' – he smiled – 'perhaps my association with you has prejudiced me in favour even of your wilder ideas. The question is, can I help?'

'I was working round to asking if you would, in the capacity of a witness,' said Antony. He glanced from Roger to Jenny and added carefully, 'And as a bodyguard too, perhaps. Bellerby conspired with me to deceive Uncle Nick into believing that I'd only talked to our clients in his presence, but of course the other people I want to see are completely outside the case unless this guess of mine is right so I can't involve our instructing solicitor.

85

Derek would help, of course – I didn't tell you Uncle Nick has roped him into the defence team too – he's a good chap but I'd rather trust you in a tight corner.'

'I'm at your service.'

'Good. I expect Uncle Nick will kick like a horse, but there's nothing really he can do about it.'

Roger grinned at that. 'Your wish is my command,' he said.

'What about Meg?'

'I shan't be neglecting her, if that's what you mean. She's thoroughly enjoying playing housewife, and during the week I'm at the office anyway.'

'Well, tomorrow morning there's just one thing I want to do, and that is to see Father William. But though he'd talk in your presence, I know, as easily as he would to me alone – he has a great admiration for you, Roger, did you know that? – there's no question of my using anything he tells me as evidence, so there's no point in dragging you along. But in the afternoon I want to try to find Mrs Porson. She may still be at the address in the telephone book, because it isn't all that long since her husband died.'

'Hanged himself in prison,' Roger put in reflectively, 'after you'd discovered where he was hiding out. You don't think that may cause a certain awkwardness between you and his widow?'

'Yes, but that doesn't worry me too much. Sykes thought at the time she knew at least something of her husband's activities, so there's just a possibility she may be able to help me. Anyway I'd like you along if you can spare the time, just in case she's willing to and has anything useful to say.'

'Tomorrow afternoon then? I'll make the time,' Roger promised. And if both of his hearers were perfectly well aware that the prospect of violent action would have appealed to him more than a quite talk with a widow, even if her husband had been what Sir Nicholas would have hated to hear referred to as a professional hit man, neither of them made any comment. Antony retrieved his glass and sat down at last, and the conversation wandered to other subjects, with special reference to whatever might be in the wind as far as Meg was concerned.

When Roger had gone, a little earlier than usual, 'Because I expect Meg will be home before I am,' Jenny made no immediate attempt to clear away the used glasses and coffee cups. She had uncurled herself now, and was sitting as her husband had so often seen her, completely relaxed and with her hands clasped loosely in her lap.

He came back to his place on the hearthrug and stood for a moment looking down at her. 'Well, love?' he asked.

'Tell me something, Antony. These ideas of yours about what may have happened in the Mayhew case –'

'What must have happened, love,' he corrected her. 'If our clients are innocent, of course.'

'Do you think you can prove it?' she asked, but he was perfectly well aware that was not the question that was really in her mind.

However, he gave it his consideration and answered as truthfully as he knew how. 'On the whole I rather doubt it. Unless something turns up,' he went on, 'and we can't rely on that.'

'Things have a habit of happening when you stir them up,' said Jenny, her eyes fixed on his face.

'Does that mean you agree with Uncle Nick, and with Sykes too, that I should let well alone?'

'No, it doesn't!' (I know you too well, my darling, I have watched you over the years. You understand what fear is, but it's something you can never admit to yourself, let alone to me.) 'I was just wondering,' she went on casually, 'would you have told me . . . all this . . . if Roger hadn't forced your hand?'

'As a matter of fact, yes I would. But I won't deny it was a help his being there to – to push me in off the deep end as it were. And I won't deny either that I nearly didn't tell you, I said to Uncle Nick at the beginning that we needn't worry either you or Vera. But then when I talked to Dorothy Mayhew today and realised that her husband had done his best to keep from her what the consequences for himself and young Harris might be . . . well, I remembered my own good resolutions that I'd never again try to keep you in the dark about anything at all.'

'I'm glad of that.' Suddenly the smile she gave him was dazzling. 'And I shan't be the least bit anxious about you,' she added, coming to her feet, 'so long as you have Roger with you.'

'Of course not.' He knew better than to believe a word she was saying, but he was reassured to realise, as he watched her carry the glasses over to the tray, that the serenity that he valued so much seemed so far undisturbed.

Thursday, 9th October

I

To give Father William his correct title would have been to address him as William Webster, the nickname having been bestowed on him in connection with his subsidiary occupation which was what is commonly known to the general public as a fence, to the law as a receiver of stolen goods, and to his clients simply as a buyer. As far as anyone could prove, however, he owned and ran a jeweller's shop in Bedford Lane, designing and constructing a great many of the pieces he sold there in his own workroom. Some time ago he had been connected with one of Maitland's cases that happened to have caused even more trouble than usual, and in fact had been instrumental in saving both Antony and Jenny's lives before it was over. In the circumstances, Maitland could hardly be blamed for having an affection for the old man, though it is doubtful whether in any event he would have been able to resist the attractions of so amiable a character.

The best time to catch Mr Webster was obviously first thing in the morning, so Antony set out on foot immediately after breakfast, leaving Jenny to phone Mr Mallory with his explanations, which had necessarily to be vague. He wasn't sure what time he would reach chambers either, and considered his wife would be better at conveying this fact without causing something in the nature of a volcanic explosion than he himself would have been.

There had been changes since first Antony visited Father William's shop, as was only to be expected. The neat brass plate by the door said now only *Webster's*, but for all Maitland could recall of the narrow window as he'd first seen it there might have been no change in it at all. Mr Webster got his effects delicately, and didn't approve of clutter. Maitland pushed open the door without hesitation.

This morning, as Antony described it to Jenny later, there was a willowy-looking female floating around the showroom with a feather duster. No sooner had he told her that he would like to speak to Mr Webster than the door at the back of the shop opened a little wider and Father William himself came in.

'Why, Mr Maitland!' he exclaimed, his blue eyes widening as though in complete surprise. He was small and whitehaired, and looked not a day older to Maitland's eyes than he had done the first time they met, though he knew the man well enough now to realise that the air of benevolent simplicity was not to be trusted, except insofar as the benevolence was concerned which he was pretty sure was genuine, at least towards himself. 'You're alone today,' he added, stating the obvious. 'But as I remember it Mrs Maitland's birthday was last month, so this I suppose must be some other matter of business.'

'Yes, if you can spare me the time.'

'Certainly I can. Rose will look after everything for me. I don't want to be disturbed, my dear, while Mr Maitland is here,' he added. 'He is a very special customer. But I'm sure you can look after anything that comes up without my help.'

He didn't wait for her assurance but led the way through the door by which he had entered, past the workroom, past the tiny office, and into his own living quarters at the back. His living-room was no more luxurious than Antony remembered, but there were a couple of reasonably easy chairs, and to these Father William led the way. 'Is there anything in the way of refreshment I can get you?' he asked. 'A cup of coffee, perhaps?'

'Thank you, Father William, but I'd rather just talk if you don't mind.'

He paused there and William Webster took advantage of the silence to say reminiscently, 'You told me once that you only came to me when you were in trouble, Mr Maitland. I had hoped that since Superintendent Briggs's retirement – '

'That's a delicate way of putting it.' He laughed suddenly, recalling the scene in Sir Nicholas's study at Kempenfeldt Square, and Father William's gentle pleasure in the situation. 'I suppose I ought to tell you, the answer to that is yes and no.

Briggs won't trouble us again, but the new Assistant Commissioner has been indoctrinated over the years with a good many of the same beliefs the Chief Superintendent held. It's quite ridiculous, because I've never even met the chap, but according to Sykes – who is now Superintendent, by the way – he's apt to view my activities with some suspicion. However, there's no trouble . . . for the time being at any rate,' he added honestly. 'I just thought . . . you hear everything, Father William. I can't go into details naturally, but you may have seen the newspaper account of the Magistrates' Court hearing of the case against Chief Inspector Mayhew and Detective Constable Harris of Scotland Yard.'

'Naturally I did, and read it with great interest,' Father William confirmed. 'Do you mean to say that you are acting for them?'

'Not alone, my uncle is leading the defence.'

'Now you do surprise me. I don't remember that the newspaper mentioned that.' Those vividly blue eyes of his were innocent but there was no doubt that his interest had been caught. 'You know, Mr Maitland, that I have no particular reason for feeling charitable towards the police, but am I to understand you feel some injustice has been done?'

'You know me well enough, Father William, to realise I'm very rarely absolutely sure about a thing like that,' said Antony ruefully. 'But, yes, I do think that's what's happened, and if it has –'

'You intend to do something about it,' said William Webster. 'Do you mean that you have Sir Nicholas's approval?'

'Not exactly, though I've brought him to see there's nothing he can do about it now. But that isn't really the point.'

'No.' The old man was obviously thinking back to the newspaper account he had read. 'As I remember it, all the witnesses changed their stories, and a surprise one turned up, a man who had been thought to have absconded.'

'You've a good memory, Father William.'

'So the two accused men were acquitted . . . is that the right phrase to use of the Magistrates' Court hearing? Upon which they immediately made statements, or rather I suppose one of them did and the other corroborated what he said, that they had been framed by the investigating officer in an attempt to extort money from them. Have I got that right?'

'Absolutely right.'

'But there was no jewellery involved as I understand it. It is usually in cases of that kind that you consult me.'

'Father William, I've learned over the years that you've ways of finding things out. My theory is that there's a whole criminal organisation with any number of different activities. This is just one of them, but I think they got the idea of going into the protection business when that racket was broken up a couple of years back. The times fit perfectly. So I've been wondering . . . can you help me? I have in mind the outfit Porson belonged to, but of course that's only because it's the only one I know about. There's more than one organisation of that kind centred in London, I believe.'

Father William leaned back in his chair and placed his fingertips together. 'Should I be offended?' he wondered.

'For heaven's sake, Father William, no! You know perfectly well I'm here because I trust you. You've helped me more than once in the past, and that's not a thing I'm likely to forget.'

'It is gratifying,' said Mr Webster thoughtfully, 'to realise that it is still possible to – to get a rise out of you on occasion. And certainly I will do what I can to help, though it is hardly my line of country. However, as you say, I do keep my ears open, so if there's anything I can tell you . . . I remember reading about Edwin Porson's suicide, of course.'

'Do you know . . . have you heard anything about his associates? All I know is what Sykes told me at that time, and I think I can quote him pretty accurately because naturally I was interested. He said that they had had a hand in almost every kind of racket you could think of that might prove profitable, either directly – as would be the case if they were organising the protection racket – or because they were hired for some specific job, as Porson was when I encountered him. I gathered too that they were by no means selective in what they did. I mean, individually. Porson, for instance, was certainly chosen for any job where marksmanship was needed, but I don't think he was at all unwilling to involve himself in any other sort of criminal activity if the occasion offered.'

'It strikes me, Mr Maitland,' said Father William thoughtfully, 'that the person you should be talking to again is Superintendent Sykes.'

'I have, and I shall see him again tomorrow. But the trouble is he isn't at all inclined to be helpful.'

'Now I thought he was a friend of yours.'

'That's why. He likes Mayhew and wants to help him, but he jibs at giving me any information that he thinks might run me into danger.'

'But my regard for you, Mr Maitland, is, I am sure, no less than his. Why should I be more willing to assist you in this way?'

'Because Sykes is a policeman and has been all his life. This is police business, and though he's welcomed my meddling in the past – that's what Uncle Nick always calls it – if there's any danger to face it's their business not mine. What I can't make him see is that I'm much less likely to be in danger if I've something to go on, if I've some idea of what I'm looking for, than if I just blunder into the whole affair blindfold. I think you might be capable of appreciating the difference.'

'Yes, I see what you mean. Well, there are one or two things I can tell you, though I'm afraid my information will fall a long way short of what you need.'

'Let's wait and see. For instance, the two men who were originally accused, Stokes and Barleycorn, both with the Christian name James, I believe. Have you ever heard of either of them?'

Father William smiled. 'Small-time crooks,' he said, 'I don't think either of them is likely to be organising anything.'

'Yes, but what do you know about them?'

'Jim Barleycorn was in a small way of business up to about two years ago.'

'I know that. At least I know he had a *modus operandi* that was very easily identifiable, but the police never had any proof after the first time, which was when he was still in his teens.'

'Whisky and military bands,' said Father William reminiscently. 'A man in his profession should be above such weaknesses.'

'The thing is he didn't just take his gains round to the nearest pawnshop, none of them ever turned up again.'

Father William ignored that. 'Do you remember Joseph

Carleton?' he asked. 'He was in a small way of business, and a receiver of stolen goods into the bargain.' As usual the old man produced the phrase as though it were unfamiliar to him. 'Not that Joe wasn't quite capable of dealing with the odds and ends Jim Barleycorn took him.'

'But you said until two years ago.'

'You know the answer to that yourself, Mr Maitland. He was employed by this firm of confectionery manufacturers that was mentioned in the newspaper report.'

'I suppose you're going to give me the same answer about Stokes,' said Antony grumpily. 'And I must say from what I've heard of him he doesn't sound as if he knows enough to come in out of the rain.'

'What did you hear of him?'

'That he was a pickpocket, but he wasn't content with the cash he found in his victim's wallet, he'd try to use the credit cards as well. And he's been employed as Barleycorn's partner, but what went on behind the scenes?'

'I can only give you rumour as it has reached my ears,' said Father William slowly. 'It was said that they had thrown their lot in with some people of rather less limited intelligence.'

'Who?' The question came sharply, and William Webster waved an admonitory finger at his companion.

'Not so fast, Mr Maitland, not so fast. What I'm telling you is something I don't know of my own knowledge, which I believe is a phrase to which you lawyers are partial. The . . . you've used the word organisation several times.'

'It's the one my uncle prefers. The word gang offends him, and racketeers even more so.'

'I am quite of his opinion.' Mr Webster nodded approvingly. 'As I understand it you believe that some organisation already in existence jumped in to – to –'

'Cash in,' Antony prompted him.

'Yes, exactly. To cash in on the money which some small shops were willing to pay for protection, after the publicity which attended the breakup of the previous project along those lines.'

'That's exactly what I do think, and naturally the one that Porson belonged to came to my mind, because it's the only one I know definitely is in existence. I've had clients from time to time who were obviously part of some such set-up, but they're not talking. They know better than that.' He broke off suddenly as a thought struck him. 'Father William, perhaps I shouldn't have come here today.'

'How far have your inquiries proceeded?' asked Mr Webster placidly.

'I've seen only our clients, and Mrs Mayhew, of course.'

'Then all, I think, is well. Things might be different if you had already been in contact with some of the criminal fraternity, but as it is I am sure we can safely proceed. Though I'm afraid you may be disappointed at the scantness of my knowledge of these matters.'

'If you're sure – '

'Quite sure, Mr Maitland. Presently I shall let fall in conversation with Rose that we're negotiating the sale of a piece of jewellery . . . a necklace perhaps for your aunt, which Sir Nicholas I imagine could well afford if he so wished.'

Antony grinned. 'No doubt he could, and no doubt it would give *him* a good deal of pleasure. But I can just see Vera's face. She's as down-to-earth a person as ever I knew.'

'You forget I had the pleasure of meeting Lady Harding, though only very briefly. But Rose knows nothing of her, so we may as well take the precaution, unnecessary though I think it to be. In my line of business I hear from time to time this and that about the various criminal organisations in this town.' ('I bet you do,' muttered Antony under his breath, and received another reproving look.) 'It was the wildest of guesses on your part, but you may well be right that the one to which Porson belonged when he was alive is the one that Jim Barleycorn and his friend joined. As your friend Superintendent Sykes told you they have a finger in every unsavoury pie in London, and I can think of no one more likely to have jumped into the breach, if I may put it that way, when they saw a new opportunity for profit.'

'Do you know anything about them?'

'If you will have patience, Mr Maitland.'

'I'm sorry,' said Antony meekly. 'You were telling me –'

'Some of my – my clients,' said Father William carefully, 'are not as discreet as would be wise. There is a boastful streak in many human beings, and I'm sure your profession has taught you that in their own interests it would better be kept in check.' He paused, looking rather challengingly at his companion, but Antony, who knew well enough what he meant in this instance by clients, held his peace. 'The operation you speak of has been in existence for many years, for ten years at least I should say. It is organised so far as I understand it rather like a business, with each department independent of the others. Where it differs from an ordinary business enterprise is in the secrecy that is involved. Each department has its head, who cannot fail to be known to the people he employs . . . women as well as men, I'm sorry to say. But as in any other business there is – shall I call him the Managing Director? And only the department heads know who he is. Which makes me think you are wrong in believing that Porson might have been called on for any sort of criminal activity. His expertise was marksmanship, certainly, but his "department" would have been concerned only with assassination.'

'That makes sense, though it also makes things more difficult. I gather employment by this company gives some guarantee of protection if there is trouble.'

'That, I think, is a recent development, and it is probably – if I too may be permitted to guess – the result of your own encounter with Porson. A number of my own clients for instance have spent some time behind bars, the result I'm sure of their own indiscretion. But none of them talked out of turn, from which I gather that there was some promise of re-employment and perhaps a reward of some kind when they were returned to society.'

'I see. Then this business of nobbling the witnesses on Barleycorn and Stokes's behalf is something new?'

'Yes, I think it is.'

'A matter of – of company policy, or something particular to their case?'

'You will understand, Mr Maitland, that I know nothing at first hand of this matter,' said Father William. 'But from what little I have heard there are deductions that may reasonably be made.' (It was quite obvious that he had already known a good deal more than Antony had told him.) 'For instance, Stokes and Barleycorn were receiving a very high reward for their work, while the sums flowing into the confectionery company's accounts must have been larger. If those two men had been convicted of murder and the Treasurer – Kingsley I think his name is – had stayed away, as in those circumstances would have been prudent, that sum of money would have been lost to the organisation for ever. I'm sure I need not explain further what I'm trying to tell you.'

'Just . . . greed?'

'Yes, I think so. But we must not forget that the two men were charged with murder. The reward for silence may have seemed too far in the future, if they had been convicted, to have ensured their not telling what they knew.'

'That makes sense so far, Father William, and I'd worked some of it out for myself. But they went a step further. Mayhew and Harris would have been in enough trouble if they'd left it there without the further accusation that Stokes and Barleycorn brought against them.' It was obviously no good trying to be discreet with Father William, for all his disclaimers he knew altogether too much. 'I made a further guess about that, that someone connected with the – the company we've decided to call it, haven't we? – is known to them. To Mayhew and Harris, I mean. That at some time something might have been said or done that might later be remembered and would lead to the discovery of the truth. I know you're as bad as Uncle Nick, and don't like guesswork, but can you think of any other reason for what was done?'

'Frankly, Mr Maitland, I can't,' said William Webster slowly. 'It seems to be the old story . . . something one of them knew, but didn't realise he knew. If I'm able to gather any more information I will certainly let you know.'

'By telephone then. I won't come here again, and I don't think you should come to Kempenfeldt Square until this is over.' He got to his feet and smiled down at his companion. 'You said – am I quoting you rightly? – that you had no cause to love the police.'

'Any friend of yours, Mr Maitland.' Mr Webster paused to gesticulate widely before struggling out of his chair. 'Besides,' he added, 'I don't approve of all this organisation. It makes it difficult for honest men to make a living.'

There was no answer to be made to that. Antony merely smiled again. 'And remember,' said Father William as he led the way to the door, 'as we go through the shop we will be arguing rather half-heartedly about the price for this necklace. I'm sure you will not object to so much dissimulation.'

It need hardly be added that Maitland, already a little worried about the possibility of having put his old friend in danger, made no objection at all. He was only glad that Father William hadn't suggested a tiara. The thought of Vera decked out in such a thing might have proved too much altogether for his sense of humour.

II

He had arranged to meet Roger for lunch at Astroff's, where a table was always kept for them until one o'clock, and he wasn't too pleased in the circumstances to find that Sir Nicholas intended to join them. They walked round to the restaurant together in good time, and Antony had the opportunity, which he would very much have liked to avoid, of bringing his uncle up to date with an account of his meeting with William Webster.

By the time he had finished they were already seated and their usual waiter had provided them with drinks. Sir Nicholas sipped his meditatively and surprised his nephew by commenting only, 'Not a bad morning's work.'

'Nothing we can use,' Maitland protested.

'I think I understand that as well as you do.' (The cold tone was much more what Antony had been expecting.) 'As for this predilection of yours for consorting with the criminal classes –'

'Uncle Nick, you know as well as I do that Father William can be trusted. As far as anybody knows he's nothing but a respectable jeweller.'

'You know and I know and the police know . . . but as usual you have succeeded in distracting me from my point,' Sir Nicholas complained. 'I was about to observe that as a confirmation of these rather wild ideas of yours what he had to tell you was not without interest. However, as you point out, it will do us not the slightest good in court. It appears to me, Antony, that much in the same way as news passes from one member of our profession to another there is a sort of criminal

97

grapevine –'

'That's exactly why I went to see him, Uncle Nick.'

'So I suppose. But he couldn't help you, you say, with the question that must concern us most . . . who is the man at the top who gives the orders?'

'Father William called him the Managing Director,' said Antony, smiling reminiscently. 'You may prefer that description to Mr X, which I gather offends you.'

'I prefer Mr Webster's description certainly, but it occurs to me, Antony, would your visit to him this morning have been observed?'

'We talked about that. Until I'm known to be interesting myself in the affair he didn't think any harm would be done, though we've agreed not to meet openly until the affair's over, even if he should find any further information to impart.' He paused to allow his uncle to get the full impact of his next words. 'Ostensibly we were discussing the price of a necklace you intend to buy as a present for Vera.'

'Good God!' said Sir Nicholas blankly. As clearly as his nephew he could visualise the impact of such a gift upon his wife. 'I hope you didn't lead him to suppose –'

'Nothing of the sort, Uncle Nick,' Antony reassured him. 'It was merely intended to lend verisimilitude to an otherwise bald and unconvincing narrative. We discussed the matter with great earnestness as we walked through the shop, so if anyone does get round to asking questions of his assistant –'

At this point Roger arrived, which was perhaps just as well. He displayed some curiosity as to how the visit to William Webster that morning had gone, but Sir Nicholas, his own curiosity having been satisfied, vetoed any further discussion of the case and they were able to enjoy their meal in peace.

After they left the restaurant they parted on the pavement outside, Sir Nicholas to turn towards the Inner Temple, while the two younger men went in precisely the opposite direction. 'I managed to find a parking place,' Roger announced (which didn't surprise his friend: it was one of Farrell's accomplishments). He deferred his questions however until they were in the car and he had manoeuvred it into the stream of traffic from a parking spot which Antony swore later gave him no more than two inches leeway at either end.

'I've just finished telling Uncle Nick,' Maitland complained.

'I promised to take Meg to the theatre tonight,' said Roger, 'so we shan't be seeing you. And you can't expect me to wait until tomorrow.'

'No, and come to think of it Sykes will be coming to dinner so you'd probably have to wait until some time on Saturday. Not that we shouldn't be glad to see you both,' he added with unnecessary formality, 'but Sykes is a cautious old bird and if I want to get him talking –'

'You don't need to explain. Just tell me what Father William had to say,' Roger insisted.

So as they drove to Fulham Antony obliged. He had often admired Roger's faculty for taking in a complicated series of facts while apparently giving the whole of his attention to his driving. 'Useful,' said Roger at last. 'And you say Uncle Nick is inclined to regard all this as a confirmation of your ideas?'

'With the added rider that it doesn't help us in the slightest,' said Antony. 'It's true enough, I suppose, but –'

'But you can do with a bit of confirmation yourself,' said Roger.

'Well, even to me it doesn't amount to anything like proof that our clients are telling the truth,' Antony admitted. 'I had a word with Bellerby when I got back from seeing Father William, and he's promised to arrange for Mayhew to be at his office tomorrow morning. I'm so afraid . . . I like Mayhew, you see, and there were occasions – one in particular – when he went out of his way to give me some reassuance I badly needed. I like his wife, too, and the lad they seem to have more or less adopted since he came to London. Which, of course, only makes matters worse from the point of view of the defence. But I don't want to believe that they're guilty as charged.'

'If you mean that you think you may be persuading yourself . . . forget it!' said Roger. 'That instinct of yours . . . where would Meg and I be if you hadn't believed I was telling you the truth the first time we met?'

'That's an argument that doesn't get us any further,' Maitland pointed out. 'I might just as well say that you're prejudiced in my favour.'

99

After that it was time to consult the street map and find the row of terraced houses where the Porsons had lived. Smallish houses, but well-kept, exactly what Maitland had thought they'd find if he'd troubled to put his mind to the subject. Edwin Porson had been an educated man, and his occupation a profitable one, but the last thing he would have wanted to do was to draw attention to any unexplained affluence on his part. Here, if anywhere, he could have the advantages of anonymity, pleasant, undistinguished neighbours, and as much comfort as he and his wife liked to arrange indoors.

It was a quiet street with little traffic about, and Roger was able to draw up almost outside their destination, number 18. But here their luck ran out. The woman who opened the door shook her head in rather a bewildered way when asked if she were Mrs Porson. Come to think of it she was younger than he would have expected. 'Was that the name of the people who lived here before?' she asked. 'We only bought the house six months ago.'

Maitland thought for a moment. 'The name and address of the person you bought it from would be on the conveyance,' he suggested. 'We really are anxious –'

But she was shaking her head. 'If you'd like to come back when Dick's home this evening, he deals with all that kind of thing,' she suggested. 'But if you want to save time, Mrs Connor's at home next door, and she might be able to tell you what you want to know. She's a nice person and has lived here for quite a long time.'

'Thank you very much, we'll try that, and not worry you again unless we can't help it,' Antony promised. 'Does Mrs Connor live at number 16 or number 20?'

'Number 16, and I know Dick would be glad to help you if he could,' she assured them. 'Only I thought perhaps it might save you time.'

'Yes, and we appreciate it.' (How long was it, he wondered, since he'd encountered what used to be known as a really womanly woman? One as young as this girl, at any rate.) They made their farewells and went down the short path to the gate, and turned in next door.

Mrs Connor was a much older woman, plump and friendly seeming, though she did express some surprise at seeing them.

100

Antony explained their errand, introducing Roger as his colleague, which he had always found the most useful description on these occasions. 'You'd better come in, then,' said Mrs Connor and backed away from the door.

She led the way to her sitting-room and turned to face them, 'What do you want with poor Connie?' she demanded

'If you mean Mrs Porson, just to find her.'

'To make trouble?'

'Nothing of the sort.' That required a small mental reservation, but he'd be very much surprised if it turned out not to be the truth.

She moved then to a chair near the fireplace, and waved them to follow her example. 'Do you know about her husband?' she asked.

'We both read the newspapers, Mrs Connor,' said Roger, feeling quite rightly that Antony might not want to go into his rather more intimate acquaintance with the man they were speaking of. 'Did you do that, or did Mrs Porson confide in you herself when he died?'

'In a manner of speaking, both. The police came here, of course, and one of them fetched me which was nice of them seeing she was so upset. It wasn't just losing him, though that was bad enough, but the way of it, and then finding out all of a sudden what kind of a life he'd been leading. As for me, you could have knocked me down with a feather.' (Which was unoriginal as well as inaccurate, considering her size.) 'I'd always thought he was the nicest man, really gentlemanly. But there, they say you can never tell what's going on in another person's mind.'

All this time she had been addressing Roger, but now Antony roused himself. 'You say she knew nothing about what had been going on,' he said. 'Can you be sure of that, Mrs Connor?'

'Sure?' She repeated questioningly. 'Come to that, I suppose I couldn't be *sure*. It's what she told me, and I thought at the time she was telling the truth. But if it had been different she'd hardly have told me, would she?'

'No, I don't think she would. Do you know anything about their friends, their close friends?'

'No one round here. I've got to say it, though it's the last thing either of them would have done, they were both a cut above the

101

rest of us. Connie and I, we'd have tea together quite often, or join up on a shopping expedition. And I always found him, as I said, most pleasant and polite. But in the evenings they'd be off somewhere, and dressed up to the nines very likely. She never talked about that, and I must say I think it was nice of her. I'd most likely just have thought she was showing off.'

'Did she ever tell you how things were left . . . financially, I mean?'

'Yes, there was some trouble about that and I think she was glad enough to have someone to talk to. Not that I understand all these legal things, something about not being able to profit from a crime, which didn't seem fair when she'd had nothing to do with his wickedness. I don't know the rights and wrongs of it, or how it was finally settled, but she didn't seem to be hard up, and the house was in her name so when she was going to be married –'

'Married? Did you say married?'

'Yes, why not?'

'It isn't very long –'

'No, but I could see how she felt. After all, however much you love someone, if you found out something so dreadful about them that would make a difference, wouldn't it?'

'Yes, I suppose it would.' The agreement was almost automatic, but there were those mental reservations again.

'Well, that's what happened. Edwin killed himself at the beginning of February and I suppose she'd already known the other man, one of the friends they used to go out with in the evening I daresay. Anyway it wasn't long before he started to call regularly, and they were married just after Easter. She left the house just as it was, said she didn't want anything to remind her, and after a couple of months it was sold lock stock and barrel to the young couple who have it now. And if you'd seen how upset she was when she heard about Edwin you'd have been glad for her as I was. I mean, what are conventions for but to be broken?'

This was so much Antony's point of view on many occasions that Roger had to hide a smile. 'She kept in touch with you?' Maitland was asking.

'Not to say kept in touch, but I can give you her address if you like.' She heaved herself out of her chair and went to a small bureau in the corner. 'There you are,' she said triumphantly a moment later. 'Would you like to write it down?'

Antony produced a tattered envelope from his pocket and began to scribble obediently. 'An address in Putney,' he said, handing the more neatly written slip of paper back to his hostess. 'But you've only headed it "Connie". What is her name now?'

'Didn't I tell you? It was a Mr Protheroe she married, and she told me he's a building contractor in a nice way of business.'

III

As Maitland seemed to have lost the power of speech for the moment Roger had to take over again to get them both out of the house with all due politeness. 'Did you hear that?' Antony demanded, once they were safely outside. 'Protheroe! The two witnesses who overheard Mayhew and Harris plotting together . . . or so they said.'

'So that's what had got into you,' said Roger enlightened. 'I'd forgotten the name, and I couldn't think what on earth was up with you. But . . . you're not relying too much on this, Antony? What I'm trying to say is, does it prove anything?'

'I'll talk it over with Uncle Nick of course, but no, I don't think it does, not legal proof. But you're missing the point, Roger. It can't possibly be coincidence, and it's enough to convince me. I *know* now that Mayhew's telling the truth and young Harris, too. Whoever worked the frame-up, I'll damned well see he doesn't get away with it.'

'Yes, I understand. There's another point you might consider,' said Roger, 'and I only mention it because I think you were a little too excited to take it in. Mrs Connor said that Mrs Porson just walked out of the house when she got married leaving everything behind her, and it was sold furnished to the young couple next door, who had probably just been married and were glad enough not to have to pay hire purchase on their furniture, as well as whatever the mortgage is costing them. I should think they'd get it cheaper that way, wouldn't you?'

'You mean something might have been left behind, something incriminating? I don't see it myself, I'm afraid. It's more likely it

103

would be like evacuating an embassy . . . Mrs Porson burning all their papers before she left.'

'Yes, I suppose you're right,' said Roger, obviously giving up the idea with some regret. 'In any case it would be no good asking the girl we saw just now, we'd only be referred to Dick again. But it's something that might be worth trying later if all else fails.'

So that was how they left it. Roger decided to treat himself to an early night, but drove Maitland back to chambers first, where he found that Sir Nicholas, having come back from lunch and re-created havoc among the papers on his desk, had also decided to go home. It was quite impossible for him to leave immediately without incurring old Mr Mallory's undying curse, but as soon as he decently could he left too and made his way back to Kempenfeldt Square. Gibbs was hovering as usual but without any message to convey, and the study door was shut. Antony went straight across the hall and flung it open, to find his uncle and aunt sharing a late cup of tea. 'I've got a good deal to tell you, Uncle Nick,' he announced. 'For once in my life I'm absolutely certain now that our clients are innocent.'

There was a moment's dead silence, during which Antony – as he related it to Jenny later – felt that it was touch and go whether his uncle told him to go out again and come in in a more seemly fashion. Sir Nicholas indeed seemed in no hurry to speak, but contented himself with looking his nephew up and down rather as though he feared he'd taken leave of his senses. It was left to Vera to make the inevitable inquiry. 'Not like you, Antony,' she said bluntly. 'What's happened?'

He shut the door carefully and went across to join them, far too restless to sit down, a fact which needed no explanation. 'You know the Protheroes,' he said. 'The couple who say they overheard Mayhew and Harris plotting together.'

'I'm hardly likely to have forgotten them,' said Sir Nicholas acidly, 'nor I think is Vera, though she's not directly engaged in the case. Witnesses for the prosecution, Antony – I trust you haven't forgotten yourself so far as to approach them.'

'No, Uncle Nick, of course I haven't. But do you know who she is?'

'Mrs Kenneth Protheroe, so far as I remember. I believe her own name is Constance. But I fail to see –'

'You will in a minute,' said Maitland, though he knew well

104

enough that his uncle hated to be interrupted. 'I should have put it differently. It isn't who she is that matters, but who she was up to about last March.'

'Are you implying that she underwent a change of identity? No doubt all this is leading up to a revelation of some kind,' said Sir Nicholas, though he did not sound hopeful.

'Uncle Nick, this is important! I've been talking about the gang Edwin Porson belonged to as being possibly involved in framing our clients, but that was just because I had to start somewhere. Only I was right! Mrs Protheroe was Connie Porson, according to her next door neighbour, and I see no reason to doubt Mrs Connor's word.'

'That is news indeed,' said Sir Nicholas slowly, 'and capable, I presume, of confirmation.'

'Bellerby's seeing to that, but to my mind there's no doubt about it. Mrs Connor's story was quite circumstantial, and she'd no axe of any sort to grind.' (Sir Nicholas closed his eyes for a moment, but made no comment.) 'Apparently she heard a great sob story from Mrs Porson after her husband was killed, about financial arrangements, and the police investigation, and of course her own innocence. But it explains her involvement in this affair . . . don't you think? If the gang gave her a pension, for instance, or compensation of some kind, she'd feel obliged to them. Sykes always thought she knew at least something of her husband's activities. Or it may have been straight out bribery of somebody they knew would be susceptible to it.'

'I thought we had agreed to refer to "the organisation",' said Sir Nicholas coldly. 'And both your aunt and I are quite capable of grasping your point without further elaboration. But what do you think I can do with it as it stands?'

'I – I wasn't really thinking as far ahead as the trial. It's just that at least we know where to look now –'

Sir Nicholas steam-rollered over this explanation, as was his habit when deeply moved. 'If you think I am going to cross-examine this woman in court about her previous marriage to a known criminal you've very much mistaken. I can think of nothing that would more surely alienate the jury, particularly as you say that she is extremely vehement about her own innocence in the matter.'

'Well, of course I understand that, Uncle Nick. Only it does make a difference, you do see that, don't you? Being sure I mean that our clients' story is really true.'

'Yes, I had grasped that point,' said Sir Nicholas, relenting suddenly, 'and it certainly is a giant step forward.' But when Antony had left them some ten minutes later he turned immediately to his wife with a rueful look. 'You know how it will be, my dear. He's exhilarated for the moment by this discovery, but it won't last.'

'At least he's convinced now, but I think you are too, Nicholas,' said Vera shrewdly.

'Certanly, I'm no fonder of coincidence than Antony is. But if you think about it you'll see what I mean. Just for the moment the certainty that he's on the right track is sufficient for him, but as soon as he realises the difficulties in our path his damnable sense of responsibility will grow to giant proportions, and he'll be in the depths again.'

'Suppose you're right,' said Vera sighing. 'But at least,' she added more cheerfully, 'I don't see how he's going to get close to any of the people, so perhaps we're both exaggerating the danger that may be involved. He can't approach Mrs Porson for information about her former husband's associates now.'

'That is certainly something to be thankful for,' said Sir Nicholas, but he sounded far from convinced. 'However, I feel more strongly as time goes on, my dear Vera, that we were wrong in persuading him to mix himself up in this affair.'

'My idea,' said Vera gruffly.

'And at the time I thought it was an excellent one,' Sir Nicholas told her. 'But at least,' he added, also brightening a little, 'Bellerby told me the case is being brought forward in the list, so there won't be much time for Antony to get into mischief before we get into court. And once there, in the unlikely event that we can do something for out clients, this Assistant Commissioner fellow will hardly be able to blame anyone but me.'

That was two rash assumptions, almost within one breath, a thing very unlike Sir Nicholas. But perhaps it was as well that he couldn't see into the future. For the moment he was content, and Vera was inclined to agree with him, with his own assessment of the situation.

Friday, 10th October

I

It had been arranged that Maitland should see the senior of their
two clients at Mr Bellerby's office before he went into chambers
the following morning, and when he got there soon after nine
o'clock Mayhew was already waiting for him. It wasn't long
before the solicitor left them alone together, and Mayhew wasted
no time in coming to the point. 'I've been talking to Gerry,' he
said. 'What's all this about someone we know possibly being
involved in . . . in what I can only call framing us?'

'Do you really want me to explain it all again?' asked Antony,
resigned.

'No, I suppose not, I understand your point well enough. The
only thing is I just won't believe that any of our friends –'

'All right then, we'll leave it there.' And try to come at it
another way, Antony thought, though he did not add that aloud.
'I think perhaps the best thing we can do at this point is to
concentrate on character witnesses. I really should have asked
Mrs Mayhew about that, but it didn't occur to me at the time.
What a delightful wife you have, Chief Inspector.'

He'd obviously hit on the right remark. Mayhew's expression
lightened immediately. 'There's nobody who doesn't like
Dorothy,' he affirmed. But then he looked doubtful. 'Are you
telling me, Mr Maitland, it's a forlorn hope. If we're reduced to
character witnesses –'

'It doesn't mean we've reached the end of everything, only it's
as well to cover all contingencies,' Maitland assured him. 'If you
can think of anyone –'

'Well, there's the Reverend Mr Mercer from St. Mark's. That's
our parish church, and besides attending fairly regularly
Dorothy's a great one for helping out when need be. Come to

think of it he'd probably speak for young Gerry as well; he's met him at our house, and seen him in church sometimes, and I don't suppose the lad would be keen on bringing up someone from the country who'd known him as a boy. There's Dorothy's father of course, a respectable enough chap as anyone can see. But in the circumstances that would hardly do.'

'No, probably not.' Antony produced an envelope, slit it open carefully with Mr Bellerby's paper knife, and was now scribbling industriously. 'Mr Mercer sounds splendid, but it would be as well if we could add a couple or more names to the list.'

'I don't know –' said Mayhew doubtfully.

'Come now, Chief Inspector, it might be important.'

'So you can look twice at them in case they've been running this racket?' Mayhew demanded.

It was obviously no good trying to dissemble, he should have remembered he was talking to a detective. 'If I admit that's part of the reason will you tell me?' he said. 'Harris did explain it fully to you, didn't he? Getting Stokes and Barleycorn off scot-free should have been enough for them, and though I don't suppose they'd have been worried at the kind of mess it left you two in why should they have bothered to press it further? Have you some friends, very familiar friends, with whom you get together regularly and talk over the affairs of the world, and your own affairs among them? Police work is of great interest to most people, and I'm not accusing any of your friends necessarily, but some scrap of information might quite innocently be passed on.'

'That's better. The trouble is I never talk about my job. Well, only to Dorothy, and then not usually until a case is closed. Only to tell her what I'm working on.'

That Antony could well believe, the Chief Inspector was naturally a silent man. 'Your job's murder,' he insisted. 'But the subject of – of crime in general might have been discussed.'

'I daresay it was. Well, I'll be frank with you, Mr Maitland, I did do a bit of thinking on the subject after Gerry spoke to me and explained what was on your mind. I feel like a traitor saying that but . . . wouldn't you have done?'

'Undoubtedly.'

'Well, I couldn't come up with anything. Think about it, Mr Maitland. Supposing I was to put an idea like that to you.'

'I shouldn't like it any more than you do, Chief Inspector. All the same . . . Sykes told me that Porson's activities were pretty generally known, though there was never any proof of his involvement that would stand up in court. His speciality was murder.'

'So it was, but I'd hardly place him among my friends or even among my acquaintances. And in any case he's dead.'

'Yes. But I've learned two things in particular since I talked to Mrs Mayhew and Constable Harris,' Antony told him. 'One is that an organisation does indeed exist such as the one for which he was supposed to have been working. My information is that it's run on the lines of a company, several different departments completely independent of each other, and that the head of the department is the only one who knows the man at the top. The General Manager, the person I was speaking to called him.'

'Who on earth told you all that, Mr Maitland?' For a moment Mayhew had forgotten his own predicament and his predominant emotion was one of curiosity.

'I don't think I'll tell you that. If we get you off you might remember, and wonder where *he* got his knowledge. But the other thing you'll find even more interesting. You know the Protheroes who are giving some of the most damning evidence against you?'

'I know of them. They didn't come forward until the disciplinary inquiry was complete so I've never seen either of them except at the Magistrates' Court hearing.'

'You probably wouldn't have been any wiser if you had. The thing is, Chief Inspector – and this ought to make you think if nothing else does – Mrs Protheroe is the widow of Edwin Porson.'

'Then –' Mayhew started in a sudden quite uncharacteristic blaze of excitement. 'But I was told she always swore she knew nothing of what her husband had been doing,' he went on more soberly. 'I can see you think it's proof enough, Mr Maitland, but if she went on playing the innocent it wouldn't help with the jury to bring that fact out into the open.'

'No, my uncle has already pointed that out to me. Though he thinks, as I do, that it would be altogether too much of a coincidence if there were no connection. But it means – even Uncle Nick agrees with me about this – that there is such an organisation involved, and they they went to the trouble of adding to the charges against you for some reason other than merely spite. They must have paid the Protheroes well, for instance, because you can't deny the risk involved for them.'

'I see what you mean.' Mayhew smiled. 'Another of your guesses that's turned out to be right. I still can't think of anybody, and I gather Gerry couldn't either. He'd been such a short time here, and the people he knows best are Dorothy and me, and though he has a girl and knows her family quite well I think he isn't keen on reminding them of his present lowly occupation. We met them once, and I can quite understand his feeling that way.'

'Do you know anything about this organisation, outside your own field?'

'Only that something exists or is believed to exist on the lines you mentioned.'

'Sykes is being cagey, but he did tell me earlier that some of the people suspected of being associates of Porson's have served prison sentences.'

'Yes, there've been cases where it was pretty evident the accused wasn't working alone, but there was no definite proof to the contrary.' Mayhew's interest was caught, and again he was only too willing to talk, but it was quite obvious that it had never occurred to him – as it had to Sykes – that knowledge might sometimes be dangerous, and he might be putting his counsel at risk. 'As to the – the different departments you spoke of, you must remember that this is still all conjecture. But in a number of different activities we have suspected that a guiding hand was at work, though I've never heard anyone carry the argument quite so far as you have done.'

'Well, suppose for a moment I'm right, as you seemed to be prepared to do a moment ago. Suppose there's one man who's the head of the whole thing. How many departments do you think he would be running?'

'I can tell you the things we suspected had some connection with each other but you must remember that it is only suspicion.' Mayhew had reverted to type and become his cautious self again.

'Why did there seem to be a connection?'

'Well, you know about Porson, he was a marksman. I could tell you half a dozen jobs I'm pretty sure he did, and the motive could well have been tied in with some of those other activities you're asking about. Victims whose existence had become inconvenient to the gang.'

'That sounds helpful. Tell me some of them.'

'Organised theft for one, and I mean in particular some special object for which there was known to be a market, most probably abroad. Art works, or valuable antiques. Smuggling is tied in with that, and I don't suppose it stops there. Hijacking too, I know you might say that was organised theft as well but the goods are of a quite different nature, and I'm pretty sure Porson was called in, at least in one instance. Dope, that ties in with the smuggling again and I think it's part of the same racket. But all this seems to argue some degree of co-operation between the departments.'

'Not necessarily. Let's stick to that way of talking about them for the moment. I'm sure my uncle will prefer it. You've organised the theft of a painting, say, a famous one which would have a ready sale to some unscrupulous buyer in America. The department heads know the managing director, remember, so that a request for assistance is made to him and he arranges with the appropriate department head for the thing to be smuggled out of the country. How does that strike you?'

'Possible,' said Mayhew rather grudgingly. 'But I must say,' he added rather more enthusiastically a moment later, 'it would be a lot safer that way for everyone concerned.'

'Well, let's hope I'm right, because I can see us taking on one Lord High Organiser, but not the heads of – I think it's five different departments you've mentioned. Is there anything else you think might be tied in, anything that shows signs of a guiding hand at the helm?'

'Yes, I think there is, but I must stress that I don't know anything to tie them in definitely with Porson and his crowd. There've been more cases than usual of arson and either proved or suspected insurance fraud, and quite definitely prostitution has been organised in a big way. We all know the kind of thing that goes on, and unfortunately always will, but this is something different. If a girl gets into trouble with the law it doesn't seem to worry her terribly; you'd almost think she was working on a salary. But neither of those things need necessarily be part of the larger organisation.'

'No, I see. Tell me, Mayhew, when these people get caught, the ones you've suspected of not working on their own, do they ever talk?'

'No, and they don't seem worried either. That's just what I've heard, but it sort of ties in, doesn't it?'

'Fringe benefits,' said Maitland rather bitterly. 'Perhaps we should add an Accounts Department to the others we've mentioned. I'm glad you've told me all this, though I don't at the moment see how exactly I can make use of it. Can we get back to the question you dislike so much, of someone you may have talked to . . . I'm not necessarily referring to any information you may have let drop, you know, I'm quite confident of your discretion. It's more likely to have been something you've heard, whose significance might only later dawn on you.'

'I don't discuss my cases with our friends, and I wouldn't mention anything I heard in the course of duty,' said Mayhew again, completely disregarding Maitland's disclaimer; or perhaps, reflected Antony ruefully, giving it as much value as it deserved.

'I understand that.'

'But sometimes, of course . . . getting together with friends we'll talk about the way the world's going, that kind of thing. And perhaps about cases I'm not involved in, but only in a general way. But I can't believe –'

'You've got to believe. If you won't think of yourself, think of young Gerry Harris. And of the effect your conviction will have on your wife.'

This time the rumbling noise which preceded Mayhew's speech sounded more like a groan. 'She fair dotes on the lad, I know, that's why I haven't had the heart to tell her how bad it may be.'

'Feeling sorry for them won't do any good,' said Maitland bracingly. 'Whereas if you'd just answer my question –'

'I thought I had. I hoped I had. Don't you think I've been brooding about this ever since Gerry told me what was on your mind? I – don't – talk – about – my – work,' said Mayhew, spacing the words out to give them greater emphasis. 'Only sometimes to Dorothy as I said, there's no harm in that.'

112

'No harm at all,' Antony agreed, thinking of Jenny and her quiet acceptance of the arguments that sometimes raged around her.

'Or of course if Gerry was visiting us and he was on some job that interested him . . . no harm in that either that I can see. And I know he understands the importance of – of discretion as well as I do. As Dorothy does.'

'Yes, I'm sure, but I'd still like you to ask her . . . is there any chance at all that someone could have got the wrong impression from something she said. She's an intelligent woman, Chief Inspector, she'll understand the importance of it in your defence.'

'She's always been very much of a homebody,' said Mayhew. 'There'd be some friends she'd meet when she was out shopping, of course, and have a cup of coffee with, or exchange visits in the afternoon. But they'd all be women, and I'd think the last thing that was discussed would be crime. To tell you the truth I think it bored her rather, even when there was something I wanted to talk over, though she always listened patiently enough. And she played bridge on Wednesday afternoons, but that would be mostly women too, except for a few older men who were retired, and lately she hasn't been able to go so often because her sister who lives in Bexhill has been ill, and Dorothy felt she ought to visit her as often as she could.'

'Well, I can understand the subject could pall with someone whose job wasn't connected with it. I often wonder,' said Maitland, trying to lighten the atmosphere, 'that Jenny doesn't rush screaming from the room at the sound of some of the legal arguments she has to listen to at home. But what about your mutual friends, Chief Inspector? Couples who visit you in the evening, with whom you're on very familiar terms.'

'You don't give up easily, do you?' said Mayhew with a half-smile. 'World affairs, yes, and politics. But there again, if we get on to crime it's only something that's been in the papers, nothing that I'm engaged in myself.'

'All right then, we'll leave it there. What about character witnesses? You've given me the name of your Vicar –'

'Mr Maitland, you know as well as I do that's pretty hopeless.'

'I'm not counselling despair, but just at the moment it seems to be the best thing we can do. The position may change before we get into court though.'

'Very well then.' Mayhew stopped for a moment to think. 'There are our next door neighbours, Rupert and Joanna Phillips; and the Somersets, Terry and Marion. I suppose we see them on an average once a week, though you know enough about my job to realise we quite often have to break engagements. Terry is an optician, and Rupert is Paul Collingwood's managing clerk. You know Mr Collingwood, I expect.'

'Yes, I've had briefs from him from time to time.'

'Well, I imagine the court would regard them both as pretty respectable; Rupert is a qualified solicitor, by the way, but he never could afford to start his own practice.'

'Yes, I should think they'll do very nicely. Then I won't bother you any more just now, Chief Inspector. I'm sorry you didn't like some of my questions.'

'That's all right, Mr Maitland, I –' Both men had got to their feet and there was a moment's silence, and then Mayhew gave one of his rare laughs. 'I knew enough about you to realise how it would be,' he said. 'I'd like to tell you now, whatever happens I'm glad you're on our side.'

He went away then, leaving Antony to report on his more recent activities to Mr Bellerby; and it was only later that Maitland was to reflect with some discomfort on what his client had said.

II

That day Maitland had remembered to warn Gibbs that Superintendent Sykes was expected to dinner, and that he was to be shown straight upstairs when he arrived. Otherwise, as he knew from bitter experience, he would have been greeted with the words that a person from the police had called, and have had to rescue the detective from exile in Sir Nicholas's drawing-room. As it was, except for a certain implied rebuke for his tardiness, he was able to get past the butler without incident; and arriving in his own quarters found Sykes and Jenny drinking sherry companionably together.

When he had helped himself and replenished their glasses he settled down to give a fairly complete account of what he had been doing since he saw the Superintendent. (Presumably Jenny had already answered all the queries as to the health of the entire family, Sykes being puncitilious in these matters.) The detective listened in silence until he came to the inquiries he had made for Mrs Porson, which he had reserved until the end. At that point Sykes sat up very straight in his chair and said stringently, 'That was inexcusable!'

'I know you did your best to discourage me,' said Antony, rather taken aback, 'but –'

'I didn't mean you. I know you well enough, Mr Maitland,' said Sykes, almost echoing Mayhew's words, 'to realise you'll go your own way whatever I say. I mean that was a point that should have been covered by the inquiry.'

'Well since it wasn't, and since by itself it hardly constitutes a defence, I hope you'll keep it to yourself.'

'You didn't need to ask me that, Mr Maitland,' said Sykes rather grumpily. Though whether his displeasure was directed towards the question, or was still reserved for the carelessness of one of his colleagues, was not for the moment clear. 'But it's enough for me and I'm very glad to hear it.'

'For me too. And it raises certain interesting speculations . . . don't you think?'

'Certainly it does,' Sykes agreed, 'and I don't imagine I need to spell them out for you. What have those two to say for themselves?'

'Mayhew and Harris? I talked to them both, and to Mrs Mayhew, though that was before I'd thought the whole thing through. They both say they never discuss their work with outsiders, and they can't think of anything they've learned that might be dangerous to these people, so that it was felt necessary to get them out of the way for as long as possible, at the same time completely discrediting them.'

At that point Jenny announced that dinner was on the table, and in deference to Sir Nicholas's views, even though he wasn't present, they kept off the subject that interested them most while the meal was in progress. Afterwards when the table was cleared (from long experience they both knew that Sykes would insist on

115

helping to 'siden up', to use his own idiom, and could only be thankful he didn't now regard it as essential to 'do the pots' as well) Jenny made coffee, and Antony produced the special cognac that he usually kept for his uncle. The Superintendent had a sedate smile for that, knowing the ways of the household reasonably well by now. 'Softening me up, Mr Maitland?'

'What a hope! No, but there are certain things you might tell me, and certain other things you might find out. I've no right at all to ask for your help, but it's not only for myself.'

'I'm as concerned as you are for my two colleagues,' said Sykes, 'particularly in view of what you've told me, and would like to clear this whole unpleasant business up if we can. Off the record, of course,' he added cautiously.

'Certainly off the record. About this man Kingsley, the one who hired Barleycorn and Stokes. Not his evidence of course, Bellerby's got the proof of that. I'm thinking more of his background, how long he'd been with that firm, and what he was doing before. There'll be a report on him from Cobbolds, of course, but it'll take time and I wouldn't mind betting you've been interested enough to ask some questions yourself.'

'A very ordinary background. His father was a construction worker, and was killed on the job quite young. They lived in Ealing as far as I can remember. His mother went back to work to keep things going, and after Martin Kingsley left Grammar School her employer, who was a chartered accountant, gave the boy his articles. I don't know whether he was exceptionally hard working, or exceptionally brilliant – probably a bit of both – but he's done well for himself since then, going from job to job and always doing a little bit better at each one. He's been at Shadwell's two years, more or less.'

'And before that?'

'The same sort of job, and funnily enough with a construction company like his father, though in rather a different line.'

Antony smiled. 'Not Mr Protheroe's by any chance?'

'No, I think there might have been questions raised about that, particularly when it was thought he'd' – he looked round, rather as though he felt Sir Nicholas might be hiding somewhere in a corner, and then went on, 'done a bunk.'

'I see.' Jenny, who was curled up on the sofa with her coffee

116

cup balanced precariously on the arm, gave her husband a sudden rather sharp look but made no comment. 'Let's talk about the foreman packer who was killed in a motor accident then. For instance, were they known to each other?'

'Only in the way of business . . . business at Shadwell's, I mean. Not previously, so far as anyone has been able to find out. And the packer, whose name was Arthur Abbott, had been with the company for fifteen years, which I'm quite sure is what Kingsley will say was the reason for giving him a hefty bonus when you or Sir Nicholas ask him that question.'

'Yes, I imagine it is. And quite a good answer too, I suppose. But about the accident, is anything more known about that?'

'Not a thing. I have a friend in that manor, so I've been able to ask a few questions without raising any hares. It was hit and run, I told you that before, and the car must have been put in a garage and left there, because there must have been damage to it and none of the repair shops for miles around has had it in for service.'

'Did anybody see what happened? What make was the car, for instance?'

'They were given six different colours, and four different makes. Probably none of them were right. I'm afraid there's no hope there, Mr Maitland.'

'They were taking no chance, were they? What about the Protheroes? Can they prove they were at Hartley's the night they say they overheard Mayhew and Harris plotting together?'

'It isn't the sort of place where you make a booking, and nobody would be likely to remember you unless you were a regular, as some of our chaps are. They say, I'm told, that they just happened to go in there because it was near the cinema they were going to, and they remembered the date exactly because it was Mrs Protheroe's birthday, and the outing a sort of celebration. It's just a matter of their word against Mayhew's and Harris's, but in view of the other evidence there's no doubt who'll be believed.'

'When Porson killed himself –?'

'I know what you're going to ask me, Mr Maitland, and I can't answer you. There was a lot of legal hoo-ha, but the only job we could prove against him was the last one, so there was no question of confiscating what money he had. Mrs Porson was all innocence, made no objection to their accounts being gone over, and I can tell you she was left quite well off. I imagine too there was a pretty hefty payment from the chaps he'd been working with, to keep her sweet as you might say. But that, if it was made, was after the inquiries were finished.'

'Was there any indication where the payments into his account came from?'

Sykes looked at him for a long moment. 'You're getting on to dangerous ground, Mr Maitland. The job he did in Yorkshire was on the side as it were, and you know quite well who paid him for that.'

'Yes, but from things you said, and things I've heard from other people, I've been assuming that the gang would employ him if they had any dirty work to do that needed his particular skills. When that happened, how was he paid?'

'In cash, apparently.'

'Didn't that raise any queries with his bank?'

'Why should it? There are dozens of people who pay in large sums that way, shopkeepers for instance.'

'Yes, of course you're right. But look here, Superintendent, Mayhew's been pretty open with me about this – this organisation as Uncle Nick prefers to call it, and another person I've spoken to –'

'Father William,' said Sykes in a resigned tone, gazing momentarily at the ceiling.

'We don't need to go into that. Am I right in thinking that it's organised very much like an ordinary company, but with each department pretty well separated from the others, and only the department heads knowing the Managing Director?' When Sykes still hesitated he added persuasively, 'If you're thinking of danger, it'd be much less dangerous for you to tell me what you know, than for me to go blundering about in the dark.' As he spoke he remembered vaguely having used that argument before, though for one moment he couldn't remember when.

'I suppose it would,' Sykes agreed rather reluctantly. 'Well as far as I know the description is pretty accurate. Certainly no one knows who's in charge, nor does anyone know what you've called the department heads in many cases. And I agree with you, Mr Maitland, if I were running things that is how I should arrange it.

Safest that way.'

'All the same, you do feel there's a connection. Mayhew mentioned various activities, dope, organised theft, hijacking, smuggling, and murder. Would you agree with his reason for tying them in together?'

'If it was because he felt that one department helped the other out when necessary, yes I would. For instance, some of the killings that bore Porson's trademark were obviously done to help out in that way, though some were contract killings, as you know. I don't know that Mayhew went quite far enough, however. Prostitution has shown some signs of being organised during the past couple of years, and for some considerable time there have been investigations into possible insurance fraud and arson, though I admit neither of those two things have ever been tied in definitely with the other activities.'

'The others I can understand, but prostitution . . . I always imagined if that were organised at all it was a matter of a pimp running half a dozen girls or so.'

'Supposing someone organised the pimps,' Sykes suggested. 'This isn't a very pleasant subject to be talking about in front of you, Mrs Maitland,' he apologised.

'Don't mind me,' Jenny assured him. 'There have been worse things than that talked about in this room over the years, I can assure you.'

'The thing about Jenny is that she likes to know what's going on,' said Antony. 'But I don't quite understand. Do you mean the pimp takes a cut of what his girls make, and then someone else takes a cut from him?'

'Yes, probably in the same way as small shopkeepers may pay for "protection", and when you multiply all that . . . but it isn't quite all. I mean,' – again he glanced rather apologetically at Jenny – 'there's male prostitution as well, and –'

'Yes, I see what you mean. And you think this can be tied in with the other things?'

'I think it's very likely, and my main reason for feeling that may be a strange one, but you know how people like to talk.'

'Only too well.'

'Well, there's been very little of that. They hold their tongues, I'm not just talking about the prostitutes now, but the people in

119

all these lines we've mentioned, and if they get sent down they do their time and I've got a feeling there's a nice little present waiting for them when they come out. Porson talked, as you may know, before he hanged himself.'

'Yes, but I don't know what he said.'

'He fingered his department head, which seems as good a name as any other, but unfortunately the man had already left the country for parts unknown . . . though I could make a pretty good guess where he is. But Porson, having by then committed a murder in the presence of witnesses, knew there was no hope of anything being done for him. Come to think of it, that may have been the reason so much was done for Stokes and Barleycorn.'

'Yes, I see. Do you know any of the department heads?'

'I have my suspicions in one or two cases, but that, Mr Maitland, is something I won't tell you even as things are.'

'But at least do you know who's running Kingsley?'

'No, I don't. I agree that's something fairly new, taking advantage of the sudden vacancy as it were. He and the two men who murdered Goodbody may be the only ones concerned.'

'And you're not going to tell me either if you've any suspicions about who the Managing Director might be?'

'I don't think I'd tell you in any case, Mr Maitland, I'd have to think about that. But as it happens I haven't the remotest idea.'

Antony smiled at him. 'Oh, well, I didn't really think you would tell me in any case,' he said. 'I take it you're thinking that Stokes and Barleycorn were a special case; as a charge of murder, if it were proved, would be likely to keep them inside for a good long time, and like Porson they'd have talked.'

'That's about the size of it, Mr Maitland.'

'Then let's forget about crime for a while and talk about something else. Tell Jenny what you were telling me the other day about your adventures in Spain when you took your holiday. It's a really good story, love, but the Superintendent will tell it much better than I could.'

They talked for a long time after that and succeeded well enough in avoiding the subject that was on all their minds. It was late when Sykes left. Antony coming back upstairs after seeing him safely on his way found Jenny standing in his own favourite place on the hearthrug with a militant look in her eye. 'What are you going to do?' she demanded.

'Collect the debris of our after-dinner entertainment,' (it was rarely indeed that Jenny neglected to do this the moment their visitors left), 'and then go to bed,' said Maitland, maddeningly literal.

'You know perfectly well I didn't mean that. Has something occurred to you? When you were talking to the Inspector about the case I thought it had.'

'Superintendent,' said Antony automatically. 'My dearest love, the answer to your question is a very simple one. Nothing at all.'

'I don't believe you!'

'I meant, of course, until the case comes into court.'

'But you've had an idea,' said Jenny. 'And I know what you're going to say, that you always have ideas of one sort or another. And you'll probably go on to say that it's too vague to tell me about. Only –'

'I meant what I said, love. The idea was one that concerns our handling of the case. I shall talk to Uncle Nick tomorrow and see if I can persuade him to my way of thinking, and to Bellerby on Monday about calling some of these character witnesses whose names I've got, and that will be absolutely all until the trial. Which won't be very long, I gather – they're pushing it ahead in the list. The Assistant Commissioner is in a reforming mood, and wants everyone to know it.'

Jenny moved then and came across to his side. 'I don't want to fuss,' she said, 'but you know on the whole I'd rather you didn't get yourself killed.'

He smiled down at her. 'I've no intention of doing so,' he said lightly, but then his expression became more serious. 'All the same, love, you were perfectly right that I had an idea, and just as right when you said it was too nebulous to put into words. And I'll tell you this much, I don't like what I'm thinking. Not one little bit!'

Saturday, 11th October

I

Saturday lunchtime, when the Maitlands joined Sir Nicholas and Vera, and Mrs Stokes put out her best efforts on their behalf, was as much of an institution as their Tuesday evening gatherings upstairs. Antony spent the morning walking in the park, and for once didn't take Jenny with him as was his custom at weekends. He had come to the conclusion that the best time to tackle his uncle would be after lunch, when Sir Nicholas might be presumed to be in a mellow mood, but before they reached that stage he wanted to think things out. By the time he returned, however, rather later than he intended – thereby earning Gibbs's disapproval, which he bore philosophically – he had decided that everything he wanted to say could be compressed into about two minutes, while the request he had to make was going to require a great deal more forbearance on Sir Nicholas's part than could normally be expected of him.

Gibbs had for many years performed exactly as many or as few of his duties as he felt disposed, and that day was one of the increasingly rare occasions when he chose to wait on them at table, thus preventing any private discussion. By the time they had retired to the study, and the old man had served coffee and left them in peace, shutting the door firmly behind him, Maitland was frankly fidgeting, and his uncle turned on him with something like a snarl.

'It is becoming increasingly obvious that there is something you wish to communicate to me, Antony. I presume it's about this wretched business of Chief Inspector Mayhew.'

'Yes, it is. Can you bear it all again, love?' he added, turning to Jenny. 'I ought to tell Uncle Nick and Vera about my talk with Mayhew yesterday morning, and my discussion with Sykes last night.'

'Yes, of course I can. He's got an idea, Uncle Nick,' she confided, 'but he won't tell me what it is. Do you think that's fair?'

'That's exactly why I want you to listen all over again,' Antony protested. 'And I think we're going to need Vera's advice.'

'If that means you've got some crack-brained scheme in your head which you hope your aunt will support,' said Sir Nicholas coldly, 'I suppose this is as good a time as any for us to hear about it.' But he, like the others, had noted his nephew's look of strain, not unmingled, oddly enough, with excitement, and refrained from comment while Antony recounted his activities of the day before and his newly-formed proposals as to how they should handle the defence. 'Bellerby says we'll probably be in court as early as a week on Monday,' he concluded. 'Can you fit that in with the rest of your list, Uncle Nick?'

'Mallory will arrange it,' said Sir Nicholas negligently. 'But in spite of what you say we shall be going into court without anything at all in the nature of a real defence.'

'There is just one other thing, Uncle Nick.' He hesitated there and Sir Nicholas put the question that had been in all their minds – unspoken because of Gibbs's presence – ever since he joined them.

'If you are about to explain your demeanour when you first came in –'

'Like a cat with its fur rubbed the wrong way,' said Vera.

'– we shall of course be glad to hear you. I take it something happened while you were out.'

'How on earth did you know that, Uncle Nick?'

'It was perfectly obvious to all of us, I imagine.'

'Well, there's nothing to worry about.' His eyes were on Jenny as he spoke, feeling now that he should have reassured her before, as she was never one to ask questions out of turn. 'I was attacked in the park this morning . . . no, love, I wasn't hurt in the slightest, I'm not likely to be caught by a trick like that, you know.'

'You said –' Jenny started, and he put out a hand to cover hers.

'I know I did, love, and I meant it. But this just goes to prove what I've been thinking, you see, because it's obvious someone

123

knows I've been asking questions, and unless I'm right how could they have done?'

'Better tell us what happened,' said Vera at her gruffest.

'It was too silly for words really. There weren't many people about, there's a nasty wind blowing and I think they got discouraged, so this chap dogging my footsteps stuck out like a sore thumb.'

'If you must use such expressions let them at least be accurate,' his uncle adjured him.

'Yes, sir, I'll try.' But his eyes were still on Jenny, and his next words were addressed to her. 'There was really no danger, love. I stopped to look out across the lake . . . it was really to give him the chance he was obviously waiting for, because I was getting a little tired of his company. He came up behind me with a knife, but I know a trick worth two of that and he finished up in the water.'

'I seem to have deplored before this habit of yours of brawling in public places,' said Sir Nicholas, but Vera had her own ideas about what they had heard.

'Think it was a very good thing,' she approved. 'What did you do then?'

'Hauled him off to the nearest bobby. He was quite a little chap, and the wetting he'd had seemed to have knocked the stuffing out of him.' He might have added, he never seemed to realise I'd only one good arm, but none of his listeners would have expected him to do that. 'We ended up at Lennox Street Police Station, and I made a statement. He wasn't talking, but I'm bound to hear a little bit more on Monday in the Magistrates' Court.'

'They'll let him out on bail,' said Jenny, obviously not liking the idea.

'Don't worry, love, he won't try anything again,' said Antony confidently. 'And if you're imagining whole rows of people lined up wanting to kill me, I think after one attempt has failed that would be a little too obvious, don't you?'

'I suppose so,' said Jenny doubtfully.

'Think Antony's right,' said Vera consolingly. 'Don't you agree with me, Nicholas?'

'I agree with you so far as the danger goes,' her husband

informed her. 'I even agree with Antony that it goes some way towards proving the rather obscure point he's been trying to make. But even with these extra witnesses Bellerby is going to call, and the inquiries he will have made –'

'Uncle Nick, you've never been afraid to take a chance, in fact there've been times when you've scared me out of my wits by the line you took. This time will you do so just on my say so?'

There was a silence, just a little too long for comfort. 'The trouble is, Antony, your premise is based on even more flimsy grounds than usual.'

'*Sir, I can give you an argument, but I cannot give you an understanding.*' ('You were taking your life into your hands, quoting Johnson at him,' said Jenny. But that was later.)

For a moment Sir Nicholas stared at his nephew incredulously, then, with one of his all-too-sudden changes of mood, he laughed. '*Touché,*' he said. 'Very well, Antony, we'll walk into the lion's mouth together.'

'It means calling Mrs Mayhew,' Maitland warned him.

'A counsel of despair,' Sir Nicholas agreed. 'But I must confess to some interest in seeing this solicitor friend of theirs. However sincere Mayhew may have been in his denials, I can't believe that two men with a common interest in the law could meet so frequently without the subject of their respective employment coming up.'

'I did make myself clear, Uncle Nick? I'm beginning to wonder whether I was right about the reason for Mayhew and Harris being framed on the more serious charge.'

Another silence. Sir Nicholas might have been preparing some devastating comeback, and on the whole that was what Maitland expected. But when it came his uncle's reply surprised him.

'Very well, Antony, I've already said I will follow the line you have laid out, but on one condition: that you spend at least a little time during the next week reading through the papers Bellerby has sent me.'

II

That should have been the end of the matter till the case came on, but in the meantime two things were to occur that were quite unexpected. The first was that very evening. Meg and Roger were dining with them, Meg obviously in a state of excitement though still maintaining a highly dramatic air of mystery. 'So you won't be needing my help any more,' said Roger, perhaps a little regretfully, when Antony had finished giving them a very much abbreviated account of what had been happening.

'So far as I can see at the moment, no. I think this is a matter that can only be dealt with in a fairly orthodox way in court.'

Roger laughed at that. 'I'm not altogether clear what you're hoping to achieve, but that I should like to see,' he commented.

'You forget, Uncle Nick will be handling matters.'

But at that moment the house phone rang, and Gibbs's voice announced disagreeably that a young lady had called to see Mr Maitland. 'A Miss Alice Harper,' he added.

The house phone had been installed years ago for Gibbs's convenience but he had only consented to use it since Vera's arrival in the household, preferring to stump upstairs with his messages, with the air of one unjustly put upon. So at least there was something to be thankful for, even if he still managed to convey the very strong impression that there was something clandestine about the whole affair. Maitland turned from the phone with a puzzled look.

'Alice Harper?' he said. And then, 'Oh, I know, Constable Harris's girlfriend. Why do these things always happen to me?'

'Because you have such a nice sympathetic nature, darling,' Meg told him.

'I've never met the girl. I told Gibbs to put her in the study, Uncle Nick and Vera are out this evening. Perhaps it would be as well if you came down with me, Roger. In case she wants to weep on my shoulder, you know, and Gibbs catches us at it.'

'I'll come of course,' said Roger, 'but from what you've told me I can't think what the girl wants.'

What she wanted, as they both very soon realised when they got downstairs, was something to hope for, a thing which no one at the moment was in a position to give her. 'I'm very sorry if I've disturbed your evening,' she said. 'I came out as soon as dinner was over, but I realise it is a little late. But Gerry said you'd been kind to him, and I've heard of you of course, Mr Maitland, so I thought perhaps –'

Seeing his friend uncharacteristically speechless, Roger stepped into the breach. Alice Harper was a pretty enough girl, with fair straight hair, blue eyes that were now more than a little anxious, and a face a little too thin for real beauty. Roger, used to Meg's ways, recognised her dress immediately as a model, but she wore it with complete unselfconsciousness.

She had, however, a slightly peaked look, and as soon as he'd got her seated he told her she'd be the better for a little brandy, and Maitland roused himself out of his trance to provide it. When he came back to join the others by the fire, which had practically gone out though the room was warm (Vera was a warm-blooded creature and would never have thought to turn up the central heating, but Sir Nicholas had learned in self-protection to remember to do so), they were already talking comfortably together. Alice received the cognac with a slight look of distaste, but it was noticeable that after she had sipped a little the colour came back to her cheeks.

'I don't deserve to be spoiled like this,' she said, 'when I've no right at all to be here.'

'Mr Harris mentioned your name to me,' said Antony, not quite sure how to refer to a client who was also a police constable. 'I gather you're a friend of his, and that your parents knew his parents at one time.'

'We're a little more than friends,' said Alice simply. 'We're going to be married.'

'Oh, I see. Ah – does he know?'

'I suppose the answer to that is, Yes and No,' said Alice Harper, who seemed to have settled down to a quite alarming extent under Roger's preliminary ministrations. 'He says he can't because he has no money, and I say why should that make any difference? I'm sure you both agree with me.'

'Better a cottage where love is, or however the quotation goes,' said Antony rather vaguely. 'But at the moment we have a more urgent problem, Miss Harper, and I'm sure that's why you're

127

here.'

'Yes, of course it is. Gerry won't see me, I had to go round to his place after he'd talked to you to find out what had happened. But he says it wouldn't be fair, and my parents are so disapproving now, even mother, who was always on our side, so I just had to talk to someone sympathetic.'

'Well, I'm sure you'll understand if you think about it that there's nothing at all I can tell you at this time about our conduct of the case, except that my uncle, who is leading for the defence, is one of the most capable counsel I know. You may be sure he'll do his best for both our clients.'

'Yes, I know that but . . . will it be good enough?'

'That's something I can't possibly say at this stage.' (This was awkward, damnably awkward.) 'If I tell you something, Miss Harper, will you promise not to talk it over with your parents until they receive official confirmation?'

'Of course, but I don't understand. Official confirmation of what?'

'Of the fact that we shall be calling them as character witnesses.'

'I don't think they'll like that at all, at least my father won't.'

'The reason is that they can speak of his background, the kind of family he comes from. You see, Miss Harper, if we can create a sympathetic atmosphere –'

'Yes, I see. Well, I think mother would go along with that, she was always fond of Gerry's mother and they've kept in touch though they haven't seen each other for quite a long time I think. And I'll do my best to persuade father, though you did say I wasn't to mention it until they knew what was happening.'

'You're quite right. Telling you anything at all is an indiscretion on my part so I'd rather they didn't know about it. Mr and Mrs Green may be called as well; I believe you know them.'

'Oh, yes, all my life. They're great friends of my parents. He's a newspaper man and she's a very artistic sort of person who teaches flower arranging. I'd always taken that for granted, but for some reason it struck Gerry as awfully funny, he couldn't imagine anybody making a living out of a thing like that. It's possible they might be more helpful though because I don't think it seemed quite so dreadful to them that he'd come down in the world as I have to admit it did to mother and father.'

'I don't think you should be too hard on them,' said Maitland, smiling at her. 'After all, the Greens probably don't have an attractive daughter whose future they're worried about.'

'They've just two sons. And I know dad has always been ambitious for me, wanting me to marry well. He used to say "never marry for money, but marry where money is" . . . as a joke, you know. And Gerry's just the sort of son-in-law he'd have liked, if things had been different. I suppose it wouldn't be any good my saying the sort of person he is . . . Gerry I mean. After all I know him a great deal better than my parents do.'

'Yes, but I don't think anyone would believe a word you said.'

'Don't you?'

'That's different. Did Gerry ever talk to you about his work?'

'Not a word. Not because he was ashamed of it, I think he'd grown to like what he was doing and that's partly why this is so awful because he was hoping to make a career for himself in the police force. But he's more likely to go to prison for years and years . . . I don't understand much about the law, but I'm quite sure it will go harder with him because he was in a position of trust.'

'And you're quite sure he never mentioned any of the cases he was involved in?'

'Quite, quite sure. After all' – she gave him a rather sad smile – 'we had better things to talk about.'

'I'm sure you had. Well, Miss Harper, it's no use telling you not to worry, and I'm sure you understand why I can't go into details about the way my uncle is going to handle things, but I do assure you that everything that can be done will be done.'

'Yes, of course, and I mustn't keep you any longer.' She got up as she spoke, and as they followed suit held out a hand to each of them in turn. 'You've both been very kind to me,' she said. 'I won't apologise for coming, because talking about him has made things seem just a little bit better.'

'Of all the damnable things!' said Maitland as they went upstairs after seeing her out. 'If she feels reassured she's deceiving herself, or was it my fault?'

'I don't think you told her anything that wasn't absolutely

true,' said Roger. 'And if she's feeling a little better, isn't that a good thing? Even if it's only temporary.'

'I told her one thing that was a downright lie,' Antony corrected him, 'besides doing my best to mislead her in other ways. Character evidence is our last resource, a counsel of despair Uncle Nick calls it. But I agree with you, I suppose, it was no use pointing that out to her, even if it does make me feel like a hypocrite.'

Monday, 13th October

I

The appearance of Antony's assailant in the Magistrates' Court the following Monday morning was a brief one. His name was Matthew Adams and he looked slightly less bedraggled that morning, but still not particularly prepossessing. (Maitland had reached the conclusion that the reorganisation of the 'assassination department' had not been particularly efficient.) The prisoner gave his age as thirty-six and his occupation as that of an electrician, though he was at present out of work. His previous employers were Greenbrier and Appleby, and they would give him a good character. It was just being short of work that had led to his being laid off eighteen months ago. He made no attempt to deny possession of the knife, but insisted it was for intimidation purposes only, 'Me needing the cash, see, and him looking as though he had something on him.' He appeared aggrieved by his victim's retaliation, and altogether seemed to feel that he had more cause to complain than the man he had – or so he said – only intended to rob. The hearing finished with his being committed for trial and being granted bail in the meantime, and the last Maitland saw of him he was talking to a sympathetic-looking individual from one of the charitable trusts, no doubt intent on providing some interim help, or perhaps even trying to find him another job.

But the hearing as a whole had given Antony a little more food for thought, and a little more information to be passed on to Mr Bellerby and his firm of inquiry agents. He wasn't too pleased when he reached the street to find his way barred by a man as tall as himself, though even more slightly built, who eyed him with disfavour and said, 'Mr Maitland?' on a note of inquiry.

'You must be a friend of Chief Inspector Conway,' said

131

Antony. 'He always greets me in just that tone of voice and looks at me as though he'd found a slug in his salad.'

'I know the Chief Inspector, certainly.' The response was obviously intended to be offensive. 'Permit me to introduce myself. Sir Alfred Godalming.'

'Do you know, I was beginning to wonder about that. I know there are a number of people who disapprove of me for one reason or another, but not too many do so quite so openly. The former Chief Superintendent Briggs was an exception, and I believe you were a friend, or at least an acquaintance of his.'

'Who told you that?'

'Why, Briggs, of course.' For once the lie cost Antony no pangs of conscience. 'But surely so important a person as yourself shouldn't be wasting his time on so small a matter as this. You have just come from court haven't you? I thought I saw you there.'

'Certainly I have, but I don't agree with you, Mr Maitland, that it's exactly a small matter. Perhaps it would be as well if you would come round to the Yard and talk it over.'

'Is that a request or an order?'

'Take it as you please.'

'There's only one way I can possibly take it. You forget, Sir Alfred, you're talking to a lawyer.'

'On the contrary, I don't forget that for a moment. Am I to understand that you refuse to accompany me?'

'No, I'm interested to meet you and I think perhaps a talk might clear the air. But my uncle's chambers are nearer, or – better still – since it's lunchtime, come and have lunch with me.'

'On the whole I should prefer to talk in chambers,' said Godalming, obviously bowing to the inevitable, though not so far as to eat his enemy's salt.

'Then let's get on with it.' Maitland set off down the pavement, and the other man fell into step beside him. 'With any luck we'll catch my uncle before he goes out.'

'I have no business with Sir Nicholas.'

'I think you'll find, however, that he has a certain interest in my affairs, and frankly I should prefer to have him present until I find out the reason for this rather unexpected desire to talk to me. Besides,' he added, and turned his head for a moment to smile at his companion, 'his room is very much more comfortable than mine.'

After that they walked in silence until they reached the Inner Temple. Inquiry of Mr Mallory revealed the fact that Sir Nicholas was alone, and Antony made his way straight to his uncle's room. 'This is Sir Alfred Godalming, Uncle Nick,' he said, standing back to let the other man precede him. 'He quite inexplicably attended the Magistrates' Court hearing this morning, and now for some reason he wants to talk to me.'

Sir Nicholas got up, removed his spectacle, and placed them carefully on the disorder of papers on his desk. 'I am of course delighted to make your acquaintance, Sir Alfred,' he said courteously, obviously needing no reminder from his nephew that they only knew of the Assistant Commissioner's hostility through Superintendent Sykes's good graces. 'I knew your predecessor, of course, Sir Edwin Fairclough. We were all sorry when ill health forced him to retire, but it's a pleasure to greet his successor. Do sit down, Sir Alfred, I think you will find that chair tolerably comfortable.'

Godalming seated himself, rather as though he expected the chair to explode when he rested his weight on it. 'Mr Maitland has not explained to you,' he said, still in the chilly tone he had adopted from the beginning, 'that I should have liked to see him alone, preferably at New Scotland Yard.'

'Well, my dear sir, you can have no secrets to discuss. And I must admit to some curiosity –'

'Quite simply, Sir Nicholas, I think your nephew has been up to his old tricks.'

Sir Nicholas froze. 'I fail to understand you, sir. What can you be talking about?'

'Quite simply, the charade I have witnessed this morning. Do you deny that Maitland has attempted to convince you that the so-called attack on him was part of an attempt to influence the court in favour of your clients, Mayhew and Harris?'

'That, as you must very well know, Sir Alfred, is a matter that cannot possibly be discussed between us with any propriety.'

'That I understand. But this quite glaring attempt to influence matters –'

'What exactly are you s-suggesting?' Up to that moment

Antony had been almost enjoying himself, but now his temper was beginning to slip, and Sir Nicholas gave him a warning look.

'Why, that this will be used in an attempt to persuade the court that the original charge against Barleycorn and Stokes was correct, that they were part of a gang engaged in what is generally referred to as a protection racket, and that some associate of theirs tried ineffectually to put a stop to Maitland's inquiries.'

'I admit my nephew's tendency to meddle in matters beyond what might be considered – by anyone less conscientious – to be outside his strict professional duties is well known, but don't you think that may well be the right interpretation?' Sir Nicholas spoke before Antony could do so, and his tone was honeyed.

'No, I don't!' Sir Alfred snapped. 'I think it is a bare-faced attempt to pervert justice, and that it is no more than I should have expected.'

'P-perhaps,' said Antony, and the gentleness of his tone almost matched his uncle's, though the slight stammer betrayed him, 'you would c-care to explain that remark, Sir Alfred.'

'It is all part and parcel of what I have heard of you, Mr Maitland.'

'From Chief Superintendent B-Briggs, no doubt.'

'Exactly. And there's no need to remind me of his errors in that last case he was involved in. He took an illegal course admittedly, but only to put a stop to something that he felt should not be allowed to go on.'

'He was quite w-wrong, you know, and I'm s-sorry to see you so c-credulous. It's hardly the b-best of attributes for a policeman.'

'Let me remind you, Mr Maitland, I said I knew something of your way of doing things. Perhaps you've fogotten that I succeeded Colonel Wycherley as Chief Constable of Westhampton.'

'What the d-devil has that to say to anything?'

'Merely that on one occasion you made an arrangement with a known criminal to – to throw one of his own men to the wolves in order to save your client.'

'Wycherley told you that?'

'Yes, and laughed as he did so. He seemed to think it was an amusing story.'

'It seems,' said Sir Nicholas, 'that you were wrong, Sir Alfred, in saying that I have no concern in this matter. My nephew and I visited the Chief Constable together when we needed his help in another matter.'

'I do not think however, Sir Nicholas, that you had anything to do with the arrangement as it was originally made with this criminal.'

'There are two things to be said about that,' said Antony before his uncle could speak. 'One is that I d-didn't know the man's name or where he l-lived . . . not the s-street, I mean, only that his house was number ten, and I b-believed – though I didn't know – that it was in London. If I'd gone to the police with a s-story like that of a journey by night, b-blindfolded so that I couldn't see where we were going, do you think they'd have t-taken any notice?'

'That would have been their responsibility, not yours.'

'It would have been quite useless,' said Sir Nicholas positively.

'Don't b-bother, sir. I d-don't think our visitor is amenable to reason any more than B-Briggs was,' said Antony. 'But as for this r-ridiculous accusation –'

'You heard what Adams said this morning. You attacked him, even before you'd seen the knife.'

'Certainly I d-did, I'd a very good idea what would h-happen if I didn't, but he c-came to no harm, unless he's caught a cold, of course.'

'And you will also tell the court, no doubt, that – handicapped as you are – the element of surprise was necessary for your manoeuvre to succeed.'

That brought Antony to his feet. 'You can g-get out of here and take your insinuations to h-hell with you,' he said. The doubts thrown on his integrity had angered him, but the reference to his physical disability was altogether too much for him to swallow.

Sir Nicholas, realising that the time was past when intervention would have done any good, sat back in his chair and didn't attempt to rise when Godalming did. For a moment the other two stood confronting each other, and then surprisingly Maitland laughed and there sounded to be some genuine amusement there. 'Briggs used to sneer,' he said. 'He wasn't very good at it, and I told him more than once he ought to practise in front of a mirror.

135

You don't do it any better than he did, Sir Alfred. And now I think – don't you, Uncle Nick? – it's time we went to lunch.' He turned his back on the Assistant Commissioner as he spoke, dismissing both him and his allegations as though the matter held no further interest for him.

That wasn't quite the end of it, of course. Sir Nicholas reserved his strictures until they were safe in their own corner at Astroff's and their drinks were in front of them, and even then his comments were quite mild. 'But I do wish,' he concluded, shaking his head sadly, 'that you could manage to contain your temper. It was just that, if you remember, that set Briggs against you in the first place.'

Regina versus Mayhew
and Harris, 1975

The Case for the Prosecution

Tuesday, the first day of the trial

The previous week had been a difficult one for Maitland, his study of Mr Bellerby's voluminous documentation interspersed by a number of appearances in court. Somehow or other it had escaped his notice – though later he realised it should have been obvious – that the trial of two police officers on two such serious charges as blackmail and perjury was likely to cause something of a sensation, and it was with a definite feeling of shock that he followed his uncle into the courtroom to find the spectators' gallery packed, and the gentlemen and ladies of the press even more tightly squeezed into the press-box than was normal. They exchanged decorous greetings with Counsel for the Prosecution, Mr Hawthorne, and his junior, a man named Terrence, before joining Mr Bellerby who was fussing gently.

'I've been talking to our clients,' he informed them, 'and I must say Mr Mayhew is despondent, very despondent indeed. In addition, I understand that their bail is to be revoked.'

'I'm afraid,' said Sir Nicholas gravely, 'that was inevitable. The younger colleague, however, are his spirits as deeply affected?'

'He seems to have got it into his head that there is some cause for optimism,' said Mr Bellerby. It was difficult to tell from his demeanour which of the two attitudes he found the more unreasonable. 'However, I've made it clear to both of them that any show of feeling in either direction would be a mistake when they appear in court.'

And in fact so it turned out. His clients obeyed his instructions to the letter, and Antony was left wondering whether the impression on the jury would be one of callousness or of injured innocence. He rather thought the former, but whichever way it was there was nothing to be done about it now.

Mr Justice Lamb was presiding, which on the whole, Maitland felt, was a bit of bad luck. The judge had only fairly recently been raised to the bench, and before that both Antony and his uncle had considerable experience of appearing against him when he was prosecuting. Neither had any doubt about his fairness or his sense of justice; the trouble was he was a melancholy man, on whom the unsatisfactory nature of humanity seemed to have the most depressing effect. Any dereliction of duty on the part of the police would sadden him inordinately, and if this attitude communicated itself to the jury they might as well save their breath. Antony, whose mind was not always well disciplined but given to flights of fancy, had always compared Lamb in his mind to a huge, unhappy bird, its shoulders hunched against the unkind winds of fortune. Watching him now while Hawthorne rose to make his opening remarks he found that the scarlet of the judge's newly-acquired robes made little difference to the aura of sadness about him.

Hawthorne, having made polite references to his own colleague and to the three members of the defence team, was starting out cautiously. 'Ladies and Gentlemen of the Jury,' (the twelve good men and true were divided five to seven in the order which counsel had given them, and Maitland took a moment to wonder why Hawthorne, a man very little older than himself, should use this rather old-fashioned mode of address) 'I have no need, I am sure, to stress to you the particularly unhappy duty which has fallen to me, that of prosecuting two members of the police force, to whom you should, as citizens, be able to look for protection, and to prosecute them, moreover for two particularly unpleasant crimes. You have heard the indictment, that both the accused have been guilty of perjury . . . a serious enough charge in itself but far more serious when allied to the additional one of blackmail. In a moment I shall outline the facts for you, but first I should like you to use your imagination for a moment on the particular difficulties of my task, which may not be quite so obvious to you as its distressing nature.

'When a crime has been committed it is customary for the prosecution to be able to call the evidence of the investigating officer, backed up of course by the relevant witnesses. This case has been brought as the result of a disciplinary inquiry held by the police force itself and I shall be calling presently upon Superintendent Wakefield, under whose auspices this inquiry was held, to read to you the sworn statements of the two accused men, which form the basis of the first part of the charge. At the conclusion of the inquiries certain further evidence came to light, and the decision was made to place the whole matter before the Director of Public Prosecutions. It is, I am glad to say, not often that a matter of this nature comes before the courts. His lordship, of course, will guide us, but our task is not an easy one.

'On the fifteenth of September last a man called William Goodbody was walking home from his shop when he was cruelly set upon and bludgeoned to death. This unhappy event does not concern directly the case which is before us today, though it was in a very real sense the direct cause of all that followed. Robbery was at first thought to be the motive, but it was later discovered that his day's takings had been deposited in the safe at his shop before he set out for home, and that he carried very little money on him. Detective Chief Inspector Lawrence Mayhew was placed in charge of the investigation, and Detective Constable Gerard Harris assisted him. There were naturally other members of the Criminal Investigation Department involved in the inquiry, but as you will see none of them can throw any light on what followed.'

Mr Justice Lamb had all this time worn his usual lugubrious expression, as though the wickedness of the world was almost more than he could bear. Sir Nicholas Harding was obviously listening carefully, with an expression of amused interest. Maitland, on the other hand, had assumed a relaxed position, and might for all anybody could tell have been asleep. But fortunately Mr Bellerby, who knew him well, was not deceived by this pose for an instant, though as a matter of fact he might as well have been asleep, knowing by now the prosecution's case backwards and forwards and sideways. He opened his eyes once to observe the demeanour of the prisoners while Hawthorne's melancholy recitation continued. Mayhew had a stolid look, and Harris was fidgeting slightly, but he didn't think either attitude could have been construed as a sign of guilt.

It was a long story, interesting perhaps if you'd never heard it before, but a dead loss as far as he was concerned. Antony was relieved when the judge adjourned for the luncheon recess as soon as Hawthorne had brought his statement to a close. Not a lengthy adjournment that day, they took Mr Bellerby with them and managed no more than a quick snack.

Maitland knew already, of course, that an old acquaintance of his, now Superintendent Wakefield of the branch of the police force known as C5, had been in charge of the disciplinary proceedings; in fact, though Sykes had never said so, he suspected that the other man had been the source of most of the information that had been passed on to him. He wasn't surprised therefore when Hawthorne called the Superintendent as his first witness but it didn't altogether please him that the distressing nature of the proceedings, to which Hawthorne had paid no more than lip service, was to the witness a real cause of grief. It was possible to interpret that in two ways. The jury might feel that Superintendent Wakefield disliked the position of having to give evidence against two colleagues whom he believed to be innocent; but it was far more likely they would think he was upset at the way the defendants had betrayed the trust placed in them.

The preliminaries didn't take long. Hawthorne was an experienced campaigner, and the witness no less used to the position in which he found himself. The proceedings at the inquiry were not lingered over, Wakefield confirmed Counsel for the Prosecution's opening address on every point. 'So we have reached the time,' said Hawthorne smoothly, 'when the two men, James Stokes and James Barleycorn, were arrested for the murder of William Goodbody, and brought up the following day in the Magistrates' Court before Mr Nolan who, after hearing all the evidence, dismissed the charge against them.'

'Yes, sir, that is quite correct.'

'At that hearing, statements were made by both the accused, statements under oath such as you are making now. I have here, my lord,' Hawthorne added, turning to the judge, 'sworn copies of these depositions which I should like to introduce into evidence.' He paused briefly and his glance flickered towards Sir Nicholas, who remained impassive. 'I should then like to ask the witness to read these statements aloud, so that we may all be acquainted with their contents.'

142

Mr Justice Lamb sighed, and as Hawthorne had done – though not so briefly – glanced in Sir Nicholas's direction. 'Have you any objection to this course of action, Sir Nicholas?' he inquired courteously. (Maitland took a moment to wonder how the judge would have proceeded if such an objection had been forthcoming.)

'No objection in the world m'lud,' said Sir Nicholas expansively. 'It is our contention that these statements contain the full truth of the matter concerning the murder of William Goodbody, and we are therefore not only willing, but anxious that they should be heard.'

'Very well then.' Obviously this cheerful acceptance was almost too much for the judge to bear. 'The witness may proceed,' he added, looking from Hawthorne to Wakefield in case one of them might have misunderstood him.

Wakefield took the sheets of paper that were being proffered to him by the usher. Like Sykes he came from Yorkshire, and was indeed not unlike him in appearance; a stiffish sort of chap, as he might have put it himself if his accent had not suffered more in the transition from his native heath. He read well and clearly, but these were the third and fourth statements they had heard already about the investigation, and Maitland again allowed his attention to wander. Sir Nicholas too, although he may have been listening to what was said, seemed more intent on the parade of ducks he was producing across the back of his brief. At present they were anonymous birds, but later it was only too likely, as Antony well knew, that they would assume some of the characteristics of the witnesses or perhaps even – perish the thought! – of the judge.

At last Wakefield had finished and handed the sheets of paper to the usher. 'I think, my lord,' said Hawthorne, 'that what we have heard speaks for itself. Unless my learned friend has any questions for the witness –'

Sir Nicholas was on his feet. 'Indeed I have, Mr Hawthorne; with your lordship's permission, of course.' There was no question, as he knew well enough, of this being denied. 'One matter you did not mention, Superintendent, in your account of the disciplinary inquiry. Was no examination made of my clients' bank accounts?'

'Yes, with their permission.'

'Given quite readily, I believe?'

'Yes, certainly,' said Wakefield, so readily that Antony thought for the first time that perhaps he really had some doubts about the justice of the charge that was being brought. But if he was right about that the witness had also a sense of honesty that led him to add with an air of unwillingness, 'Though I suppose in any case we could quite easily have got a court order.'

'I am sure that in both cases they were examined with some care.'

'With great care. I can tell you at once, Sir Nicholas, we found nothing out of order, nothing unexpected.'

'With his lordship's permission I should like to consider that for a moment, in the light of the charge of blackmail. My clients are accused – are they not? – of having threatened to bring a false murder charge against the two men, Stokes and Barleycorn, unless they were paid for not doing so.'

Mr Justice Lamb leaned forward. 'You have heard the indictment, Sir Nicholas,' he moaned.

'Yes, m'lud, I am not quite so forgetful. The point I am trying to make is that, although this might have been the first venture into crime for Detective Constable Harris, a man as long in the force as Detective Chief Inspector Mayhew, who was so lost to all sense of decency as to commit the very crimes he was paid to prevent, would hardly have waited some twenty years before starting on – shall we say? – the downward path.'

Even the judge, at whom, as Antony well knew, they were directed, seemed a little taken aback by this collection of clichés Hawthorne, equally aware that his lordship was being baited, came quickly to his feet. 'My lord, I don't think this is a matter on which we can properly regard the witness as an expert.'

'In this matter I'm afraid I must disagree with my friend, m'lud,' said Sir Nicholas. 'He was himself careful to bring out the witness's experience in various branches of the C.I.D. before he was transferred to his present position. I should be grateful for a ruling on this, because my next questions also call for his opinion as an expert.'

Mr Justice Lamb looked from one to the other of them as though in an agony of indecision. 'I think, Mr Hawthorne –' he began, and then went on more decisively. 'In the circumstances, I think Sir Nicholas is entitled to an answer to his question.'

'Thank you, m'lud. Superintendent Wakefield –?'

'Yes, sir, I remember your question perfectly.' He hesitated a moment and then looked straight at his colleagues in the dock as he answered. 'I should have been surprised if I thought the charge was true, but I didn't, so I wasn't.'

There was rather a ghastly pause. Maitland was willing his uncle not to press the matter further. Sir Nicholas said, at his silkiest, 'Thank you, Superintendent, that is exactly what I wanted to hear. I should like your help a little further, however, in your capacity as something of an expert on police matters.'

'Sir Nicholas?' said Lamb inquiringly.

'At least your lordship will hear the question,' said Sir Nicholas confidently, and went on quickly before the judge could reply. 'You are aware, Superintendent, that my clients reached the conclusion . . . or perhaps I should say that Chief Inspector Mayhew reached a conclusion, because obviously his younger colleague was guided by him – that certain small shopkeepers were being asked to pay what I understand is called protection money, under threat of violence. I have some reason to think that that month Goodbody had refused the extra payment, and had therefore been made an example of. Perhaps his death was not intended, we shall never know that. But that was the conclusion my clients reached.'

'According to their statements, yes.'

'Have you any reason to believe that this was not the only type of organised crime going on in London?'

'I've every reason to believe it wasn't,' said Wakefield, suddenly throwing caution to the winds. 'You name it, someone's doing it.'

'I phrased my question badly. These different activities – could there have been any connection between them?'

'My lord,' said Hawthorne, 'I fail to see how this affects the matter.'

'Is it relevant, Sir Nicholas?' sighed Lamb.

'I can only assure your lordship –'

'Very well, the witness may answer. But then I think – and I'm sure you will agree with me, Sir Nicholas – that we have had enough of conjecture.'

Wakefield was answering almost before the judge had finished. 'I can't offer proof, sir, but I'm pretty sure one thing was linked with another. There'd be cases where one lot seemed to be helping another out.'

'Would you go a step further and agree that it's very likely the whole thing was under the direction of one man?'

'It very well could be. In fact the more I think of it –' That was as far as Wakefield got before Hawthorne was on his feet and Mr Justice Lamb was speaking, more in sorrow than in anger, but still drowning the witness's words.

'That will do, Sir Nicholas, I think. Unless you have some other line of questioning –'

'Nothing further, m'lud. Does my friend wish to re-examine his witness?'

'Indeed I do. And I trust, my lord, that I shall not have occasion to ask your lordship's permission to treat him as hostile. May I ask you, Superintendent, why – in view of what you've told us – this case was proceeded with?'

'It wasn't my decision, sir.'

'No?'

'It was the Home Secretary's decision, and he was advised, I believe, by the Assistant Commissioner (Crime), that the papers should go to the Director of Public Prosecutions.'

'And you disagreed with that decision?'

'No, it was the only one that could have been made in the circumstances. There was the evidence, you see.'

'Ah, the evidence,' said Hawthorne in a tone of satisfaction.

'Yes, sir, there was no getting away from that. But when you've known someone as long as I've known Mayhew –'

'Very commendable,' Hawthorne interrupted, and sat down rather quickly before the witness could continue. On the whole, Maitland thought it as well that Sir Nicholas let the matter rest there.

All this had taken a good deal of time, and to his further relief Mr Justice Lamb decided to adjourn early. Without any need for consultation uncle and nephew piled their various documents into Willett's eager care and after a brief session in the robing room said 'Goodnight' to Derek Stringer – another member of Sir Nicholas's chambers, but one who had chosen to remain at the junior bar – found a taxi and made their way back to Kempenfeldt Square. As usual when they arrived together Gibbs was compelled to the nearest he ever came to affability. They scooped up Vera in transit and made their way directly upstairs to join Jenny.

Even though they were so early she had everything under control. They discussed briefly the respective merits of tea and sherry, and decided on the latter. Before long they were regaling the two women with the story of their day's activities. Maitland was tempted to repeat the judge's remark regarding speculation, but on the whole decided that it would be unnecessarily foolhardy to do so.

'I always thought Wakefield was a good type,' he said instead, when his uncle had finished speaking, 'though I haven't seen anything of him really since he was transferred to London. I only hope his rather free expression of his opinion won't do him any harm with that wretched man Godalming.'

'He has a right to his own opinion,' said Sir Nicholas, 'though I agree with you he may not have been altogether wise. However – as I'm sure you'll agree with me, Antony – the satisfaction of expressing himself freely is probably sufficient compensation for its possible unwisdom.' This, as his nephew knew only too well, was an oblique reference to his own crossing of swords with Sir Alfred Godalming the previous week. He thought it as well, therefore, to change the direction of the conversation slightly.

'On the whole I was glad you were dealing with him, Uncle Nick. I told you I like him, though I've no idea what he thinks about me. He might have started to reminisce.'

'Better explain,' said Vera. 'Said something about his being transferred to London. When did you know him?'

'Ages and ages ago. When I was mixed up with what Uncle Nick is pleased to call that gang of thugs in Whitehall,' Antony explained. 'I was undercover, if you'll forgive the expression – not using my own name, I mean – and he regarded my activities with extreme suspicion which wasn't helped when I insisted on spouting poetry to him. That was my cover story, that I was a poet.'

'What sort of poetry?' asked Vera, fascinated by this revelation of the past.

'Blank verse, so far as I can remember. Don't ask me to quote it, it was bad, very bad, and thank heaven I've forgotten all about it. But Wakefield was not amused, which on the whole I consider a reasonable attitude.'

'The less said about those days the better,' said Sir Nicholas repressively. 'Particularly if you will insist on using such vile expressions. It makes me wonder whether I was altogether wise to consider our appearing together. Even in court you are only too apt to forget yourself.'

'Consider, Uncle Nick? That's hardly fair,' Antony protested. 'You bullied me into taking the brief, you and Vera, you must admit that.'

'In the mistaken belief that it might be helpful,' said Sir Nicholas, almost as sadly as Lamb might have done. 'But let us look on the bright side. Whatever the consequences for Wake-field, he did our case no harm. And if things go as you anticipate, it is hard to see how Godalming can take offence.'

'As I anticipate?' Maitland sounded horrified. 'Uncle Nick, you know I realise the risks we're taking as well as you do.'

'I know you persuaded me against my will into a course of action which I consider imprudent,' said Sir Nicholas. 'But it's no use crying over spilled milk,' he added with one of his sudden changes of mood, to which fortunately all his hearers were quite accustomed. 'There is nothing helpful to be said about the case at the moment, so we may as well forget it and enjoy our evening. Jenny and Vera, no doubt, have a good deal to contribute to the conversation if only we give them the chance.'

That was all the excuse Jenny needed. 'Meg has something up her sleeve that she isn't even telling Roger about, and both Vera and I are bursting with curiosity as to what it may be.'

'A new part in a play,' said Antony. 'I thought we'd decided that was the most likely thing.'

'I suppose so. But it must be something very special,' said Jenny, unwilling to give up her small mystery, 'because it isn't a bit like Meg to keep things to herself.'

That was enough to set the ball rolling, and it wasn't until much later in the evening, when the Hardings were on the point of leaving, that Antony reverted to the subject of the trial. 'I forgot to tell you, Uncle Nick, that Roger's doing a job for me. He

148

promised to go and see the people this evening who took over the Porsons's house. You remember I told you the girl we saw said they'd taken it over lock, stock and barrel.'

Sir Nicholas paused half way out of his chair and then came erect. 'And what do you suppose will come of that?' he asked.

'Nothing, I expect. But there is just a chance ... I ought to have done something about it before, when Roger pointed out the possibility that something might have been left behind.'

'I consider that unlikely in the extreme,' Sir Nicholas told him. 'If you're trying to convey to me that you have decided after all that the help we're endeavouring to give our clients is a forlorn hope you've succeeded only too well.'

He took his wife away then, and as the door shut behind them Antony turned to Jenny. 'Crushed again,' he said. 'The trouble is, he's probably right, but we can't afford to miss any chances.'

Jenny gave him a serious look, but then she smiled. 'The darkest hour —' she began, but didn't attempt to finish the quotation. 'Antony, if you do succeed in getting Inspector Mayhew and that poor young man who's charged with him off, will Sir Alfred Godalming be very angry?'

'If you mean will he be angry with me, I'm afraid he is whatever happens about the case,' Antony told her. 'It's nothing to worry about, you know, and you see I was quite right,' he added, knowing perfectly well where her thoughts were tending, 'they won't risk trying to harm me again, that would be to give the game away completely.'

'I'm sure you're right,' said Jenny, and even Antony, well as he knew her, could have made no guess as to how far she was telling the truth. 'Anyway, I do hope you get them both off, of course, but I can't help feeling it would be awfully nice as well to annoy that horrible man by doing so.'

'I did tell him to go to hell,' Antony told her. And did his best to amuse her, as they made ready for bed, by recounting his uncle's reaction to the remark.

Wednesday, the second day of the trial

I

Mrs Jessie Goodbody, who insisted that this was her full name and looked quite offended at the idea that it might be Jessica, turned out to be a thin, sad-looking woman, the latter attribute not unnatural perhaps in view of her recent bereavement. She was in black from head to toe, and while her examination in chief was in progress Maitland noticed that his uncle had added what used to be known as Widow's Weeds to one of his ducks; the veil succeeded in giving the bird, however, an undoubtedly sinister appearance.

She told what she knew of her husband's death in trembling tones, adding that she herself had had nothing to do with the operation of the shop. Willie was against women working, and he had been a good provider, there'd never been any need for her to do so. Of course she had been into the shop from time to time, and could confirm that he had bought stock from the Shadwell Confectionery Company, because she'd seen their boxes on the shelves. He had certainly never confided in her that there was anything wrong with that account, or any other for that matter. She could only think that he had been attacked by someone who hoped that he had the day's takings on him, or just for what he had in his wallet, though that seemed to be untouched. Certainly he had no enemies.

'And yet, Mrs Goodbody,' said Hawthorne in his most sympathetic tone, 'I am bound to put to you the contents of a statement you signed for the police, because my learned friend will certainly do so if I do not. My lord, I should like to put this statement into evidence.' (There was the usual delay while this was done.) 'And now may I ask that the usher show the witness the signature. Do you agree, Madam, that that is your handwriting?'

'Yes, indeed it is. I remember too the handwriting of the young man who wrote it down for me to sign. I thought he was being so kind, not making me go to the police station to do it.'

'Do you see this young man you speak of in court, Mrs Goodbody?'

'Yes, of course, that's him up there, and the older man who was with him too.' She was pointing at the dock as she spoke.

'Thank you. Now I'm afraid I have to trouble you to read the statement through, and as it isn't very long perhaps it wouldn't be too much trouble for you to read it aloud to us.'

'If you say so, of course,' she said doubtfully. 'But you were at the Magistrates' Court hearing when those two men were accused of killing Willie. You know I told you then there wasn't a word of truth in it.'

'Yes, Mrs Goodbody, *I* know what you said, but unfortunately it must be repeated now so that the jury can hear it. So if you don't mind –'

The statement itself was exactly as Mayhew had described it to his lawyers. Mrs Goodbody read in a failing voice, and said when she came to the end, without waiting for Hawthorne's question, 'It's just as I told you before, there isn't a word of truth in it.'

'It is not what you told the police officers who questioned you?'

'Nothing like. All I know is what I said just now in answer to your question. Nothing about being browbeaten into paying money he didn't owe, that's a wicked lie.'

'In that case, Mrs Goodbody, perhaps you'll tell us a little about the interview between you and the two accused. How did you come to sign such a statement? Was it read through to you, for instance?'

'He – the young one – seemed to be reading what he'd written, which was just what I'd told them. It was the day after Willie was killed.' She dabbed at her eyes with her handkerchief. 'I thought you'd understand that. I was so upset, I never bothered to read it. After all, you ought to be able to trust the police and I thought there was no harm in signing it when he put it in front of me.'

'No, Madam, I think that is quite clear to all of us, and may I say again how much we sympathise with you in your loss. I wonder, Sir Nicholas –?'

'A few questions only, Mrs Goodbody,' said Sir Nicholas soothingly as he came to his feet. He paused a moment to glance down at the note his nephew had pushed in front of him, *What'll you bet she'll have hysterics*? and then went on smoothly. 'As my learned friend has said we all sympathise with you in your sorrow, and I certainly will not detain you long. It is very understandable, Madam, that in the circumstances you might have signed what was put in front of you with very little care as to its contents, but is it your habit to be quite so trusting . . . even of the police?'

'I've never had anything to do with legal documents. Willie always looked after everything.'

'So that now he has been so brutally taken from you you must learn about business matters from the beginning. Have you found yourself in any difficulty over the operation of the shop for instance?' His tone, as Antony told Jenny later, was sympathetic to the point of nausea, and Hawthorne glanced at him suspiciously but made no objection. Indeed, how could he?

'No, I've left everything to David . . . David Lindley, Willie's assistant. He's had to take on a boy to help, of course, but I haven't been bothered and now I've got the shop up for sale. When I have the money I mean to travel, and see something of the world.' She seemed to recollect herself suddenly. 'And try to forget,' she added with pathos.

'That will certainly be the best thing you could do,' counsel agreed. 'I take it then you will have no difficulty about funds, there is no mortgage on the shop, for instance?'

'As to that . . . I shall have plenty for my needs.'

'You haven't answered my question, Mrs Goodbody.'

Hawthorne was on his feet. 'My lord –' But Mr Justice Lamb didn't make him go any further.

'This cannot possibly concern us, Sir Nicholas. I think you should leave this line of questioning.'

'If your lordship pleases.' (Maitland, only too conscious that he would have himself accepted the ruling with a faintly mutinous air, took a moment to admire the smoothness of his uncle's tone.) 'In that case, Madam, we must return to the interview you had with my two clients, with Detective Chief Inspector Mayhew who was the investigating officer into your husband's murder, and Detective Constable Harris who was assisting him.'

'It was just as I told you,' said Mrs Goodbody rather quickly.

'I'm wondering, you see,' said Sir Nicholas in a conversational tone, 'how these two men could have hoped to get away with such a mispresentation of the truth. They knew from long familiarity exactly what would happen when the case came to court. Are you quite sure that nothing was said to suggest to you that your husband might have been the victim of such a plot as your statement describes?'

There was a perceptible pause before the witness replied. Then, 'The statement's a lie from start to finish,' she insisted.

'I see. And – I'd like you to think very hard about this, Madam – nothing at all was said by you that might have been misconstrued?'

'Certainly not. Why should I tell them a tale like that?' she asked indignantly.

'Why indeed? On the other hand,' said Sir Nicholas, apparently addressing the ceiling, 'why should my clients invent it when they knew you could give them the lie?' He said this in his gentlest tone, and was already seated again before Hawthorne realised that perhaps another intervention might have been in order.

Finding himself on his feet with his adversary already withdrawn from the field he put, rather half-heartedly, a number of additional questions to the witness, designed to remind the court perhaps of the suddenness of her state as a widow. Sir Nicholas listened imperturbably, and drew a heavy line through the mourning duck.

The next witness was Vernon Peele who lived in the same street as the Goodbodys, and kept a shop that leaned more heavily on groceries for his income and didn't sell newspapers. He was a man who looked as though he could do with a good meal, but whether this would arouse the sympathies of the jury, or whether (as Antony did) they would consider that he had a shifty look, Maitland couldn't decide. As with the previous witness the statement that he had signed was produced and put into evidence, and then handed to him for identification. But there the resemblance ended. He had known quite well what he

153

was signing, but had been afraid not to confirm the story that was suggested to him. Certainly he had made payments into the branch at Wood Green to the credit of the Shadwell Confectionery Company, but they had been for goods received. And he knew both Mr Stokes and Mr Barleycorn quite well by sight, as they were the ones who always called for his orders. It would have been quite believable that he should have been walking home a few minutes behind William Goodbody, and if Stokes and Barleycorn had indeed been attacking him he would certainly have recognised them. The fact remained that the tale was a fabrication from beginning to end.

'Yet you signed it quite willingly,' said Hawthorne. 'I am bound to put this to you, Mr Peele, because my learned friend for the defence will certainly insist on an answer.'

'I was afraid,' said the witness simply.

'Are you implying that you were threatened in some way?'

'They said I'd be prosecuted if I didn't play ball.'

Mr Justice Lamb roused himself from what seemed to be the melancholy contemplation of the depths of depravity to which human nature could sink. 'Play ball, Mr Hawthorne?' he said.

'I think the witness is implying that a charge might have been brought against him, my lord, if he hadn't agreed to sign the statement the accused put in front of him. That is right, is it not, Mr Peele?'

'Quite right. And being as they were police I thought they could get away with it, you see. It wasn't until I'd heard what Mrs Goodbody had to say and thought perhaps they'd be in trouble themselves that I dared tell the truth.'

'You do understand, Mr Peele, that you are under no obligation to say anything that might incriminate you.'

'Oh, yes, sir, I understand that all right. The thing is it was some stuff I'd bought in good faith, and the older of the two, Chief Inspector Mayhew that is, said I'd been receiving stolen goods that came from a hijacking. Said they could prove it, and I didn't know but what that was true and what made it worse – I may as well tell you as I admitted it in the Magistrates' Court – it was a cash deal, and I forgot to declare it in my income tax return.'

'Let us get this quite clear then. The monies you paid to the

Shadwell Confectionery Company were for goods received, and you were not a witness to William Goodbody's murder?'

'That's right, sir.'

'But you were intimidated by the accused into admitting both those things?'

'Well, they had the upper hand, didn't they?'

Hawthorne's questioning went on a little longer, but at last he seated himself again and invited Sir Nicholas with a gesture to cross-examine. Sir Nicholas got up in his leisurely way. 'In connection with this statement of yours, Mr Peele, there seem to have been a good many untruths flying about.'

'That's what I've been telling him,' said the witness, with a jerk of his head in Hawthorne's direction.

'Precisely. I take it, m'lud, that as the matter has already been brought up there can be no objection to my questioning the witness about the threats alleged to have been made against him to obtain his co-operation?'

'As I understand the matter, Sir Nicholas, he denies having committed any intentional offence. Therefore I cannot see any objection to that line of questioning, can you, Mr Hawthorne?'

'No, my lord,' said Hawthorne, but he sounded cautious.

'I am obliged to your lordship. You were telling us, Mr Peele, that you were threatened with prosecution for receiving stolen goods, and for failing to declare the transaction to the Income Tax authorities.'

'Forgetting,' the witness corrected him.

'If you prefer. Where exactly had these goods come from, and what items were involved?'

'A truck had been hijacked . . . stolen,' he added quickly with a glance at the judge who had just opened his mouth to speak. 'Tins of fruit and vegetables mainly. I bought some of them from a man who said he'd been to a bankruptcy sale, and though he gave me a receipt it was just on a bit of plain paper, and I couldn't have proved where I got them.'

'That, Mr Peele, does not concern us. What I should like you to tell the court is which of my two clients made the threat?'

'Why, the older one of course. Though the young man backed him up, getting the statement typed and all that.'

'I see. Chief Inspector Mayhew is a member of the Criminal

155

Investigation Department, certainly, but his particular duties concern murder, and it is very unlikely he would have known anything at all about such a matter as you mention.'

'Well, I wasn't to know that, was I? I thought he could do me –'

'Do me?' said the judge in tragic tones, which would have done credit to Meg at her most dramatic. 'Really, Mr Hawthorne, your witness is very much inclined to give answers that I do not understand.'

'I'm sorry, my lord.'

'If my friend would permit me to elucidate the matter,' said Sir Nicholas, 'I think the witness means, m'lud, that he felt my clients were in a position to prosecute him successfully if he didn't agree to their story. Is that right, Mr Peele?'

'Near enough,' said the witness.

'Very well, we will proceed,' said Lamb in a dissatisfied way. 'Sir Nicholas?'

'Where did the interview take place . . . the interview at which the threats were made which led you to agree to sign the statement which my friend has introduced into evidence?'

'In my office behind the shop.'

'I see. I think, Mr Peele, we must ask you for a full account of what was said both by my clients and by yourself.'

'I told you!'

'You have given us a somewhat vague outline, Mr Peele. In view of your subsequent denial of your statement I think his lordship will agree that the court has a right to hear your story in more detail.'

'It was just as I said,' Peele insisted. 'I had heard from some of my friends in the same line of business that inquiries were being made about this protection racket, but no one asked me anything about that.'

'Just one moment. Suppose, for the sake of argument, that you had been the victim of a threat, that you were paying money in some way so that those threats should not be carried out, would you have been inclined to admit as much when the police questioned you?'

'Not on your life I wouldn't. Asking for trouble that would have been.'

Hawthorne bounced to his feet, but Counsel for the Defence had already turned to Mr Justice Lamb. 'I agree, m'lud, hardly a proper question. May I proceed?'

'I suppose you must, Sir Nicholas,' sighed Lamb.

'Well then, Mr Peele, as I understand it my clients came to see you and you took them into your office, presumably so that you could be private there.'

'That's right.' The witness was definitely more cautious now.

'Perhaps you will tell the court exactly what was said and how the interview proceeded.'

'Well, as to exactly, I don't pretend to remember all that well. But they asked me whether I'd heard there was a protection racket in the district, and told me William Goodbody had been killed for not paying up.'

'And by the words "protection racket",' said Sir Nicholas concealing his distaste for the phrase well enough, 'I think his lordship would like you to confirm to the court that you intend to convey that money had been obtained from some of your fellow shopkeepers by threats of physical violence.'

'That's what I said, isn't it?' (Mr Justice Lamb was seen to discontinue his note-making for the moment, sigh, and cast up his eyes to heaven as though pleading for strength; a gesture so reminiscent to Antony of his uncle's attitude in similar circumstances tht he began to feel a real sympathy for what Sir Nicholas was going through.)

'With his lordship's permission I think we should take that as assent,' said Counsel for the Defence hopefully. The judge nodded dumbly. 'And what do you tell us happened next at this interview with my clients, Mr Peele?'

'Well, I was horrified of course because I'd never thought of such a thing in connection with Goodbody, just that it was an ordinary mugging, you know.'

'Robbery with violence?' asked Sir Nicholas quickly. He had got the measure of the witness now and Maitland thought that Hawthorne was on the whole grateful to him for forestalling the judge's intervention.

'That's right.' But even in agreement the witness sounded vaguely belligerent. 'That's what I thought and that's what I still think for that matter. And if you can tell me of anyone else it was happening to I'll be surprised.'

That last rejoinder was one the defence could well have done without. A lesser man than Sir Nicholas might have hurried to his next question, but he was too experienced to underline the matter in that way. 'So you told them that you yourself had never been threatened,' he said. 'From what you told my friend that didn't end the conversation.'

'No, it didn't! They said they didn't believe me, and they said the people responsible were Mr Stokes and Mr Barleycorn. And they said again that was why Goodbody had been murdered, and they knew those two had done it only they couldn't prove it without my help. And I said I wasn't telling lies for anybody, let alone going to court and swearing to them, and they said – it was the older man that was doing most of the talking – that unless I gave them a statement saying I'd been – I think the word he used was victimised – unless I gave them a statement like that, and said as well that I'd been walking home on the night of the murder and actually seen what happened, they'd get me for receiving stolen goods and fiddling my tax. Which was a thing I'd forgotten about, being as innocent in both matters as a newborn babe,' said the witness, using, it must be admitted, about as unlikely a simile as he could have found. 'But there, *he* seemed to know all about it' – again he jerked his head in the direction of the dock – 'and I wasn't to know whether he was telling the truth. And a Chief Inspector, he's not someone to tangle with. I've been respectable all my life, and the wife wouldn't have liked to see me doing a spell in prison.'

'So you agreed to the proposition . . . just like that?'

'I'm not saying there wasn't a bit of argument back and forth. But when all was said and done, what was a chap to do?'

'And these scruples of yours about lying, about lying under oath . . . what happened to them?'

'I didn't have any choice, did I?'

'I think, Mr Peele, there are a number of steps you could have taken. For instance, you mentioned that a Chief Inspector is an influential man, but he has superiors in the Force, any number of them. You didn't think of going to them with the truth?'

'My word against theirs, wasn't it, and there was two of them? Who'd have believed me?'

'There is a saying that truth is great and will prevail,' said Sir Nicholas, and Maitland, glancing down at the pad on which Derek Stringer was taking the note, observed that his colleague had automatically started to write *Magnum est veritas*.

'Well, I couldn't rely on that, could I?'

'In this instance, I think you may find you're mistaken. I put it to you that what you have told us here today is a string of lies. For instance, you have just made two contradictory statements: that nothing was said at your interview with my clients about obtaining money from your fellow shopkeepers with menaces, but then a moment later that they had told you they believed this practice to have been the motive for Mr Goodbody's murder.'

'All these questions! A chap gets confused,' said the witness sulkily.

'Not, surely, if he is telling the truth. You have already admitted to us that in certain circumstances you are quite prepared to lie under oath. The truth was contained, was it not, in the original statement you made to the police?' After the quiet tone he had been using the last words came like a whiplash, and the witness went back an involuntary pace, almost as though he had indeed been struck.

'I'm telling you the truth now,' he said doggedly, 'as I'd have done all along if it hadn't been for the threats that were used. And you may not feel so cocky,' he added spitefully, 'when those two crooks you call your clients get theirs.'

'I'm sorry if my questions offend you,' said Sir Nicholas smoothly, 'but a man who has admitted to a willingness to lie under coercion should hardly object to the suggestion that he's doing so now rather than at an earlier date.'

'My lord!' Hawthorne was on his feet again. 'I think my learned friend should explain to us exactly what is in his mind.'

'Well, Sir Nicholas?'

'I shall be only too pleased to do so, m'lud. You have heard the Crown's own witness, Superintendent Wakefield, admit to the possibility – I will put it no higher than that – that criminal activities in London, and possibly to a lesser extent throughout the country, are being organised on a grand scale. If such an organisation exists it would obviously be to its advantage to look after the welfare of its members. A criminal is apprehended and spends some time in prison, during which period he has no worries as to the welfare of his family, and most likely is given a bonus of some kind when he returns to civil life. Under such circumstances a sentence could be accepted philosophically. But in the case of Barleycorn and Stokes a rather more serious matter was involved . . . murder. If such a charge went forward who could tell whether they would hold their tongues about the other activities of which they were aware? Steps must be taken to assure their acquittal, and those steps unfortunately involve the present charges against my clients.'

(Regretfully it must be admitted that during this oration Maitland, forgetting his own good intentions, succumbed to temptation, scribbled 'Speculation, Sir Nicholas?' on his pad, and pushed it in front of his uncle.)

'Well, Sir Nicholas, as I invited your comment I suppose I cannot complain that these remarks should have been reserved for your address to the jury. As must Mr Hawthorne's reply,' Lamb added, looking sadly at Counsel for the Prosecution, who was showing some signs of restlessness. 'Have you any further questions for the witness, Sir Nicholas?'

'None at all, m'lud. A man who by his own admission regards the truth so lightly –'

'Yes, Sir Nicholas, you will have the chance to expand on that theory later. Mr Hawthorne?'

'A few more questions, my lord.' But they were only, Maitland thought, what must have been expected in the circumstances, stressing the fact that the witness was telling the truth now, and couldn't be blamed for the false statement he had made – and which incidentally, as Hawthorne stressed, had not actually been sworn to. Many people grew confused under cross-examination . . .

Mr Justice Lamb adjourned at this point for lunch, obviously taking the gloomiest view of what he was going to be offered to satisfy his hunger. For that matter Antony couldn't be said to have enjoyed his meal either; he spent almost the entire time endeavouring to smooth his uncle's ruffled feathers, and even Derek's well-meant intervention didn't help in the slightest.

160

II

After the luncheon recess the first witness Hawthorne called was perhaps the least controversial, Charles Shadwell. The only surprise about him was that he was the founder and head of an apparently successful confectionery business. He looked exactly as he had been described to Maitland, like the sort of person to leave things to other people. And perhaps after all that was his secret, he knew how to delegate authority and to whom. He confirmed under Hawthorne's questioning that he had known nothing of the Wood Green account, but there had been nothing odd about that, he was accustomed to leave all such matters in Martin Kingsley's hands. Kingsley also dealt with all matters concerning the staff, and until the police inquiry was made he – Shadwell – had known nothing of either Stokes or Barleycorn. Of course if the police had pursued their inquiries further the accounts department could have given them the necessary information.

When his turn came Sir Nicholas contented himself with obtaining the witness's agreement that in view of his position in the company it was not odd that Mayhew and Harris had taken his word for the fact that there was no account at Wood Green. He admitted to knowing the name of Arthur Abbott and as he had been employed in the packing department for so long he supposed he had exchanged a word with him now and then, but it was only after the hit and run accident that the man's name had impressed itself upon him. This time Sir Nicholas attempted no comment, but went straight on to a question as to how long Martin Kingsley had been employed by the firm. 'Nearly two years,' the witness replied. 'Since the first of January 1974, to be exact.'

Sir Nicholas thanked him, Mr Hawthorne had no further questions, and he stood down thankfully.

Martin Kingsley followed on his employer's heels, and here too the description he had had was, thought Maitland, a good one. A smooth character if ever there was one, dressed with some care – or dressed for the occasion – and obviously quite capable of handling efficiently even the rather heavy load that Charles

161

Shadwell had placed on his shoulders.

His evidence followed the expected course. As far as staff was concerned he had inherited a number of salesmen from his predecessor, but he felt that more could be done if a bigger area were covered. James Stokes and James Barleycorn were among the first people he had taken on, and they had proved eminently successful. Two of the best men he had in that capacity. The controversial account had been opened for the convenience of the local tradesmen, some of whom actually had their own accounts at the same branch, and others were within easy distance so payments could be made without resorting to the help of the post office. It was a pity he had been away at the time the matter came up. Any of his friends could have given the police his holiday address, but he hadn't happened to mention it at the office, nor was he in the habit of talking about his private affairs there, so it was unlikely that anyone would have known who to appeal to.

This time Sir Nicholas left the questioning to his nephew. 'Something that can't possibly get you into trouble,' he commented acidly when they discussed the matter at lunchtime.

Mr Justice Lamb regarded him sorrowfully as he got to his feet, so that the expression his colleagues had used when his lordship was still at the Bar came vividly to Antony's mind, poor Lamb! 'There are just one or two matters, Mr Kingsley,' he said, 'that require clarification. For instance, Mr Shadwell has told us you deal with all staff matters, so I must presume that you knew the chief packer, Arthur Abbott, now unfortunately deceased.'

'I knew of him, of course, but personally only slightly.'

'When orders come in through the salesmen how are they dealt with?'

'They are handed to Abbott, or now to his successor, and he allocates the work of filling them.'

'And then?'

'The list of what has gone out is passed to the accounts department – you understand that sometimes items are out of stock – and the statement sent out in the usual way.'

'You are aware, of course, that certain accounts, including those that were paid directly into the bank at Wood Green, were always dealt with by Abbott?'

'I can't say I ever noticed that.'

'You may take it from me that this is true, and we are in a position to bring evidence to that effect. Can you explain why that should have been so?'

'I suppose that Abbott, like the rest of us, had his own foibles.'

'You don't think it was a coincidence that he was killed at the exact moment when his evidence might have been needed?'

'It was unfortunate, but hardly a coincidence. Hit and run accidents happen every day.'

'If it *was* an accident.' (Funny that Hawthorne hadn't objected so far.) 'Another of the jobs you undertake is to prepare the list of bonuses at Christmas, is it not?'

'Certainly. That would naturally form part of the Treasurer's job, and as in this case I combined the role of Personnel Officer it was very natural that I should do so.'

'Then I'm sure you can explain to us' – Maitland was cordiality itself, and had no idea that he was parodying his uncle's manner – 'why at Christmas 1974 his bonus was almost double what it had been the previous years.'

'That's quite simple.' (Damn the man, he'd thought of every answer in advance.) 'He had been with the firm a long time, much longer than I had myself, and I felt the amount previously allocated to him had been inadequate. What I gave him was merely what I felt was his due.'

'Nothing to do with the fact that he put up the orders for Mr Goodbody and Mr Peele among others, for instance?'

This time Hawthorne did get up rather quickly, but before he had time to speak Mr Justice Lamb turned his melancholy regard on Antony. 'You said you had one or two matters to clarify, Mr Maitland, and I think your questioning on this line has gone far enough.'

'If your lordship pleases. Mr Shadwell has also told us,' he went on, turning to the witness again, 'that you were instrumental in taking on Barleycorn and Stokes as salesmen.'

'Certainly I was, but I have already told the court that.'

'What can you tell us about them?'

'They were extremely efficient as salesmen.'

'Is it customary to employ two men working together in that capacity?'

'It happens sometimes. In this case I took on James Barleycorn

163

first; he is a bright man but not over fond of using his pen. It was at his suggestion that Stokes went along with him to write down the orders they received.'

'I see.' Maitland's tone could not have been more sceptical. 'They were employed by you then at very much the same time as you opened the account in Wood Green?'

'Yes, it was a new departure for us to expand in that area.'

'You obtained references for them, I suppose.'

'I did, though I must tell you that I am more accustomed to rely on my own judgement than on other people's. James Barleycorn had been unemployed for some time, but was able to give me a letter from a gentleman for whom he had occasionally done gardening work.'

'A gentleman who has since gone abroad with his family, no doubt.'

'As it happens, yes.' Even this didn't shake Kingsley's composure.

'You relied then on a document handed to you by Barleycorn himself, not on personal contact with his previous employer?'

'That's correct.'

'And in the case of Stokes –?'

'He had a part-time job as a waiter. I did ask at one or two of the most recent places he mentioned, and the reason for his leaving had always been seasonal, nothing wrong with his work. Frankly I had already made up my mind, because I wanted Jim Barleycorn and it seemed to be' – he paused, considering his next phrase, and then smiled as though his choice of words amused him – 'it seemed to be a package deal.'

'And it worked out so well that they were making, I understand, a considerable amount of money between them?'

'That is so, and a still more considerable amount for the firm, of course.'

'Do you have signing authority on the firm's account, Mr Kingsley?'

'Naturally I do. I'm not quite sure what you're suggesting –'

'I think you know very well. And if you're going to add,' said Antony, suddenly too angry with this plausible man to maintain his bland approach, 'that my question implies an insult, you're quite right, it does.'

164

'My lord!' That was Hawthorne again. 'I appreciate the fact that in view of their clients' plea of Not Guilty my friends for the defence have no choice but to attack my witnesses, but –'

'Have you finished your questioning of Mr Kingsley, Mr Maitland?' Lamb asked.

'Not quite, my lord. There is just one other matter.'

'Very well.' Difficult as it may have been the judge seemed saddened by the reply, so that Antony thought suddenly, if we can't change his mind he'll sum up dead against us. But he did not voice his thought, instead he sketched a bow to the bench which might with a little imagination had been construed as an apology, and then turned back to the witness again.

'Mr Shadwell informed us that you joined his company at the beginning of last year,' he said, making the words a question.

'On the first of January, which happened to be a Tuesday,' said Kingsley readily.

'And may I enquire as to your previous employment?'

'I was with Greenbrier and Appleby.'

'Ah, yes, the building contractors. A large firm I believe.'

'They have branches all over the country, but their head office is in the City.'

'What position did you hold with them?'

'I started as Chief Accountant, but was later promoted to being Company Secretary. The new Chief Accountant reported to me.'

'Why did you leave their employment?'

'I decided that a smaller firm would give me a little more variety. A little more scope for – for such talents as I possess.'

'And a little more remuneration?'

'That was not the point.'

'No, it's difficult to see how it could have been. Could Mr Shadwell, successful though I am sure he is, compete with a giant corporation like Greenbrier's?'

'I have already said that was not my consideration.'

'In fact you took a drop in salary, did you not?'

For a moment Antony's imagination, always lively, presented him with a picture of the witness, cartoon fashion, with a large question mark in a balloon over his head. Can this be proved or can't it. Better not take the risk. 'I took the job at a slightly lower remuneration', he said.

165

'Thank you, Mr Kingsley, I felt sure that must be so. And one final question: it would be interesting to know how much monetary value you put on the additional scope for your abilities that the new position offered you.'

There was a moment's dead silence before the witness said in a lower voice than he had previously used, 'My new position carried a salary five thousand pounds lower than the previous one.'

Maitland sat down amid a sudden clamour from Hawthorne about irrelevant matters introduced solely to confuse the issue, with which he was all too sure Mr Justice Lamb – and probably the jury as well – agreed.

The rest of the afternoon was taken up with the examination by Mr Hawthorne and cross-examination by Sir Nicholas of Messrs Barleycorn and Stokes. James Barleycorn was called first and had little to say beyond the story he had already told at the Magistrates' Court hearing. He and his sidekick ('sidekick, Mr Hawthorne?' moaned Lamb) had both been glad to get regular employment, which wasn't so easy these days, but he'd discovered in himself a certain aptitude for selling, and the results, even when divided between them, had far exceeded their expectations. He was quite sure that whatever Mr Kingsley had said he would not have been dissatisfied with their work.

Barleycorn was a big, burly man with tightly curled hair receding from a high forehead and wearing a respectable but tight-fitting navy blue suit. Maitland found it easy to imagine him in the role of First Murderer, but it was obvious that he was an intelligent man (too intelligent, you might have thought, to be unemployed for so long) and he told his story well. He had known Mr Goodbody, of course, and both he and Jim Stokes had been distressed to hear of his death, and had discussed it between themselves. But how the police had picked on the two of them as good prospects for blackmail in that connection he couldn't think. Still, sure enough the suggestion had been made: pay up or we'll see you face a murder rap. (Hawthorne explained that one before the judge could intervene.) However, three thousand quid was three thousand quid and anyway he didn't believe in giving in to threats like that. Maitland said afterwards that he could see the words, conscious of my own innocence, trembling on the witness's lips, but wisely perhaps he refrained from using them. Instead he said, 'It was a bad business but it seemed to us the truth would have to come out . . . which is what happened, so we up and told the court then and there exactly why the charges had been laid.'

The foremost of Sir Nicholas's ducks now held a blackjack. He laid down his pencil and got to his feet in a leisurely way. 'To go straight to that last statement of yours, Mr Barleycorn, why did you refrain from speaking in your own defence until the case had been dismissed?'

'Why, because our lawyer – I daresay you know him, a chap called Harrison – told us to hold our fire.' ('To reserve their defence, my lord,' said Hawthorne by way of explanation.) 'Those were his very words,' Barleycorn agreed. 'The police have got a good case, he said, so reserve your defence, he said, and it will sound much more effective at the trial.'

'But when Mrs Goodbody disowned her statement . . . how do you suppose my clients intended to get round that difficulty? According to her present story she had no idea what it contained.'

'I don't think, my lord,' said Hawthorne, 'that it is up to the witness to answer a question like that, though I shall have my own explanation of the matter to offer the jury when the time comes.'

'Quite right, Mr Hawthorne, quite right. Perhaps you will proceed, Sir Nicholas, but without putting these unanswerable questions to the witness.'

'If your lordship pleases. And now, Mr Barleycorn, perhaps you can give us some idea of your activities during these past years. I believe at one time you were employed by a public house.'

'Yes, I was.'

'As a barman, a waiter?'

'As a bouncer. A chucker-outer,' he added, looking at the judge, 'in case your lordship doesn't know what that means.'

'Thank you, Mr Barleycorn.'

'Did you enjoy your work?'

'It was all right.'

'Why did you leave?'

'They said I got too rough with one chap. He was carrying on,

167

might have smashed the place up, something had to be done.'

'I see. And before that again –?'

'Sir Nicholas.' Mr Justice Lamb was leaning forward again. 'You are coming perilously near what I fear may be an attack on the witness's character. I'm sure I don't have to remind an advocate of your experience of the consequences of this action on your part.'

'No, m'lud.' Sir Nicholas sounded positively cheerful. 'Your lordship, I take it, means that I shall be laying my own witnesses open to being attacked in their turn on the grounds of character. As far as my clients are concerned the words of the indictment have already done whatever can be done in that direction, but as for the remainder of the witnesses . . . if my learned friend chooses to attack them in this way I shall be only too happy to see the results.'

'Very well, Sir Nicholas. So long as the matter is perfectly clear.'

'I'm obliged to your lordship. Mr Barleycorn, you have at least on one occasion been in trouble with the police, I believe.'

'Only once, and that was a long time ago.'

'A matter of breaking and entering?'

'I didn't take nothing.'

'I'm sure the court will have the fullest sympathy with you in this matter,' said Sir Nicholas dulcetly. 'You had made your inquiries and believed the occupants of the house to be away, I understand.'

'Well, so they should have been. But there wasn't no harm in what I did expect for a drop of whisky drunk while I was listening to some of their records. And I knew better than to get into trouble the same way twice.'

'I'm sure you did. The police have had occasion to question you again since then, however? A liking for whisky and . . . military bands isn't it? . . . might also be regarded as a sort of trademark.'

'There's some people as would imitate anything rather than think for themselves.'

'How true, Mr Barleycorn. Perhaps you will tell us now about these last few years when you have been unemployed. How have you lived?'

'There's help for those as need it.' Mr Barleycorn's vocabulary was going rapidly to pieces. 'And there've been odd jobs to do here and there.'

'Perhaps you could describe some of them for us,' Sir Nicholas suggested.

'I can't rightly remember.'

'Have all the people you worked for gone abroad?' There was nothing but sympathy in counsel's tone now, and he sat down as he finished speaking.

After that Mr Stokes's story was something of an anti-climax, and it was obvious to Antony – though he realised this might have been wishful thinking – that he had been carefully coached by his companion in what he should say. The only difference was in his answers to Sir Nicholas's questions about the nature of the offences with which he had been charged in the past. 'But I've been going straight ever since I was married,' he said, 'and was very glad to get some regular employment at last. And never a bit of violence in my record,' he added, with a rather apprehensive glance at where Jim Barleycorn was sitting in the body of the court. This wasn't hard to believe: he was about half the size of his partner, upwards and downwards and sideways, and had a naturally ingratiating manner that didn't endear him to Maitland at all. At last he was allowed to go and to everyone's relief the judge adjourned until the following morning. It was not quite so early as the previous evening and both Antony and his uncle were glad there was nothing to take them back to Chambers. They shared a cab to Kempenfeldt Square, and Maitland – rather expecting squalls – was relieved when Sir Nicholas's only remark concerning the case was, 'Do you want to take on the Protheroes tomorrow morning?'

'I suppose they're Hawthorne's grand finale. Don't you think you ought to deal with them yourself, sir?'

'For some reason Hawthorne seems to be inclined to give you a little more latitude than he allows me. I can only account for this by curiosity,' said Sir Nicholas rather coldly. 'He's wondering – and I'm not at all sure that I blame him – what you'll be up to next. So if you care to oblige me –'

'Of course I will, Uncle Nick. Only' – he grinned – 'what do we do if Mrs Protheroe has hysterics?'

III

He declined Sir Nicholas's invitation to come in and tell his aunt what had been happening today on the grounds that Roger and Meg were coming to dinner, and sure enough when he got upstairs the Farrells had already arrived. 'You look battered, darling,' said Meg when he went in (she was the only one of his friends and acquaintances who ever dared to comment upon a thing like that). 'Has it been a very dreadful day?'

'Not too bad. Uncle Nick bore the brunt of it, and among other things brought out the rather shady backgrounds of those two saintly gentlemen, Stokes and Barleycorn, to admiration; in the course of the proceedings daring Hawthorne to try the same thing with our witnesses when we reach them.'

'But isn't that a good thing?' said Jenny. 'I mean, to take their word rather than Chief Inspector Mayhew's and that poor young constable who's charged with him seems a bit thick.'

'Yes, but you're forgetting Mrs Goodbody, who's playing to the gallery like nobody's business, not to mention Peele, the man who originally said he saw them commit the murder, and the Treasurer of Shadwell and Company with whom I had the pleasure of dealing. He had to admit he took a drop in salary when he went there; you could almost see him calculating whether I could prove that or not, but he was a damned smooth fellow and pretty convincing I should say. I'd had my doubts about Shadwell, as I may have mentioned to you before, but he is patently honest, just a *laissez faire* type. And then there are the Protheroes to come. Uncle Nick wants me to deal with them.'

'Well, Roger's got something to tell you about that,' said Meg. 'Something that may help,' she added encouragingly, so that Antony smiled at her.

'I'm past believing anything can help,' he confided. 'I suppose you mean you went to see the people who took the Porsons' old house as I asked you, Roger, and I'm very grateful to you for that. They vehemently deny knowing anything at all about her previous husband's criminal connections, and if I persist I shall only convince the jury I'm persecuting her, and consequently swing them round to her favour.'

'There's a chance, just a chance, that what I have to show you may change that a little,' said Roger cautiously. He glanced up at Antony who, not afraid in this instance of distracting his witness, had taken up his usual stance on the hearthrug. 'Drink your sherry and give us all a refill,' Roger told him. 'Then I'll tell you.'

Antony obeyed, but grumbled between sips that he wasn't sure whether he was being encouraged or warned not to expect too much. When the second round of drinks was poured he took up his former position. 'All right,' he said, 'let's have it!'

'I went out there at lunchtime,' said Roger, 'and as luck would have it I caught them both at home. Margery and Dick Hartley – they haven't been married very long as I expect you gathered. He works as a salesman in one of the big department stores and as he has to work on Saturdays today was his day off. She remembered me luckily and took me on trust . . . no explanations. They bought the house furnished, which they said was a bit of good luck because it was cheaper that way, but I gather Mrs Porson – or should I call her Mrs Protheroe now?' – had cleared things out pretty well, all their personal belongings, I mean. The bureau, for instance, had been completely cleared, not so much as an overlooked bill or receipt, still less any letters. But there was a bookcase and she hadn't taken any of the contents.'

'If you think,' said Antony, 'that the jury will accept any deep psychological implications drawn from their choice of literature –'

'Wait for it, darling. You're always telling me to be patient,' Meg complained.

'Yes, I'm sorry. Go on, Roger.'

'I have to admit that didn't sound very helpful. They'd never seen Mrs Porson except when the sale was completed, and they asked her then – at least Dick did – what they should do with the books. She said she didn't want them; they went with the house like the rest of the furniture and they could do what they liked with them, keep them or give them away.'

'Thank goodness for that, anyway. If anything's coming of all this,' said Antony, still not entirely convinced, 'I don't want either of us to be had up for pinching the possessions of one of the witnesses.'

'No, there's no question of that. The books are a bit over their heads, I imagine, over the Hartleys' heads, I mean . . . and come to think of it that's a coincidence, that they should have the same

171

name as the restaurant where the Protheroes are supposed to have overheard Mayhew and Harris concocting their nefarious scheme.'

'Coincidences happen, though it's a common enough name.'

'So it is. Anyway, as I said, there was nothing on the shelves that interested them so they'd bundled the whole lot into a carton and stored them in the attic. The bookcase was still there, partly filled with paperbacks, and partly accommodating some ornaments, but they were willing enough to let me see what they'd taken out of it.'

'I said we were going to go all psychological,' said Antony despairingly, but it was noticeable that his eyes were bright with interest. 'So Dick brought the carton down, and you emptied it on the sitting-room floor. What did you find there?'

'Philosophy mostly, which is odd when you think of it though you told me that Porson was an educated man. Also some military history, but that didn't go back very far, mostly modern stuff. And a few novels, but not the kind of thing Margery Hartley likes. I gathered from a glance at the present contents of the bookshelves that her taste runs to romance, or the plucky little heroine type of thing.'

'Get on with it,' Antony urged him. 'You shook them all out in turn to find if there was anything left between the leaves, and with one of them you struck lucky.'

'Don't spoil the story, darling,' Meg rebuked him. 'That's exactly what happened but –'

'Don't worry,' said Roger quickly. 'There was something and I've got it sealed in an envelope and both Margery and Dick have signed it across the flap to say where and when it was found. I made a note of what it said, so you needn't open the envelope until you do so dramatically in court . . . if that's how you want to play it, of course. And Dick's quite ready to add his evidence to mine about the finding of it, so I think you'll find that tied up tightly enough.' He produced as he spoke a large manila envelope which he had been hiding down the side of his chair. 'It's rather too big, but I couldn't find anything smaller that would fit.'

'Bless you,' said Antony fervently. 'At least . . . what's in it?'

'A letter addressed to Mrs Edwin Porson, and postmarked in Arkenshaw on February the third of this year. It's been cut open neatly, and the note inside is on paper that seems to have been torn from a spiral-bound notebook, the size that would fit easily in a man's pocket. There's no date on it and no address, and it begins without any salutation. I wrote down what it says for your benefit, but it's quite short and I'd no difficulty in memorising it. *You'll have read in the papers what happened. When I can get away I shall go abroad. Get in touch with you-know-who for funds and arrangements to join me,* and it's signed with a squiggle that could very easily be an E.'

Antony was staring at him with his mouth open. 'So she knew what her husband was up to and we can prove that she knew. We can also prove – or can we? – that the person Sykes calls the Managing Director was also known to her, which according to my theory means that before he died Edwin Porson was the head of his department. That figures, as a marksman they don't come any better than he was, though I learned from Sykes that he'd named a chap – who'd conveniently disappeared in the meantime – as the man from whom he took his orders. And I suppose he didn't give away the top man in the organisation because he still wanted his help for his wife. But of all the damned cautious fellows . . . he might have been a bit more explicit.'

'Doesn't it help, darling?' asked Meg anxiously.

'Yes, of course it does, it's marvellous, and I'm more grateful than I can say, Roger. I should have taken your advice in the beginning. All the same, I'll have to go down later and talk to Uncle Nick. We've got to think how best to play it. I could produce it tomorrow and give her the hell of a shock, but if she's the woman I think she is she'll bounce right back with the name of some friend – possibly her present husband, she must have known him before Porson died – and say that was who was meant by you-know-who. It's enough proof for me, heaven knows, but then, as you are both aware, I already have my own ideas on the subject. But if she sticks to the story that the first thing she knew about her husband being a professional hit man was what she read in the papers while he was holed up in Arkenshaw we shan't be any better off.' He turned and used his left hand to take his glass from its place near the clock, and raise it to his friend in a mock salute. 'But I'm more grateful than I can say, Roger, and you couldn't have treated the matter better if you'd been trained

173

to the law from childhood. If you'll give me the copy of the note I'll go down and talk to Uncle Nick and Vera after dinner, and decide how we should use this new bit of information.'

'It seems to me a very odd thing,' said Meg severely, 'that the word of two honest men, two policemen with nothing at all against them in their record, shouldn't be taken against that of a bunch of crooks.'

'Don't blame me, *darling*,' Antony pleaded. 'Nobody's saying Mrs Goodbody's a crook, or Vernon Peele, though it's as obvious to you as it is to me that they were either bribed or intimidated into changing their stories. I wouldn't give you a penny as a bet on Kingsley's honesty either, but accepting a job at a smaller salary can hardly be construed as a crime, while as to Stokes and Barleycorn, they've records it's true, both of them, but not very impressively evil. If we had to rely on their word alone it might be different, but the other three will carry the day.'

'Now that you know this Mrs Protheroe consented tacitly at least to what was going on,' said Meg, 'surely, darling, that makes a difference.'

'To me and to you, yes, but to the jury who are trying as hard as they can to keep a collectively open mind ... even if they believe it, she may be able to convince them that she turned over a new leaf when she married. We know nothing to Kenneth Protheroe's detriment.'

'I see that, of course, but it seems very unsatisfactory to me,' Meg complained.

'To me, too, if it's any consolation to you. Wait till I've talked to Uncle Nick, Meg: he may see things more clearly than I do.'

So he went downstairs after dinner and found Sir Nicholas and Vera discussing the day's events, as he might have expected. Vera immediately supplied him with cognac which he accepted with a rather guilty feeling, knowing well enough that the party upstairs were regaling themselves with a rather inferior brand. He told them Roger's story and not surprisingly Vera was the first to comment on it.

'Good work,' she said approvingly. And then, 'Woman must be a fool. Should have destroyed it.'

'A mistake easily enough made,' said Sir Nicholas thoughtfully. 'The question is, Antony, what are we going to do with the

174

information?'

'That's up to you, sir. It's what I came downstairs to find out.'

'You're forgetting, my dear boy, we're playing this hand according to your rules.'

'Hitting below the belt, Nicholas,' said Vera in her gruff way. 'Antony only wants your advice.'

'He shall have it. You say this boy, Dick Hartley, is quite willing to appear as a witness for the defence?'

'So Roger says.'

'Then you will still treat Mrs Protheroe with kid gloves tomorrow, exactly as we planned, except that I think in view of Roger's discovery, that you might bring out – very gently – her previous association with Porson. Don't get carried away; leave it at that, no innuendos, no snide remarks.'

'Snide, sir?' said Maitland, catching to perfection Lamb's querulous tones.

There was a moment's silence and then Vera laughed, and presently her husband followed her example. 'I hesitate to blame your aunt for corrupting the purity of my speech, Antony. Perhaps we may put my fall from grace down to what I have had to bear from the Crown's witnesses in court today.'

'That seems very reasonable, Uncle Nick. But after I've dealt very gently with Mrs Protheroe –?'

'When our turn comes we'll call young Hartley, and then we'll open the envelope. That will be after the weekend, with any luck, but at least it'll be nearer the time when the jury have to consider their verdict, and there's some small chance they may remember it.'

'Cynical,' said Vera, but she nodded her approval of this course of action.

For form's sake Antony argued a little, but his uncle's ideas synchronised only too well with his own instinctive view, and by the time he had finished his brandy and left to go upstairs again, they were all in complete agreement.

Thursday, the third day of the trial

Kenneth Protheroe was a stout man, and not very tall, with dark hair that receded well from his temples; and though he declared himself to be a builder by trade it was perfectly obvious that he had a businesslike head on his shoulders and under Hawthorne's gentle probing he admitted to owning his own firm in the contracting business. 'Nothing large, mind you,' he insisted. He was obviously an educated man, but there was still a faint trace of some regional accent, so faint that Antony – who had an ear for such things – couldn't begin to identify it. Protheroe had also a benign, rather cherubic look, which didn't please Maitland at all. There was no denying it, the man looked honest, and if he gave his evidence well and firmly it would go a long way with the jury.

Hawthorne had obviously no worries on that score, he was giving the witness his head. After the preliminaries were concluded it needed only one question to get things going. 'We should be obliged, Mr Protheroe, if you would give the court an account of certain events which took place on the twenty-third of September last.'

'That's easily done. And why I remember the date so well is because it was the wife's birthday. I thought, to tell you the truth, I'd take her uptown to some really good restaurant, but there was a film she wanted to see and as it was playing at a cinema near Victoria we decided to have a quick snack before the show, at Hartley's Restaurant. That's how we came to be there. It's not a big place and the tables are fairly close together.'

'Close enough for you to hear your neighbours' conversation?'

'If you stopped talking yourself to listen, which is what I did, and shushed Connie too, when I realised that what they were talking about was a bit out of the way.'

'One moment, Mr Protheroe. The people you are speaking of who occupied the neighbouring table – do you see them in the court?'

'Yes, of course I do.' He looked straight at the dock. 'The prisoners,' he added. 'Of course I know their names now, but I didn't at that time.'

'And what was the first thing you overheard that roused your interest?'

'It was the older one that was speaking. He has a deep voice but it carries well. Should I quote his exact words, sir? I don't want to offend the court.'

'If you remember what was said exactly, Mr Protheroe, I think you must leave the court's sensibilities out of consideration and tell us what you heard.'

'He said, we've enough on the buggers now to charge them if they won't play ball.'

'That remark immediately caught your interest?'

'Of course it did.'

'What did you conclude from it, Mr Protheroe?'

'Well, the reference to a charge made me think they must be police officers, and the implication of the rest of the sentence was perfectly clear, that in return for some consideration or other no charge would be brought. I glanced across at the men and took a good look. They'd finished their meal and were sitting over coffee. So I gave Connie – my wife – a sort of warning look and she fell silent, listening too. Do you want me to tell you what was said?'

'That is why you were called as a witness, Mr Protheroe.'

'Well, I can't remember word for word, but I do remember exactly what they meant. The younger one replied, "Do you think they will?" And the one who had first spoken said, "It's a murder charge," as if that settled the matter.'

'I think, my lord,' said Hawthorne, 'that it might perhaps be in order for the witness to use the prisoners' names in recounting this conversation. It will be less confusing. So long as the jury clearly understand that at the time he was quite unaware of who they were.'

'Anything that will simplify matters,' sighed Lamb, 'would I am sure be welcome to us all. Have you any objections, Sir Nicholas?'

177

'None at all, m'lud. The witness's story will be no more and no less true because my clients are identified by name.'

'Very well, Mr Hawthorne. You may proceed with your questions.'

'I'm obliged to your lordship. Very well, Mr Protheroe, you did not know at the time what you have since learned, that the elder of the two men you overheard is called Mayhew, and the younger Harris.'

'Gerry Harris?' said the witness in a questioning tone. 'I heard the other man call him that.'

'Gerard, to be exact,' Hawthorne told him. 'But I think we'll stick to the surnames to avoid confusion.'

'It was obvious they had discussed the matter before. Harris said, "The only thing that worries me is Mrs G.'s evidence. Peele's different, we scared him pretty badly and he knows exactly what he's supposed to say. But her statement is nothing like what she told us. Won't she contradict it?" '

'And what had Chief Inspector Mayhew to say to that?'

'He laughed and said something like, "You don't know the Mrs Goodbodys of this world. Just being in court will be enough to intimidate her: she'll be frightened to deny what she's put her name to. Besides, if she thinks those two really killed her husband she'd be glad to go along with us anyway." '

'And then?' Hawthorne prompted him when he fell silent for a moment.

'Mayhew went on, "You're new to this, but you can take it from me that's how it'll be. But even if it doesn't go as I expect there's still Peele's testimony, and it would be the easiest thing in the world to suggest that she'd be intimidated by some associate of Stokes and Barleycorn into changing her evidence again." So the other one – Harris – thought about that for a minute and then he said, "Yes, I see all that, but supposing Kingsley returns and backs up their story of being genuine employees? It was a bit of luck for us, Mr Shadwell not knowing about the Wood Green account, but that would spoil things, wouldn't it?" And Mayhew laughed again; he seemed to be in a good humour. "Kingsley isn't due back from his holiday for another fortnight," he said, "and once they've been committed for trial he could give all the evidence he liked on their behalf, but he'd be taking a big risk in doing so . . . a risk of being tarred with the same brush. In any case this isn't the first time I've done this sort of thing. You can take it from me none of this is going to happen. Stokes and Barleycorn will pay up, and that'll be the end of it, so no more questions out of you, my lad, or I'll begin to regret I took you in with me." "You need me now that your other partner's been transferred," Harris said. "And don't think I'm not grateful for the opportunity – it's the sort of thing I've been looking for." '

'And that was all?'

'Yes. They finished their coffee, paid their bill and left. I wasn't going to spoil Connie's birthday treat, so we finished our meal and saw the film and then sat up half the night at home talking over what we'd heard. But we didn't know any of the people concerned; neither of us are particularly interested in reading about murder, and it was difficult to see what we could do about it. I mean, at that point it was all so vague. But we did keep an eye on the newspapers after that, and when we saw that the case against two men called Stokes and Barleycorn who were accused of murder had been dismissed in the Magistrates' Court, we thought it was time to come forward.'

'Thank you, Mr Protheroe, that's all very clear, and I'm sure we all appreciate your public-spiritedness.' Hawthorne hadn't quite finished with the witness, however. He took him through the whole story again, which perhaps was sensible as the more serious part of the case against the prisoners rested solely on his and his wife's evidence. When at last he had finished, Maitland got up to cross-examine.

'I do not know how the court may regard the matter, Mr Protheroe, but assuming your story to be true it is still something of a mystery to me why you and your wife were so long in coming forward with this valuable piece of evidence.'

'I hoped I'd explained all that. We're ordinary people, unused to police matters. Naturally Mrs Protheroe was nervous about getting involved.'

'But the murder charge against Mr Stokes and Mr Barleycorn had already been dismissed. You knew nothing, I suppose, of the police disciplinary inquiry that was going on behind the scenes?'

'Naturally not, but it was obvious that those two men – the prisoners – committed perjury, and we thought our evidence

179

should be available if it was needed. I regret now that we delayed so long because of my wife's scruples, but it hasn't really made any difference, has it?'

Maitland glanced down at that moment. One of his uncle's ducks was wearing a barrister's wig, and Counsel for the Defence was busy adding what could only be intended to be a gag to his portrayal. Maitland was smiling as he looked up again; Sir Nicholas had obviously realised only too well how the word 'scruples' applied to Mrs Protheroe would have affected his nephew. 'Another point in your story that seems strange,' said Maitland slowly, 'is why Chief Inspector Mayhew and Constable Harris should have discussed so private a matter in a public place.'

'They were sitting at a corner table and probably thought they couldn't be overheard. When we first went in my wife was chattering away as women will, and by the time we stopped talking to listen I'm sure they were too taken up with what was being said to notice the fact.'

'An answer for everything,' said Maitland admiringly. 'What was the date of your marriage to Mrs Protheroe?'

'April of this year. The twelfth, to be exact.'

'She had been recently widowed, had she not?'

'Yes, but we were not strangers to each other. Both she and her husband had been friends of mine, and in her unhappiness she turned to me. It seemed obvious to try to lessen our grief by sharing it.'

'Thank you, Mr Protheroe, I've no further questions.'

Neither had Hawthorne it seemed, though he did look faintly puzzled. Mrs Constance Protheroe was called, and confirmed her husband's evidence in every particular, though giving, when she came to recounting the conversation they had overhead, the gist of what had been said between the two policemen rather than attempting to reconstruct their dialogue. Hawthorne anticipated Maitland's question as to why they had been so late in coming forward with the information, and was told that it was all the witness's fault, Ken having been eager to do something, but she had felt nervous about the possible results of their intervention. 'Such as finding yourself giving evidence like this,' said Hawthorne sympathetically. 'I'm sure we can all understand that, Mrs

180

Protheroe, but it hasn't been such an ordeal after all, has it?'

'No,' she agreed doubtfully, and eyed Maitland's tall figure as he got up to cross-examine with some trepidation.

She was still a young woman, perhaps in her early thirties, and something near to being a beauty. But what had he expected after all, Porson's taste had been excellent in other matters, why shouldn't it extend to his women? She had assumed for the occasion a fluttery manner which he was convinced wasn't genuine, but it had its dangers. One wrong word ... he remembered only too well his uncle's warning.

No use repeating Hawthorne's question about the lateness of their evidence being given, but no harm perhaps in asking her also why the two prisoners should have chosen so public a place for an incriminating conversation. This time, however, the judge himself intervened without waiting for a protest from Hawthorne.

'I think, Mr Maitland, that that is something you cannot expect the witness to be able to explain.'

'If your lordship pleases.' The meaningless phrase came out automatically, but he had seen the quick flare of anger in the woman's eyes at the mention of his name, and thought, that's torn it! before going on in an even tone to his next question.

'Your marriage to Mr Kenneth Protheroe took place, I believe, on the twelfth of April last. He has also told us that you were a widow at the time. What was your previous husband's name?'

'My lord, is this relevant?' asked Hawthorne.

'Is it relevant, Mr Maitland?'

'Extremely so, my lord, as you will see when our side of the case is presented.'

'Then you may continue,' the judge told him.

'I'm obliged to your lordship. What was your previous husband's name, Mrs Protheroe?'

'Edwin Porson.' She had had time to consider the futility of evasion.

'And at the time of your re-marriage he had been dead almost exactly two months?'

'You ought to know,' she spat at him. 'He'd never have been in prison if it hadn't been for you. There'd have been no need for what he did.'

'I'm sorry to make you recall such unhappy things, Mrs

181

Protheroe. Your late husband was a professional killer, was he not, a marksman? And under arrest for murder at the time he hanged himself?'

'You seem to know all about it. That's what they said, but *I* never knew, never quite believed it was true.' She turned and looked appealingly at the judge. 'If he did something wrong, am I to blame? I admit that's why I didn't want Kenneth to go to the police, but I didn't think anyone would be so unkind.'

'I'm very sorry indeed, Mrs Protheroe,' said Mr Justice Lamb, looking as though he were about to burst into tears. 'This questioning was certainly uncalled for, and in my estimation quite unforgiveable. Have you any further questions, Mr Maitland, questions that directly concern this witness's evidence?'

'No, my lord. I am quite sure there would be no shaking that story, it has been far too well rehearsed,' said Antony and sat down beside his uncle. 'I'm sorry, sir, I blew it,' he said, and for once Sir Nicholas let the colloquialism pass without rebuke.

Hawthorne, perhaps wisely, declined to re-examine and that ended the case for the prosecution.

The Case for the Defence

Thursday, the third day of the trial (continued)

Sir Nicholas's opening address was very brief, consisting mainly of a re-hash of Superintendent Wakefield's evidence insofar as it could be construed as being favourable to the defence. He concluded by affirming his clients' innocence. 'It is unfortunate, members of the jury, that the case against them rests in this instance not on mistaken testimony, as is so often the case, but almost exclusively on stories which are deliberate fabrications. I trust however that we shall be able to prove to your complete satisfaction that Chief Inspector Mayhew and Constable Harris are the victims of a conspiracy, and, in addition, explain the reason why it became desirable to certain criminal elements to have them disgraced.'

But even this short discourse had brought them to the luncheon recess. Stringer, as so often happened, had fish of his own to fry, Mr Bellerby had a client to see and his clerk would have arranged sandwiches in the office. Sir Nicholas glanced at his watch and declared firmly that there was time to go to Astroff's so long as they let the waiter know quite clearly the time they had to be back in court. Antony followed his uncle in some trepidation.

But as it turned out, his fears were groundless. 'My dear boy,' said Sir Nicholas, 'it was always a possibility that the woman would recognise your name. After that –'

'I needn't have thrown it in her face that I believed they'd rehearsed their story.'

'You did no more than I did later in my opening address,' Sir Nicholas assured him. 'As I said, there are no two ways about

183

this case. Either our clients are lying or all the prosecution witnesses have been carefully orchestrated.'

'But so many of them!'

'How many times, Antony, have you reassured a client that however black things looked when the prosecution had finished presenting their case, there was still our side of the story to come? Think about that and drink your scotch and perhaps you'll feel better.'

It would have taken more than the rather watered-down whisky that had been set before him (their favourite waiter seemed to know by instinct which days they were in court, and adjusted matters accordingly without any further instructions) to make Antony feel better at that moment. When they got back to court, as he knew only too well, Mayhew and his young co-defendant would be giving evidence on their own behalf, and he was very much afraid that both of them would be badly mauled in cross-examination.

And in the event this dismal prognostication – almost worthy, he reflected wryly, of Mr Justice Lamb himself – proved to be only too accurate. Sir Nicholas took each in turn through his evidence. Harris, whom he called first – because Hawthorne won't be expecting us to do it that way – was reasonably eloquent, but Mayhew, who had talked so freely at their original conference, had now retreated into his usual taciturnity, and every sentence had to be dragged from him almost by force. And with each of them Hawthorne went through their stories again step by step in cross-examination, and of each statement, 'What proof can you offer the court of that?' he asked. Both of them remembered having visited Hartley's Restaurant on the night in question, Mayhew obviously because Harris had reminded him of his wife's absence that day, though in any case it was quite likely that they would have done so as they were working hard on the inquiry and it was a convenient place to slip into for a quick meal. But the worst of Hawthorne's attack was reserved for Mayhew, when the afternoon was already well advanced.

'So it comes to this then: all the prosecution witnesses are lying, even when their evidence confirms what the others have said, but you and your younger colleague alone are telling the truth?'

'Superintendent Wakefield wasn't lying,' said Mayhew

stolidly.

'No, I'm sure of that. He confirmed the evidence of the other witnesses –'

'Repeated, not confirmed,' Mayhew corrected him. 'He didn't know the truth of it and didn't pretend to.'

'You are referring, I presume, to the more fanciful part of his evidence. That, may I remind you, was pure speculation.'

'Speculation that had some backing,' Mayhew insisted. 'It's common knowledge that someone in the criminal world's been running things.'

'Knowledge, Mr Mayhew?'

'You must be aware, sir, that there's things we know in the Force that can't ever be proved.'

'Yes, exactly. But don't you think the array of witnesses against you goes some way towards providing the proof that what they're saying is true?'

'I wouldn't take the word of those two – Stokes and Barleycorn – not if they were to swear it on a stack of Bibles.'

'You're forgetting I think, Mr Mayhew, that their story has independent corroboration.'

'Independent, fiddlesticks!' said Mayhew, which Maitland mentally applauded though he recognised it wasn't particularly wise. 'Someone wanted us out of the way and arranged matters to be sure we didn't have a leg to stand on.'

'Perhaps you can suggest who that somebody may be.'

'If I knew that he'd be standing here instead of me.'

'You're telling us you don't know?'

'I don't know,' said Mayhew belligerently, 'but the whole story isn't in yet.'

'We shall await its unfolding with interest,' said Hawthorne rather satirically. 'Meanwhile . . . how many times have you played this trick before, Mr Mayhew?'

'I don't know what you mean.'

'Obtained money from innocent people of perhaps a less-than-respectable background, under threat of prosecution for some crime or other.'

'Never!' It seemed for a moment that Mayhew had nothing more to say, but before Hawthorne could open his mouth to form another question he began to speak again more quickly than before. 'But I'll tell you this, if I wanted to play that game I wouldn't have to use people that were innocent. There's enough crime goes on to keep you busy in that racket for a lifetime if you were so minded.'

'You have been very free with the word know, Mr Mayhew. Would you admit that temptation sometimes exists to provide evidence when you know the guilty party, as you say, but are unable to prove it?'

'It's . . . frustrating,' said Mayhew after seeking for a moment for the right word. 'But it's not a thing I'd ever try, nor young Gerry Harris either.'

'Well, we shall see in due course what the jury feel about that. I have no further questions, my lord,' he added. 'Perhaps Sir Nicholas –?'

'Only one thing, m'lud,' said Sir Nicholas, rising to his feet in his leisurely way. 'I should like my client to repeat what he has already told the court, that the charge against Mr Stokes and Mr Barleycorn was brought in good faith, and on evidence which he believed to be good and sufficient.'

'That's right, sir,' said Mayhew relapsing in taciturnity. 'That's just how it was.'

'You would not in any event have been foolish enough to – to –'

'To rig the evidence,' Mayhew completed the sentence for him obligingly. 'No, sir, I wouldn't.' And with that Sir Nicholas let him go.

Mr Justice Lamb, however, had had enough of the matter for one day, and adjourned in a failing voice until the following morning. Mr Bellerby scuttled away to have a word with his clients. 'Though I don't really see that he can find anything particularly consoling to tell them,' said Antony, almost as gloomily as the judge might have done, as he left the court with his uncle.

'If this idea of yours is right –'

'Yes, Uncle Nick, but is it?'

'You were confident enough when you discovered that Mrs Protheroe was the former Mrs Porson,' Sir Nicholas pointed out.

'Confident of our clients' innocence, yes.'

'And you're beginning to doubt that?' Sir Nicholas's tone had taken on a sudden sharpness.

'No. No, I don't think so. But two things are worrying me. I may be quite wrong in the conclusion I have reached as to who is the Managing Director of the whole show. And even if I'm right he may not react as I expect, and the result I'm hoping for . . . it's all a toss-up, which is why, though Meg and Roger know everything that's happened, I haven't said a word to them about the conclusion we – I've reached.'

'It's the only chance we have,' Sir Nicholas agreed, which in his nephew's present mood was just about the last thing to prove comforting.

Friday, the fourth day of the Trial

The first witness the following morning was the arresting officer of the man who had attacked Antony in the park nearly two weeks before. There was a good deal of argument back and forth about the admissability of the evidence, but Sir Nicholas could be very persuasive when he wished to be, and in this instance he was quite well aware that the same objections would be made several times during the course of the day, and put out his best endeavour. 'I wish to impress upon the court that there have been in this affair a series of so-called coincidences that can be explained in only one way.'

'By assuming your clients' innocence, no doubt,' said Hawthorne, forgetting for the moment to address the court.

'Precisely,' said Sir Nicholas, having turned his head in the direction of the judge in token apology. 'I hope your lordship will be willing to let me proceed.'

'Am I to take it,' said Mr Justice Lamb despairingly, 'that Mr Maitland has been on one of his fact-finding expeditions?'

'I'm afraid that was his intention, m'lud. You may know that he has something of a reputation in these matters, and it is our contention that the attack which the witness will describe was the direct result of his being known to be concerned with this case.'

'Then I suppose it must be admitted, though I do not necessarily agree that your interpretation is the right one. But please be brief, Sir Nicholas; this matter seems to be dragging on interminably.'

'If you need Mr Maitland's confirmation, m'lud –' Sir Nicholas paused invitingly and the judge responded as he had hoped.

'Heaven forbid!' he said piously.

So the story was told of the complaint that had been received, and the arrest and subsequent committal for trial of the man called Matthew Adams. As no harm had been done the lesser charge of attempted robbery, to which the accused admitted, had been substituted for one of attempted murder.

'There is just one more small matter,' said Sir Nicholas with an apologetic look in the judge's direction. 'This Matthew Adams, can you give us any further particulars of him?'

'He's thirty-six years old and an electrician by trade, but he had been out of work for nearly eighteen months, or so he said.'

'I see. And his previous employers?'

'Greenbrier and Appleby. He lives in London, but the last job he did for them was on the modernisation of an old house in Derbyshire.'

'Thank you,' said Sir Nicholas. 'Another small coincidence,' he remarked, to nobody in particular.

'I don't quite understand you, Sir Nicholas,' said the judge.

'I hesitate to bring up the matter, m'lud. You may think it more fitting to be spoken of in my closing address.'

'You may stress it then, of course, and I have no doubt you will if it is to your clients' advantage,' said Lamb, with the first glimmer of humour that Antony had ever observed in him. 'But in the meantime, I should like you to explain –' He made no attempt to finish the sentence.

'Merely this, m'lud. Greenbrier and Appleby are in the same line of business, though on a much larger scale, as Mr Kenneth Protheroe. They are also the former employers of the prosecution's witness, Martin Kingsley.'

'A coincidence,' said the judge consideringly. 'Have you any questions for this witness, Mr Hawthorne?'

'None at all, my lord. I cannot see that the matter has any relevance whatever.'

The next witness was called: the detective from the traffic division who had tried unsuccessfully to find the driver of the car that had killed Arthur Abbott. 'I suppose this is another of your coincidences, Sir Nicholas,' said Lamb when he had got tired of hearing the details of the investigation.

'Yes, m'lud. The relevance here is even more obvious than it was in the case of the last witness's evidence. Mr Abbott was the chief packer at the Shadwell Confectionery Company. Mr

Kingsley if you recall mentioned him in the course of his evidence.'

'An accident might happen to anybody.'

'Certainly, m'lud, and I admit I have no proof that that isn't what happened. But you must agree that it is another of those coincidences we spoke of.'

'Why should anybody want this man dead?'

'My next witness will explain, m'lud. With your lordship's permission, of course.'

'I suppose we must hear him,' said Lamb, resigned.

He needn't have worried. The next occupant of the witness box was there very briefly. This was the man who had succeeded to Arthur Abbott's job at Shadwell's, and all he had to tell them was that Abbott had been very much in the way of choosing what work he would do, which was generally felt by the men under him to be in the interest of doing as little as possible. Certainly there were certain jobs that he always reserved for himself, and among them was the putting up of the orders for Mr Goodbody and Mr Peele. He would also, of course, make up the list that was sent to the accounts department.

'So that if there was any discrepancy between what was supplied and what was charged for, Abbott would be the only one to know,' said Sir Nicholas, rubbing it in.

The witness agreed, and again Hawthorne, somewhat disdainfully, declined to cross-examine.

Even briefer was the evidence of William Goodbody's assistant, David Lindley, of having seen a letter on Shadwells' letterhead saying their account was in arrears; and that of one of the ledger clerks at the branch bank to which his payments were usually made, who told the court that Mr Goodbody had made a deposit on the usual day, though it was for a lesser amount than usual. Both told their stories and were dismissed without questions from the prosecution.

After that there was Richard Hartley, the present owner of the house that had been Edwin Porson's. He proved to be a pleasant-looking young man of a rather engaging naivety, which displayed itself in the pleasure he obviously took in finding himself involved in what was obviously for him an unusual and rather exciting situation. Sir Nicholas took him through the

190

preliminary questions with practised speed and then asked, 'You bought the house you are living in from a Mrs Protheroe, I believe?'

'Yes, we did, though in fact we were living there for a short time before the sale was completed. I understand the lady had been recently widowed, and probate had not yet gone through. The house, she told us, had been in the joint names of herself and her husband.'

'The lady concerned is, I believe, at present in court. Can you identify her for us?'

'I don't know. I only saw her the once and I'm not very good at faces.'

'Just look around, take you time, Mr Hartley, and see if anybody strikes you as familiar.'

Dick Hartley did as he was told, and then said rather hesitantly, 'I think that lady over there. At least I'm more sure of the gentleman sitting next to her, who was with her at the solicitor's office, though he took no part in the proceedings.'

'Mr and Mrs Protheroe,' said Sir Nicholas with satisfaction. 'Perhaps you will be kind enough to stand so that the witness may be in no doubt.' (Not that there was any real importance about it, Maitland thought, but perhaps his uncle was right after all in emphasising the length of the connection between Kenneth and Connie Protheroe.)

'Yes, those are the two people. But I thought –'

'Mrs Protheroe owned the house by virtue of her marriage to a man since dead,' Sir Nicholas explained. 'And now, m'lud, I have an envelope here which I wish to introduce into evidence. May I then ask the witness if he recognises it?' A few minutes later Dick Hartley had the envelope in his hand. 'You will see, m'lud, that it is sealed, and signed by the witness and two other people across the seal.'

'I have already observed as much, Sir Nicholas.'

'Then, Mr Hartley, do you recognise this envelope as having been sealed in your presence and signed by yourself and your wife and a gentleman who visited you on behalf of the defence in this case?'

'Oh, yes, that's my signature all right, and Margery's, and Mr Farrell signed it too.'

'Perhaps you would describe Mr Farrell's visit to us.'

'He'd been before, with Mr Maitland. They just saw Margery that time, and she couldn't help them because they were looking for a Mrs Porson. But this time Mr Farrell was alone, and he asked us whether the people we bought the house from had left anything behind them. Margery told him that we'd bought the house furnished, but everything of a personal nature had been cleared out except a small bookcase. The books in it didn't interest us, and at the completion Mrs Protheroe told us to keep them, she didn't want them, so we just put them in a packing case and stored them in the attic.'

'But you examined them that evening in Mr Farrell's presence?'

'Yes, we did. We took each one out in turn and shook it, and an envelope with a note inside it fell out of one of them. I looked at the envelope and its contents, so I can identify them both, and then I found an envelope big enough to contain them and we sealed them inside and signed it, as you see.'

'Thank you, Mr Hartley. I may add, m'lud, that both Mrs Hartley and Mr Roger Farrell are waiting to give evidence if you feel it necessary.'

'I hope there will be no need for that, Sir Nicholas.'

'Then if the usher would be good enough to let the jury see the envelope I think we can all agree that it has not been tampered with since it was sealed in Mr Hartley's presence. I have heard, though I admit I have never tried it myself, that envelopes can be steamed open, but I am very much of the impression that if such a thing had been done the ink of the signatures would have been smudged. What do you think, Mr Hawthorne?'

Counsel for the Prosecution smiled at his adversary. 'Like you, Sir Nicholas, I have no experience in steaming open other people's correspondence,' he said. 'However, I agree that there are no signs of its having been tampered with.'

'Thank you. I wonder, m'lud, if I might take the liberty of asking my learned friend to open that envelope himself and tell us exactly what he finds in it?'

'If that is your wish, Sir Nicholas, and if Mr Hawthorne is agreeable.'

Mr Hawthorne was not only agreeable but by this time obviously curious. The usher produced a paper knife and Counsel

192

for the Prosecution slit the envelope open neatly. 'One further word for your lordship,' Sir Nicholas interpolated at this point. 'I should like to stress that though I have been told of the contents I have not myself seen them nor have either of my colleagues on the defence team.'

'That is understood, Sir Nicholas,' said the judge, 'and I am sure the jury will take note of the fact.'

By this time Hawthorne had the inner envelope in his hand. He held it up so that the court could see it. 'It is addressed to Mrs Edwin Porson, my lord, at the address the witness gave us as his own. The postmark is a little smudged, but quite legible. It was posted in Arkenshaw, Yorkshire, on the third of February this year. The small sheet of paper inside seems to have been torn from a notebook, one of the kind with a spiral binding. It has no address, no date, no salutation.'

'Yes, yes, Mr Hawthorne. You are going to read it to us,' said Lamb impatiently.

Hawthorne held up the scrap of paper and read from it slowly: *You will have read in the papers what happened. When I can get away I shall go abroad. Get in touch with you-know-who for funds and arrangements to join me.'*

Mr Justice Lamb was frowning. 'Is this note not signed in any way, Mr Hawthorne?'

'Only by an initial, my lord. It is not very clear, but my guess would be that it is the letter E.'

'A note to the present Mrs Protheroe, written from Yorkshire as long ago as last February,' said the judge thoughtfully. 'Perhaps, Sir Nicholas, you would be kind enough to explain the significance to us.'

'I should like your lordship's permission, and that of my learned friend, Mr Hawthorne, to ask Mrs Constance Protheroe whether she can identify the handwriting.'

'Yes, yes, that will be quite in order. Have you any further questions for your witness, Sir Nicholas?'

'No, Mr Hartley has done his part nobly. Unless Mr Hawthorne . . . I see he has no questions for you, Mr Hartley, you may stand down and join the other witnesses.'

There was a little confusion while Connie Protheroe was recalled, reminded of the continuing efficacy of her oath, and handed the note which she took reluctantly. She stared at it for a long moment. (Somebody else wondering how much can be proved, Maitland thought.) 'It's Ed's handwriting, my late husband's,' she said at last. 'He'd gone away on a job, I'd always thought he was a salesman of some kind. And then I read in the newspaper that he was wanted for murder. It was the first I ever knew of his real work. It was . . . I'm sure you can understand, my lord, it was a terrible shock.'

Mr Justice Lamb had himself taken over the questioning. 'If you were indeed unaware of his activities —'

'I was, oh, I was.'

'— that is something with which we can all sympathise. But the note is written by a very cautious man, and we should like you to tell us who you thought he meant by the expression you-know-who.'

Again she hesitated for a moment. 'I could only think . . . Ken was always such a good friend of both of us. He would have helped me, I know, when I showed him the note, though he was no wiser than I was, and of course he'd been just as shocked and surprised when the news broke. All we could think was that perhaps Ed would get in touch with me some day, and then he hoped that Kenneth would help me to join him.'

'Very well, Mrs Protheroe, though I find his caution in not naming your present husband a little difficult to understand.'

'That was Ed all over,' said Connie Protheroe.

'I see. Have either of you any questions to add?'

Hawthorne shook his head.

'Your lordship has covered the matter to my entire satisfaction,' said Sir Nicholas.

'I am glad of that,' said Lamb. 'If you'll allow me to say so, this matter on which you seem to have placed so much importance doesn't seem to have got us very much further forward.'

'I must bow to your lordship's greater wisdom,' said Sir Nicholas, with an insincerity that perhaps his nephew, alone of all the people in the courtroom, recognised. 'Would you wish me to call my other witnesses to the finding of this note and the sealing of the envelope?'

'No, Sir Nicholas, I should not. I am quite sure Mr Hartley has told a completely truthful story. It is the emphasis you place on

194

the matter that I question.'

'I am sorry to hear that, m'lud.' Sir Nicholas was noticeably downcast. 'It seemed to me that the identity of the person whose name Porson so carefully concealed might be of interest to the court.'

'Mrs Protheroe has explained that, Sir Nicholas. May I ask if you have any more witnesses to call?'

'Certain character witnesses, m'lud, on behalf of both my clients.' His demeanour, as clearly as his words, made this an admission of defeat.

'Very well, we will hear what they have to say. But I think' – he glanced up at the court clock – 'on Monday morning perhaps, Sir Nicholas. If we take the luncheon adjournment now it will be very late when we get back, and I'm sure none of us wish to prolong this sitting unduly just before the weekend.'

'Your lordship is considerate as always,' said Sir Nicholas, and again Antony was pretty sure he was the only one to have detected the hint of irony in his uncle's tone.

Saturday and Sunday,
the weekend recess

They had been out to dinner with Roger and Meg at their house in Chelsea on the Friday evening, with Meg playing up for all she was worth to her unaccustomed role as housewife. In the normal way that would have been enough to keep Antony amused, but that evening he was silent and uncommunicative, though he did deign to give them a brief description of the day's events, adding reflectively, 'Uncle Nick's a cunning old so-and-so, but he's not in the mood just at the moment to have that pointed out to him.'

'You mean,' said Roger, 'that he's left everyone with the impression that the defence has shot its bolt.'

'He wouldn't like that way of putting it, but that's just what I do mean. In effect, the defence's case is finished and the character witnesses are just being thrown in to show we've tried everything.'

'I think it was very clever of him, darling,' said Meg, but she caught Jenny's eye at that moment and decided that any further teasing was not at the moment in order. So she changed the subject rather violently to the description of an investment she had just made on Roger's advice, a matter which they all – even her stockbroker husband – found extremely dull, but safe.

As for Jenny, she was worried, but she'd know when Antony was ready to talk and the time hadn't come yet. So she held her peace and nothing more was said about the subject until they had finished breakfast the following morning and the house phone rang. Maitland answering it heard with a further sinking of his spirits Gibbs's voice announcing that Mrs Mayhew had called to see him. 'Have my uncle and aunt finished breakfast?' he inquired sharply.

'Sir Nicholas and Lady Harding went back to the study about

196

a quarter of an hour ago,' Gibbs told him. As usual his tone was faintly admonitory, though on this occasion it was difficult to see why.

'Then ask Mrs Mayhew to wait. I'll come straight down,' Maitland told him. And paused only to tell Jenny where and why he was going before setting off downstairs at top speed. Mrs Mayhew, he was relieved to find, had not been consigned to the rigours of the drawing-room but was seated comfortably enough on a chair at the side of the hall. He greeted her saying, 'Just one more minute, I want to speak to my uncle,' and disappeared into the study.

'Mrs Mayhew's here, Uncle Nick,' he announced without ceremony. 'Can I bring her in here? It may be no more than she's worried about her evidence, but I've a nasty feeling there may be something else.'

'Leave you to it,' Vera offered.

'No, of course you won't. You know about as much of all this as we do, and you know we always value your advice.'

'Can't think why but I'll stay, of course,' said Vera obligingly.

'If you're really puzzled, my dear, I can explain it to you,' Sir Nicholas offered. 'Antony knows perfectly well that in our frequent disagreements you are sometimes known to take his side.'

'Try to be fair,' said Vera seriously. 'Bring the poor woman in, Antony, and let's hear what she has to say.'

Maitland glanced at his uncle, received a slight confirmatory nod, and went out into the hall again to summon their visitor. Her face seemed thinner, he thought, and her mouth was turned down at the corners. His premonition of bad news was only too likely to be right.

And sure enough once the greetings and introductions were over and she was comfortably settled on the sofa it all came out. 'I know I shouldn't be troubling you, and perhaps I should have gone to Mr Bellerby. But as Laurie has spoken so often of Mr Maitland I knew I could trust him. And you of course, Sir Nicholas, will know better than anybody what I ought to do.'

'What is the trouble, Mrs Mayhew?' inquired Sir Nicholas gently.

'You know I was at the court all day yesterday in case you were

197

ready to call me as a witness. The post hadn't come when I left home, but it was waiting when I got back and I've laid awake all night wondering what I ought to do. It was a statement, you see, but not from our bank – in fact I though it had been delivered wrongly until I looked a second time at the address. It was ours all right, Mr and Mrs Mayhew, it said. So I opened it.'

'An account you knew nothing of? Perhaps you could give us some details of it, Mrs Mayhew,' said Sir Nicholas.

'Yes, that's what I'm here for. It showed a balance of fifteen thousand pounds. We never had that much money in our lives.'

'If you husband is of a saving disposition –'

'Don't you understand? The accounts we hold, the ones I knew about, the ones we use, cover everything. Laurie's whole salary is paid into them, he couldn't have possibly saved so much money out of the little he takes for his own expenses, and anyway why should he? We have some small savings as I told Mr Maitland when I saw him, but this is different.'

'Have there been any recent transactions?'

'No withdrawals. The money was paid in on the eighteenth of September, that's when the account was opened.'

'All in one sum?' He glanced quickly at his nephew and then went on in a milder tone. 'That makes it more of a puzzle, Mrs Mayhew, but perhaps less troublesome for us in the circumstances. It's a pity your husband's bail was revoked when the trial started, or he would probably have been able to explain the matter to you. As it is I'll talk to Mr Bellerby and find out what he has to say.'

'But what have I to do?'

'I think in the circumstances it will be necessary to be quite open with the prosecution about this. But I'm sure we shall find it is capable of explanation. So will you leave the matter in our hands, and either I or my nephew will be in touch with you later in the day?'

'Yes, of course. I'm grateful for your kindness. But do you really think . . . I wish I could have been in court to hear the other witnesses.' She turned a little to face Antony more directly; he had remained standing a little outside the group round the fire. 'You must have thought me incredibly naive, Mr Maitland, when we talked before. Laurie always made light of what might

198

happen but since then I've realised how terribly serious it is, and that the judge is likely to take a very poor view of his being a police officer. It won't go so hard with Gerry, of course, they'll say he was under Laurie's influence . . . won't they?' she added with a sudden doubt in her tone.

'I'm afraid none of us is in a position to make predictions, Mrs Mayhew,' Sir Nicholas told her, 'but certainly I should expect Constable Harris's youth to be taken into consideration.' He got up as he spoke and rather hesitantly she followed his example. 'My nephew will show you out,' he said. 'I know it's hard for you but you must try not to worry. You must be as calm as possible when you tell the court on Monday of the quiet life you and the Chief Inspector have led, and what a good husband he has been to you.'

'Thank you, yes, I'll do my best.' She started towards the door with Antony at her heels. 'And you will let me hear from you later in the day, Mr Maitland, won't you?'

When Maitland came back to the study he closed the door carefully and crossed the room until he was standing just behind the sofa. He looked then from Sir Nicholas to Vera and said the one word, 'Well?'

'Oldest trick in the world,' said Vera. 'Paying money into a person's account to make it seem they've accepted bribes.'

'I know, a sort of insurance policy. And the deposit being made only three days after the murder means that as soon as it was known that Mayhew was the investigating officer this plan was concocted.'

'I don't see anything strange about that,' Sir Nicholas told him. 'You said yourself, Antony, that murder is a serious charge, and the members of the organisation might be expected to take a smaller sentence in their stride in the hopes of better things to come, but Stokes and Barleycorn would certainly need some reassurance long before it came to an arrest. Again, as you said yourself, to prevent them talking out of turn.'

'Yes, but that's assuming Mayhew's innocence.'

'Are we back to your doubts again?'

'No, I didn't mean that. I meant, how is the prosecution going to explain this one payment? If Stokes and Barleycorn paid nothing, and anyway were not asked for as much as that –'

'I can think of at least two explanations they can give,' said Sir Nicholas, 'and if you stop to think for a moment you will see what I mean. The money may have been built up over the years in another account and transferred by Mayhew himself in a lump sum for safety's sake –'

'Or it may have been a payment from the real murderer for framing Stokes and Barleycorn for what he had done,' said Antony slowly.

'Precisely.'

'But you don't believe either of those things happened. You haven't changed your mind either ... not about what really happened, I mean?'

'No, Antony, I haven't changed my mind. But we shall have to go through the motions of consulting Bellerby and having him consult Mayhew for a possible explanation, which I'm sure won't be forthcoming. And as the matter has been placed in our hands we have no choice but to give this further piece of evidence to Hawthorne. He'll certainly want to recall Mayhew and I don't see how we can refuse.'

So the weekend was not so quiet after all. Mr Bellerby clucked distressfully over the statement, Chief Inspector Mayhew had no explanation to give, he'd never even been in the branch concerned. The manager's weekend relaxation was disturbed as well as that of a number of his staff, and as far as the cashier who opened the account could remember – so large a cash transaction had naturally been unusual – the money had been paid in by a woman who said she was Mrs Mayhew and gave all the correct particulars. It was to be a joint account, with either herself or her husband as signatories. The card with her own signature was on file, but the one she had taken away for her husband to sign had not yet been returned. The one bright spot was that the woman had been a redhead, not young but well turned out and well, though discreetly, made up. Nor was the signature anything like the one Mrs Mayhew produced for them. Antony did what he could to comfort her with this information, and left her with a promise that they would do the best they could with the matter in court.

It was late on Sunday when he sought his uncle out again alone, though he had, of course, seen a good deal of him in the meantime, as was customary on weekends, and very necessary on this occasion. Vera had already retired, and Sir Nicholas was looking along the bookshelves for some reading matter to take upstairs with him when he heard the door open and close and turned to see his nephew at his elbow. 'Have Roger and Meg gone?' he asked, as casually as he could.

'Yes, a few minutes ago. Uncle Nick –'

Sir Nicholas pulled down a book at random. 'If you want to talk we may as well sit down,' he said, and went across to his usual chair. He would have liked to add, You look tired to death, but that was a forbidden subject, though it had been obvious for several days now from his nephew's appearance and the stiff way he held himself that his shoulder was even more painful than usual.

Antony followed him but didn't attempt to sit down. Instead he stood looking down at his uncle, just in front of the chair that was now recognised as being Vera's. 'Uncle Nick,' he burst out, 'do you think we're doing the right thing.'

'As officers of the court –'

'I don't mean about that stupid statement. I know the rules as well as you do. I mean, supposing these people react as we think they may, have we the right to inflict so much suffering on anybody?'

'Think of it another way, Antony. Have we the right to let Mayhew and young Harris go to prison for years?'

'No, of course we haven't.' He tried to smile but it was a miserable failure. 'Talk about being between the devil and the deep blue sea,' he added bitterly.

'I don't really think we have any choice in the matter,' said Sir Nicholas. 'As for the unhappiness that may be caused . . . now or later, does it really matter? Just think about the future for a moment.'

'You're always telling me to do that lately, Uncle Nick.'

'Because you've lost your sense of perspective,' said Sir Nicholas. 'The situation is none of your making.'

'No, of course. I'm sorry I bothered you, Uncle Nick. I'll see you in the morning.'

He went upstairs to find Jenny just disappearing through the kitchen door with a tray of coffee cups and empty glasses. She obviously did no more than put it down on the table, but came out immediately, smiling at him. 'You were longer than I thought you would be, Antony.'

'I had a word with Uncle Nick.'

She looked at him hard for a moment and then made for the living-room door. 'Was it helpful?' she asked as she went.

'I suppose it was. He told me not to be a fool,' said Antony, translating his uncle's remarks rather freely.

Jenny had reached the hearthrug but she didn't attempt to sit down, instead she turned to face him. The room was warm and there was no need, she thought, to make up the fire even if her husband had at last reached the mood for confidences. 'You're not worried about that horrible man, Godalming, are you, Antony?' she asked.

'I haven't given him a thought for days,' said Antony truthfully. 'It's like – like the forces of nature, there's nothing to be done about it. He's made up his mind and nothing I can say or do will change it.'

'Then it's the case,' said Jenny. 'Uncle Nick hasn't changed *his* mind?'

'Nothing like that. Both he and Vera have accepted my arguments with rather unnerving readiness. But you know, love, however things go it's not going to be pleasant.'

'There's nothing you can do about that. And even if things were different, even if two men's freedom didn't depend on it, it's better to know the truth. Just think if it were you –'

That was a long speech for Jenny, and for some reason he found it almost unbearably touching. 'My dear and only love,' he said, 'that would be quite impossible.' He reached out his left hand to pull her towards him, and then tilted her chin so that he could look down directly into her clear grey eyes. 'Not so long as I'm married to you,' he said, 'but that poor devil –'

They talked for a long time after that, and when they went to bed it was Jenny who lay awake, and her husband who slept far more heavily than he usually did at her side.

Monday, the fifth day of the trial

It was only too obvious the following morning that Hawthorne considered that the case for the defence had already been presented, and that the remaining witnesses were no more than a formality, except, perhaps that Mrs Mayhew's evidence, as it had been revealed to him, very properly, by the defence, might now be turned to the prosecution's advantage. True, Sir Nicholas and Maitland between them had produced a few surprises, but nothing to discount the evidence of such respectable citizens as Mrs Jessie Goodbody and Vernon Peele. Not to mention Kenneth Protheroe; on the whole it was most likely that the jury would consider his wife more sinned against than sinning, and take her corroboration of his evidence at its face value. But it was the defence's job to give him a run for his money, and he listened indulgently as Sir Nicholas called his first witness, the Reverend Mr Mercer, the Vicar of St. Mark's Church.

That Mr Mercer was in earnest couldn't be doubted, that he had a genuine respect for the elder of the two defendants was also evident, but there was nothing he could say that would in any way counter the evidence before the court. Maitland did his best with what was extremely unpromising material, and Hawthorne didn't feel it necessary to point out to the jury that it was the reverend gentleman's duty to be charitable.

Though Hawthorne didn't realise it, the next witness was of more interest to the defence. This was Rupert Phillips, the managing clerk to Paul Collingwood, a solicitor long known to both Sir Nicholas and his nephew as he had an extensive criminal practice. Sir Nicholas put him through his paces quietly. Yes, he had been a friend of the Mayhews for many years, and had the greatest respect for both of them. This charge had completely taken him aback, and from what he knew of Laurie – Chief Inspector Mayhew, he should say – he simply could not believe in his guilt. He had always found his friend reticent where his professional duties were concerned, though after a case was over they would often re-hash it, both naturally having an interest in law and crime. 'I wonder,' said Sir Nicholas, 'did Chief Inspector Mayhew ever mention to you the possibility that a great deal of the crime in London, and some in the provinces, was being organised by a single man.'

'We talked about the subject in a general way,' said the witness. 'After all, everybody knows that organised crime exists.'

'I meant something rather more detailed than that. A blanket organisation, if I may put it that way, covering a number of different activities, but organised by one man.'

Rupert Phillips thought for a moment. 'I've heard some such possibility spoken of, and now you mention it I think it might have been by Laurie. But he always said the police know a lot more things than they can prove, and that I suppose would be one of them.'

So they went back again over what had been said before, how long he had known the Mayhews, how often he saw them, what he knew of their life style. It all added up to the picture of a very respectable couple, without doing anything to counter the case against the accused. Hawthorne tried rather half-heartedly to draw an admission from the witness that Chief Inspector Mayhew had shown an inordinate interest in crime and criminals, but as Phillips pointed out, such interest as he displayed was not to be wondered at, considering his job.

Hawthorne let him go then to join the other witnesses who had already given their evidence and were seated at the side of the court. Sir Nicholas called for Mrs Dorothy Mayhew, who was to be his next witness.

After he had taken her through the preliminary questions he turned to the bench. 'M'lud, since you recessed the court on Friday last a certain piece of information came into our hands through this witness, who was very naturally distressed and puzzled as to what she should do. I may say that I have discussed the matter with my learned friend, Mr Hawthorne, and he agreed that we would introduce the matter at this point. It consists of

204

this bank statement, which I should like to put into evidence, and came into Mrs Mayhew's hands when she got home on Friday evening and examined the day's post.'

There was the usual slight delay while the statement was labelled as an exhibit, handed to the judge, and then to the members of the jury. 'The witness will tell you, m'lud, that she knew nothing of the account until this statement arrived. You will see that it was opened by a single deposit on the eighteenth of September last, and my friend and I have agreed, subject to your lordship's approval, that my client, Chief Inspector Mayhew, should be recalled after Mrs Mayhew has finished her evidence, and also the cashier from the bank who opened the account, and who can describe the lady who did so and give details of any other circumstances which seem to be relevant.'

'If Mr Hawthorne is in agreement that seems a very satisfactory arrangement, Sir Nicholas. May I ask if Mrs Mayhew brought the statement directly to you?'

'To my house, m'lud. She asked for Mr Maitland but we saw her together.'

Mr Justice Lamb turned to the witness. 'I can well understand your distress, Madam,' he said. 'May I congratulate you on the correctness of your behaviour.'

'I didn't know what to do, my lord,' she said. (It was touch and go, Antony told Jenny later, as to which of them was the more likely to burst into tears at this point.) 'But I know Laurie wouldn't have done anything wrong, so I thought it was better to get everything out in the open.'

'An admirable attitude,' the judge concurred. 'You have some questions for this witness, Sir Nicholas.'

'Indeed I have, m'lud. How long have you been married, Mrs Mayhew?'

'Going on for twenty years.'

'And have you in that time ever heard your husband express any dissatisfaction with his career?'

'Well, there've been times when promotion seemed a bit slow in coming, the same as would be the case with anyone. And I won't say it's always been too easy, though the pay is better now, and there were only the two of us, you see.'

'How are things arranged between you, in the matter of

finances, for instance?'

'We had joint accounts. Laurie's salary went straight in, and the bank transferred a certain amount for savings. We had it all worked out, so much went for housekeeping and the mortgage, so much for clothes and entertainment, and whatever Laurie needed in the way of daily expenses, some of that of course he got back.'

'You lived quite comfortably, then?'

'Oh, yes.' She didn't sound terribly enthusiastic, but Mr Bellerby had obviously primed her well because she went on without prompting. 'On weekends we'd mostly have friends in in the evening, or go to see them. In the summer there was always the garden, or we might go to the zoo, or out to Kew Gardens. I won't say it wasn't difficult sometimes with the irregular hours Laurie had to keep, but our friends understood the way it was. On the days he wasn't working late he didn't feel much like doing anything, just a quiet evening at home, though if it was an anniversary or a birthday we might go out for dinner somewhere nice. And, of course, there were always his holidays to look forward to. Lately we mostly go abroad for a fortnight, that was about what the money would run to. He enjoyed that, he always said when he retired we'd travel.'

'And you managed to fill your days quite happily, when he was working the long hours you've described to us?'

'Yes, I never complained, and no one could say I did. And for the last couple of years –'

She broke off there and didn't go on until Sir Nicholas had prompted her gently. 'Yes, Mrs Mayhew?'

'There was Gerry . . . Gerry Harris. The one they say helped Laurie frame those two men. I told you we never had any children of our own and I don't think it worried Laurie, but I always . . . but that's all in the past. My family worked for Gerry's when they had their place in the country, and when he came to London Dad gave him our address. He's a dear boy and has become . . . the son I never had.'

'We know, because he has told us himself, that his family circumstances changed at about the time he should have been going to university, and that he joined the police force because he couldn't afford training for a legal career. How would you say he felt about that?'

'If you mean did it make him bitter, not a scrap of that in his nature. He liked his work, and after his transfer to Central he always said, I've got my foot on the ladder now.'

Better leave it there. Sir Nicholas thanked his witness and sat down again and neither he nor Maitland was surprised to see Hawthorne on his feet.

'I won't detain you, Mrs Mayhew, I know how distressing all this must be for you. I gather from what you said to my friend that you saw a great deal of Detective Constable Harris when he was off duty.'

'Yes. I think he became as fond of us as we were of him.'

'He was ambitious you say?'

'Well, he wanted to get on. That was only natural, wasn't it?'

'Quite natural, particularly in the circumstances.' (Did she see the sting in the tail of that or didn't she?') 'Would you say he admired your husband, looked up to him as a model perhaps?'

'Yes, but if you're trying to say he'd have gone along with any funny business because Laurie asked him to you're quite wrong. He wouldn't have done . . . and nor would Laurie of course,' she added.

'Thank you, Mrs Mayhew. If my friend has any more questions –'

Sir Nicholas, however, had no intention of re-examining. The rest of the time until the luncheon recess was occupied with the cashier from the bank who had opened the account that had only just come to light. Nothing new emerged from her evidence, and as Maitland remarked afterwards anyone coming into court at the moment she took the stand couldn't possibly have guessed whose witness she was. Hawthorne went so far as to ask whether she recognised anybody in court, but she didn't, even when he asked Mrs Mayhew to stand for a moment. 'Nothing like her,' said the witness firmly. And added, with a rather apologetic look in the other woman's direction, 'I told you she was very smart and up to date in her appearance, and of course there was the colour of her hair. I couldn't have forgotten that.'

'You had forgotten about the matter sufficiently, however,' Hawthorne insisted, 'as not to connect it with the case now proceeding. I'm sure you read at least some mention of that in the papers, and the name Mayhew is not exactly a common one.'

'I remember the opening of the account because it seemed rather odd to make such a large deposit in cash, and that impressed on me the appearance of the person who paid it in. But there'd been no further transactions; I'd forgotten all about it until people started asking questions over the weekend, and I certainly didn't remember the name or the fact that the second signature card hadn't come in until I was shown the statement.'

'I see. Well, perhaps Chief Inspector Mayhew will be able to explain the matter for us,' said Hawthorne, obviously quite convinced to the contrary. But they had to wait until the afternoon for that.

Mayhew, recalled to the witness box and asked by his counsel whether he knew anything of this extra account said flatly, 'It doesn't make sense to me.'

'You can assure us that you didn't have the money in an account at a different bank, perhaps the result of many years' savings, and had it transferred at that time.'

'My current account and my deposit account were both at the same bank. Ours, I should say, because they were both joint accounts. We have saved, well the court has seen that, but there's no way I could have just put by a sum like fifteen thousand pounds in addition. And I assure you, Sir Nicholas, if an uncle in Australia had died and left me that much money there's no way I could have forgotten it.'

'How long have you been in the police force, Chief Inspector?'

'Just upon twenty-three years.'

'Then I'm sure you've come to some conclusion in your own mind about this business; we should like you to tell the court what you think, and how you would explain this unexpected development.'

The rumbling cough that Mayhew gave before he answered was very clear, and conveyed to Maitland at least that he had given considerable thought to the matter. 'I don't know if anyone believes me, I'm pretty sure Mr Hawthorne doesn't, but I'm not guilty of any of the things I'm accused of. Knowing that, as I do, there's only one conclusion I can come to: that Constable Harris and I have been deliberately framed. This money must be part of it, and I can see two possible ways it could be explained to work to my disadvantage.'

'Perhaps you would tell us what they are,' Sir Nicholas suggested.

'Somebody might be trying to prove I extorted money over a number of years, only as I haven't there was no way of producing a bank statement that showed periodic deposits. The prosecution may suggest, however, that this was done, and that I had the money transferred in a lump sum with some idea of concealing the fact. On the other hand –'

'On the other hand, Chief Inspector?'

'It could be suggested that I knew who had murdered Mr Goodbody, and had been bribed to shift the blame to Stokes and Barleycorn. Either way I'm proved the villain, I don't see that it matters much which line Mr Hawthorne chooses.'

Neither Counsel for the Prosecution nor Mr Justice Lamb had intervened while this exchange was going on. It seemed the defence was to be allowed some latitude, in consideration of their production of a controversial bank statement. 'Those are precisely the conclusions to which my colleagues and I have come,' said Sir Nicholas, 'and which I shall put to the jury when I address them later. That is all I have to ask you, Chief Inspector, and I would like to thank his lordship for his consideration.'

'I suppose in a way,' said the judge sadly, 'your client may be regarded as an expert witness. Have you any questions, Mr Hawthorne?'

'My friend and his client between them have already – have already taken the wind out of my sails,' said Hawthorne, and for once Lamb did not request an explanation. 'I suppose if I put either of those possibilities to you, Chief Inspector, you will give me the same answer, that you have been framed.'

'I don't see any other possibility,' said Mayhew seriously. 'Mr Maitland had a theory about why it had been done,' he added cautiously, 'but it seemed a bit far fetched to me.'

'Well, no doubt the defence will explain the matter to us in due course,' said Hawthorne, amused. 'I have no further questions for this witness, my lord.'

'Sir Nicholas?'

'No, m'lud.'

'Have you any more witnesses to call?'

'Just one, m'lud. Or two at most. If this unexpected matter

hadn't arisen I should have called the first immediately after Mrs Mayhew.'

There was a short pause while Mayhew returned to the dock, and then his place was taken by Colin Harper. It was obvious from the beginning that he was in something of a rage, and as soon as he had answered as briefly as possible Sir Nicholas's initial questions he turned deliberately away from counsel to address the judge. 'My lord, I should like it to be clearly understood that I'm here under protest. A *sub poena* was issued, and I have come in response to that. But I know nothing whatever of the case, and I am quite certain that nothing I can say will be of help to you.'

Mr Justice Lamb looked more depressed than ever. 'Sir Nicholas?' he said in a failing voice.

'I explained to your lordship that I should be calling certain witnesses as to character. Mr Harper, though he has only known Constable Harris for the past two years personally, is well acquainted with his family. I'm sorry of course to inconvenience the witness, but as the matter is so serious –'

'I really think you must do your best to answer counsel's questions, Mr Harper,' said the judge despairingly.

'I am in your lordship's hands,' said the witness rather ungraciously, and turned back to look at Counsel for the Defence. 'You gave your profession as that of an architect, Mr Harper,' said Sir Nicholas conversationally.

'I did. What has that to do with the matter in hand?'

'You mustn't question counsel, Mr Harper,' the judge admonished him.

'Nothing directly,' Sir Nicholas replied. 'I merely wish to impress upon the jury your respectability. But now, come to think of it, the fact interests me for another reason. I called you with one thought in mind, that you could perhaps speak on behalf of the younger of my clients. But it occurs to me that you may be acquainted professionally with some of the other witnesses in this matter, and with his lordship's permission I should like, very briefly, to ask what – if anything – you know of them.'

'I don't quite understand what you mean, Sir Nicholas, but certainly if there is any point upon which the witness can enlighten us –' said Lamb obligingly.

'Mr Kenneth Protheroe is a builder, I believe, trading under the name of Protheroe and Company. Have you any knowledge of his firm?'

'He has been the contractor for a number of private houses for clients of mine. His company's work is satisfactory, and I know nothing about him personally.'

'And Greenbrier and Appleby?'

'I fail to see . . . but I must bow to his lordship's ruling, I suppose. I imagine everyone in the country is familiar with their name, everyone that can read a signboard, that is. They're an extremely large firm of contractors and nobody in my profession could fail to have had some dealings with them.'

'I see. Well, Mr Harper, as you cannot help us in these matters I am sorry to have taken up your time with them. May we now come to the reason you were called by the defence? Your acquaintance with the Harris family –?'

'Goes back many years. I have a house in the country near their estate, or the estate that was theirs, I should say. I knew the defendant Gerard Harris as a boy, he was no better and no worse than most boys, I suppose, but I'd seen nothing of him for a number of years until he came to London, to Scotland Yard I understood, and came to my wife and me with a letter of introduction from his mother.'

'How did he impress you?'

'A personable young man. Well-mannered.'

'And on further acquaintance?'

'He was obviously pleased when my wife and I encountered these friends of his, the Mayhews. The meeting was accidental, I may say, but I think he wanted to impress me with the possibilities there were for a promotion in the detective branch of the police force, even for a constable.'

'You saw no more of them, however?'

'We'd nothing in common.'

'Very well then, let us get back to Detective Constable Harris. You saw him from time to time, I understand.'

'My wife insisted on entertaining him more often than I thought necessary, as a courtesy to his mother with whom she had remained in correspondence. I'm afraid these periodic meetings didn't lead to any intimate knowledge of the young man, nothing that would help you.'

'He is a friend of your daughter's, I believe.'

'If so, without my consent, though he has met her at our house, of course.'

'What was your objection . . . what would have been your objection to the friendship if you had known of it?'

'I should have thought that was obvious. A young man with criminal tendencies –'

'Are you telling me you discerned such tendencies in him from the beginning of your acquaintance?' Sir Nicholas was coming perilously close to cross-examining his own witness, but again neither the judge nor Counsel for the Prosecution intervened.

'From the beginning, no.'

'I'm sorry to press the matter, Mr Harper, but surely your opinion of Gerard Harris can be no worse than that he is a young man led astray by an older colleague whom he admires?' Hawthorne had a frown for that, the judge looked puzzled, Maitland was quite simply holding his breath.

'It might be if I hadn't heard what he said to her.'

'To your daughter, Mr Harper? On what occasion?' When the witness did not reply immediately he went on, almost as though the answer had no interest for him, 'When they were discussing marriage perhaps?'

'There can be no question –' He broke off there, seeming to recollect himself, and then added deliberately, 'He said to her that the financial side of things needn't worry her, he had a second activity in mind that would be very profitable, in addition to the job he held. If she'd marry him they'd never want for anything. It's quite obvious now what he meant.'

'Colin!' Dorothy Mayhew was on her feet, and because everyone in the court had been so taken up with what the witness was saying, her sudden intervention brought a moment's complete silence. 'You promised,' she said. 'You told me you'd arrange matters so he'd get off lightly. And now you're making it sound as if he's as guilty as we want them to believe Laurie is.'

Harper was looking at her blankly. 'That is Mrs Mayhew, isn't it?' he asked, looking in a bewildered way at Sir Nicholas.

'Indeed it is,' said Counsel non-committally.

'Young Harris introduced us, but I can't for the life of me think

212

what's got into her.'

'How can you say such a thing?' Dorothy Mayhew demanded indignantly. 'You know you promised that whatever happened to Laurie it would just seem as if Gerry had been led astray, him being so much younger, and he'd get off lightly.'

'I'm afraid, madam,' Sir Nicholas put in, 'Mr Harper is not the only witness who has given incriminating evidence against Mr Harris.'

'But he told me . . . he promised,' she said again. 'The witnesses would say just what he told them.'

'I'm sure they did, Mrs Mayhew.'

She stood a moment, obviously trying to absorb the implications of this. 'He promised,' she repeated. 'He told me he'd arrange matters so that Gerry wouldn't seem to be very much to blame, and now he's saying . . . ' She began to sob hysterically. Mr Justice Lamb opened and shut his mouth once or twice and finally managed to articulate, 'Sir Nicholas?'

Counsel for the Defence said smoothly, as though he had rehearsed the speech beforehand, 'With your lordship's permission I think we should ask Mr Harper to stand down for a moment, and recall Mrs Mayhew to the witness stand.'

As for Maitland he had taken only a quick glance at the dock, but it had been long enough for him to see Harris's bewilderment, and the suddenly dawning realisation on Mayhew's face of what his wife had said. He looked down at the pad in front of him, fighting the impulse to put up his left hand to cover his eyes. After a moment he began to draw on the blank sheet of paper in front of him, his pencil moving almost automatically to depict a high wall that looked as if it had been put together from a child's building blocks.

Monday, after the Verdict

I

After that there was, of course, no question but that they should all dine together that evening, whether Mrs Stokes chose to take offence or not. 'She took it quite well on the whole,' said Vera complacently, when Jenny questioned her on the subject.

'Then Uncle Nick can tell us,' said Jenny with some satisfaction, 'just how he pulled it off.'

Sir Nicholas took one look at his nephew, and decided that this wasn't the moment to demand explanations from him. He recounted the day's events up to the point of Dorothy Mayhew's outburst, at which point he added coldly, 'I have to admit that the only words that fit the occasion are Sensation in Court.'

At that point Antony roused himself. 'It's no good trying to blame me for it, Uncle Nick,' he said. 'You played the hand yourself, and unless I'm very much mistaken you enjoyed every minute of it.'

There was a brief pause while Sir Nicholas appeared to examine his conscience. 'You may be right, my dear boy,' he admitted, with one of his bewildering changes of mood. 'But now let us consider the outcome.'

'Too many people got hurt.'

'What happened?' said Jenny. If it would have done any good she would have forgotten her curiosity and willingly seen the whole thing buried fathoms deep, but that was no use, she knew. Antony wouldn't forget what had happened in a hurry, she could tell that, but better get the whole thing into the open.

'Quite right,' said Vera, almost as though she had divined the younger woman's thought. 'Can't leave us in the dark, anyway.'

Sir Nicholas went back to his story. 'I must say for Mr Harper, he kept his head. He insisted he had no idea what she was talking about, and had only met her once. But he'd no choice but to vacate the witness box and let her take his place, and the whole story came out in a rush with almost no prompting from either Hawthorne or myself. Harris had introduced his new friends to each other, and a couple of days later Colin Harper had called on her again while Mayhew was on duty. The acquaintance had quickly ripened into a full-grown love affair; he's an attractive man and it would have taken a stronger character than hers to withstand him. Money was evidently no object, he took a small studio flat as a meeting place –'

'I expect we shall find he had it all along,' Maitland put in. 'I don't suppose she was the first or only one.'

'You may be right. In any event that's where they used to meet. He took her shopping, encouraged her to wear her new clothes when they were together, and to make up a little. He encouraged her to talk about the cases her husband was involved in, and when he was sure she was completely infatuated he let her know little by little that he had other interests besides his professional one. My impression is that he was aching for someone to confide in, which is, after all, a natural human instinct, and as her dependence on him grew she was the only one he could trust.

'Or thought he could,' said Antony.

He half expected a demand from his uncle as to who was telling the story, but it did not come. Sir Nicholas only said, 'Precisely,' and went on without a pause. 'He told her all about his organisation, which was not unlike the outline Sykes gave to Antony at the beginning, or the further speculations that Antony made on the subject. He was quite right about that, Antony, I mean, the department heads each knew the people under them, and knew Colin Harper, but none of them knew each other. At last – it was after Mr Goodbody's murder, so we can safely make the assumption that the two things were cause and effect – Harper suggested to Dorothy Mayhew that if her husband were out of the way they could spend very much more time together. He wouldn't go so far as to divorce his wife, because she would understand that a respectable environment was very important to him. He had to keep up appearances. But Mrs Harper was used to his absences and would never query them. Dorothy could wear

215

her new clothes and new make-up all the time, and live in considerably more comfort than she'd ever have been able to as a policeman's wife.'

'Must have been a very silly woman,' said Vera rather gruffly.

'Very true, my dear, I think she was. All the same you can imagine the attraction for a rather drab person like her, leading what she may have felt was rather a dull life, having undreamed of affluence dangled in front of her. But Harper had his blind spot too. He hadn't reckoned with her affection for young Harris, who, as she told us, had taken the place of a son to her. Harper had promised her, she told us, that he'd arranged with the Protheroes, who were in the organisation up to their necks of course, that their evidence would be that they'd overheard Mayhew endeavouring to subvert his younger colleague, so that Harris would get off much more lightly. But he had never had any intention of doing that, there was his daughter to consider and he didn't think a police constable, even in the detective branch, was anywhere near good enough for her. So the Protheroes gave their evidence as originally arranged, and he made very sure that Harris was represented by them as a full partner in the crime. She wasn't in court when they gave their evidence, of course, but she heard what he said and it was just too much for her. Once she began to talk there was no stopping her.'

'What you hoped,' said Vera.

'Antony thought that was what might happen, and I agreed with him . . . though only after some argument, you remember.'

'And if she hadn't cracked?' Vera persisted.

'We should have called Mrs Mayhew's brother-in-law from Bexhill to say his wife had died eighteen months ago and he hadn't seen Dorothy since. Bellerby dug that up for us. She'd obviously concealed the fact from her husband so as to have an excuse for her more frequent absences.'

'And what had this Mr Harper to say?' Jenny asked.

'Not a word, though from the rather sick look he had when the police took him in for questioning I gather there's evidence to be found now they know where to look for it.'

'That's what Inspector Sykes always says,' Jenny agreed.

'And while we'll never know the whole story there was no question of the case even being put to the jury after all she'd had

216

to say. Lamb directed them to acquit, which they did, and your husband, my dear Jenny, seeming to have withdrawn himself from the proceedings, I was left to face our clients with only Bellerby's support. Neither of them, in spite of their vindication, was in a particularly happy frame of mind.'

'Could have foreseen that,' said Vera. 'Even the young lad Antony says he wants to marry the girl, or she wants to marry him, or perhaps both. And neither she nor her mother can be very happy in the circumstances.

'They will pick up the pieces,' said Sir Nicholas, 'as Mayhew will, and start again. I can only hope that the two young people will be able to console each other to some extent, but I'm afraid Chief Inspector Mayhew is in for a rough time. I think he may ask for a transfer rather than face his colleagues here again.'

'Not a good idea,' said Vera positively. 'Friends here, doesn't want to run away from them.'

'Well, we shall see. There are so many people involved that the police will have a difficult time clearing everything up. Enough charges of perjury to keep them going for twelve months. As for young Harris, I have an idea about his future; if you agree, my dear, and if Antony thinks it's a good one.'

'What is it?' asked Jenny, sensing unerringly an attempt to distract her husband from his brooding.

'That we should find him a place as a clerk in someone's chambers – I'd give him one myself if we had a vacancy – and whatever help we can in reading for the Bar. What do you think, my dear?'

'I think it's a marvellous idea,' said Jenny firmly, not waiting for Vera's more abrupt agreement. 'And what about that horrible man, Godalming? Is he going to apologise to Antony for what he said?'

'I think it very unlikely,' said Sir Nicholas, smiling slightly. 'However, for the moment it seems he can have no further cause for complaint, which brings me to Superintendent Wakefield. You will remember he gave evidence for the prosecution, but did his best for the defence when I gave him the opportunity.'

'You don't mean that may harm his career?'

'I think it might. However, he came over to talk to Mayhew while I was doing so, and I gather he's just about reached the age when retirement wouldn't be altogether out of the question. He seems to think it would be a good idea and to be quite happy about the prospect.'

'In that case, is Inspector Mayhew going to be all right? I mean, if the Assistant Commissioner is such a one for bearing grudges he may blame him just because you and Antony helped him.'

'I think with this prosecution in the background Mayhew should be in a pretty strong position as far as his job goes. Personally, it's a different matter, but as I told you, Antony, there's nothing either you or I can do about that. We couldn't let him go to prison for a thing we were sure he hadn't done, nor could we ignore Harris's point of view.'

'Yes, but . . . isn't there any other way we could have fixed it?' Maitland at last seemed willing to break his silence. 'Without hitting him over the head with his wife's infidelity in open court. I know it was my suggestion, but –'

'But you couldn't think of anything else, and neither could I . . . then or now. It was a poor hope at best, and we must be thankful that it succeeded. Yes, I said thankful,' he added more sharply. 'Supposing you hadn't realised what was going on and by some miracle we'd got a Not Guilty verdict in some other way, what would have happened in the long run? Sooner or later he'd discover that his wife was unfaithful to him without any assistance from you.'

'I suppose you're right, Uncle Nick. In fact I know you are. But,' he added rather drearily, 'I can't help wondering what he's doing tonight.'

'Gerry Harris and Alice Harper, having put her mother to bed with a sleeping draught, are doing their best to comfort him,' said Vera positively.

This was so unlike her that Antony stared at her, and after a moment began to smile. 'Don't tell me you've been concealing a crystal ball from us all these years, Vera,' he said. 'And if you're going to start making as wild guesses as I do about things, goodness knows what Uncle Nick will say.'

'He'll blame you,' said Vera, returning his smile. And there, for the moment, they let the matter rest.

II

Roger and Meg came in after dinner, and ordinarily Meg, having read the newspapers, would have been full of questions, but one look at Antony's face convinced her that this was not the moment. Instead she suggested some music. Vera, knowing her nephew's tastes well enough, opted for Mozart, and the remainder of the evening passed peacefully. Only when Sir Nicholas and Vera had gone did Meg venture a question, and by that time Maitland was as ready as he ever would be to talk about the matter.

'I know you and Uncle Nick did something very clever,' said Meg, 'and I know you told us you were sure Chief Inspector Mayhew and Constable Harris were innocent and why you believed that, but you never did tell us that you'd decided on who was responsible for what happened to them.'

'As to being clever,' said Antony, 'it was all Uncle Nick's doing and I daresay when he thinks it out he'll never forgive me.' He smiled again. It was only for the second time that evening, but Jenny, seeing his expression lighten, breathed a sigh of relief. 'You should have heard him. If ever he accuses me of raising the devil again I'll remind him of it, you can be sure of that.'

'But you put him up to it,' Meg protested, 'and what you haven't told us is how you knew.'

'It was all so vague. I knew – or most of the time I thought I knew – that Mayhew and Harris were innocent, but who was really responsible for framing them I just couldn't be sure. I was all wrong from the beginning, you see, about why they were being framed for blackmail as well as perjury. I mean, clearing Stokes and Barleycorn of a charge of murder was part of it, but I didn't realise that Mrs Mayhew would be glad to be rid of her husband, or that Colin Harper had an additional motive for involving Constable Harris, to get him out of his daughter's way.'

'You couldn't have realised all that,' Roger pointed out, 'until you'd made up your mind who was responsible.'

'No, that's right. And when I said it was vague that was almost an exaggeration. I was working from the wrong premise, thinking the reason for framing our clients was because one of them knew

219

something detrimental to the man who was running things, without realising what he knew. Obviously I was suspicious about Phillips, because, being in the legal profession himself, it was ten-to-one that Mayhew talked more freely to him than he might have done to some other of his friends. It was only when one after the other of the witnesses for the prosecution began to admit to some connection with the building trade that I began to wonder about Harper. There was Kenneth Protheroe, who had his own small firm, and there was Martin Kingsley who had left employment with Greenbrier and Appleby to take a job that paid considerably less. Finally, but this was later, there was the man who attacked me, who had been employed by Greenbrier's and was probably known to Martin Kingsley. Well, architects employ builders, or is it the other way round? Anyway it was rather a lot of coincidences.'

'What on earth put you on to Mrs Mayhew? I don't see that at all,' Meg complained.

'It seemed reasonable to suppose that I'd been attacked at that particular time because I started making some inquiries on behalf of Mayhew and Harris. But when it happened very few people knew that. Our clients, of course, and Mr Bellerby, but as far as I knew they were all for it. Also Father William, but I have every reason to know he's well disposed. The only other person was Mrs Mayhew, and unlikely as it seemed I began to think back on our talk together, and I couldn't help but realise that she was far more concerned for Harris than she was for her husband. There was also the fact that she seemed to believe nothing very dreadful could happen to either of them, which when you come to think of it was ridiculous. Obviously she could have passed the information on to Rupert Phillips, who was a friend of the family. Mayhew himself might have done so, for that matter, though I didn't think he was in the mood to talk about the charge with anyone. If Mrs Mayhew had done it she must have made an opportunity to see Phillips alone, and the only reason I could think of for that was that her connection with him was closer than we knew. But she could hardly have been carrying on an affair with one of their next-door neighbours without Mayhew tumbling to what was happening.'

'They might have been just good friends,' said Meg idiotically.

'Stuff and nonsense!' Antony's spirits were reviving rapidly. 'If she was going to betray her husband it was for somebody she cared about. We brought out in court, and Superintendent Wakefield helped that, that the police were suspicious that some one person was organising crime on a large scale and that somehow Mayhew and Harris might have got in his way. But that wasn't nearly enough, in view of all the people willing to perjure themselves. So we had just two cards up our sleeves, the presumption that an affair was going on between Colin Harper and Dorothy Mayhew; and that she had a rather excessive maternal affection, not shared by her lover, for young Harris.'

'But all those witnesses,' said Meg in a wondering tone.

'Yes, how do you think they'd have been persuaded to go along?' asked Roger.

'As Uncle Nick isn't here I'll make a guess about it,' Antony offered. 'With Stokes and Barleycorn it was obviously self-interest. As for the Protheroes, I don't know about him, but she knew what her previous husband had been up to even if she hadn't taken an active part in any criminal proceedings. I imagine she was well paid off after he killed himself, and there'd be more money forthcoming for both of of them as the price of their evidence. I have to assume that Colin Harper was a good judge of men, and he had obviously met Martin Kingsley in the course of business. When there seemed to be an opening for a protection racket he got in touch with him, got him to apply for a job that was open with a firm that dealt with small shopkeepers – and I expect Shadwell's were very pleased to get him – and start the line going. Mrs Goodbody and Vernon Peele were innocent bystanders as far as the criminal activities were concerned – I don't know whether they were paid or threatened to give the evidence they did. That will all presumably come out in due course but it's the police's business, not mine. And that's all there really is to say about one of the nastiest cases I remember.'

'In that case,' said Jenny, 'I think it's time we turned the tables on Meg and made her do some of the talking.' Antony turned to look at her and was immediately comforted by the familiar serenity with which she returned his gaze. 'It's perfectly obvious she's bursting with some news of her own, and I only hope she's told you about it, Roger, because I've a sort of feeling –'

221

'She has,' said Roger. 'It's a new play, of course, and you needn't worry, either of you, it was bound to happen sooner or later and I'm quite reconciled to the fact that she'll be going back to work.'

'Of course he is, darlings,' said Meg. 'And I know you sometimes think I'm horrid, Antony, but I really do realise there are times when Roger would like a full-time wife. But this is a chance I just couldn't let slip by.'

'A play is a play is a play,' said Antony.

'Oh, no, darling, not this one,' Meg assured him. 'It's something quite, quite different.'

But they had all heard that before.